CAST O

FAMILY
SECRETS

*Five extraordinary siblings. One dangerous past.
Unlimited potential.*

Marcus Evans—The Navy SEAL had superhuman strength, but was he really one of the genetically engineered Extraordinary Five?

Samantha Barnes—Someone wanted the beautiful ambassador dead, but could she trust the powerful, passionate soldier who vowed to protect her?

Jake Ingram—He knew the truth about Marcus, and the danger his long-lost brother was in....

Agnes Payne and Oliver Grimble—The corrupt Coalition scientists helped bring the Extraordinary Five into the world, and now they want payback....

About the Author

VIRGINIA KANTRA

Don't we all dream of the perfect hero? So you can imagine how excited Virginia Kantra was when her editor offered her a crack at Marcus Evans, a man designed before birth to be physically perfect in every way—stronger, faster, more powerful and more incredibly gorgeous than your average hero. He even has a sense of humor. "I fell in love. A dedicated Navy SEAL, a decorated war hero, he seemed the perfect man to guard elegant Ambassador Samantha Barnes during her brief visit to Washington. Perfect. Except, of course, for this one tiny defect, this niggling compulsion....

"What woman could resist a challenge like that? What writer could?

"So here I am, participating with some of my favorite authors in what I think is one of the sexiest, edgiest, most out-there series yet—FAMILY SECRETS."

HER
BEAUTIFUL
ASSASSIN

VIRGINIA
KANTRA

Silhouette Books

Published by Silhouette Books

America's Publisher of Contemporary Romance

Special thanks and acknowledgment are given
to Virginia Kantra for her contribution
to the FAMILY SECRETS series.

 SILHOUETTE BOOKS

ISBN 0-373-61372-5

HER BEAUTIFUL ASSASSIN

Visit us at www.silhouettefamilysecrets.com

Printed in U.S.A.

FAMILY SECRETS

Henry Bloomfield (d.) m. Violet Vaughn 2nd m. Dale Hobson

Susannah Hobson

Extraordinary Five

Jake Ingram

Connor Quinn (d.)

Gretchen Wagner m. Kurt Miller

Marcus Evans

Faith Martin

Gideon Faulkner

"Uncle" Oliver Grimble m. "Aunt" Agnes Payne

Ingram Family

Clayton Ingram m. Carolyn Cook

Zach Ingram
m.
Maisy Dalton

Evans Family

Russell (Russ) Evans
m.
Lynn Van Allen

Charles Evans
m.
Sarah Alexander

Seth Evans

Drew Evans

Laura Evans

Honey Evans

Holt Evans

———— Birth Family

- - - - - Adoptive Family

m.   Married

d.   Deceased

For my writer buddies,
Suzanne Brockmann, inspiration of all things SEAL,
Candace Irvin, source of all things Navy,
Evelyn Vaughn, creator of he's-not-
genetically-engineered-he's-just-that-good
Matt Tynan, and for all the FSC authors who held
my hand, answered my e-mails, provided
character sketches and shared information.

And for my husband who cooked and my children
who left me alone while I finished this book....
Thank you!

Prologue

He was a big, badass Navy SEAL in command of a squad of warriors, and he didn't know what to do.

Lieutenant Marcus Evans hated that.

He wasn't too crazy about the fact that at any moment the ship they were on could smack into a mine and blow up, either.

Of course, it wasn't his ship; the frigate was on its way to a routine refueling in the Persian Gulf when it had picked up his team after a successful recon mission. But these were his men.

Marcus made eye contact with each of them, trying to be as honest and reassuring as he could.

"The captain's lowered the APUs." The auxiliary propulsion units. "Chances are we can tiptoe out of the minefield along our own wake."

"Backward." That was Garcia, the weapons specialist, dark and skeptical.

"Yeah."

"In the dark."

"They've focused all floodlights on the starboard bridge onto the surface."

"It's not the surface mines I'm worried about," said Buzz, the squad's explosives expert. "It's those suckers under the water. We kiss one of those, they'll see the fireworks all the way to Baghdad."

"Maybe Clark here could go up there and offer them his X-ray vision," Petty Officer First Class James Robinson said.

He meant Marcus. Aka Clark aka Clark Kent aka Superman.

James Robinson was one of the few men entitled to use the nickname to Marcus's face. But then, they'd pulled each other through BUD/S training. Clark and Jimmy. They could have been paired together as Ren and Stimpy or Tom and Jerry or even Dr. Evil and Mini Me.

Although unlike Dr. Evil and his sidekick, they looked nothing alike.Robinson was a brilliant, wiry, black enlisted man, and Marcus was none of those things.

Marcs smiled wryly. "I think if I get in their way right now, they'll just toss me overboard."

"Might as well," muttered Garcia. "We couldn't be any more out of our depth."

Marcus sympathized with his men's frustration. Hell, he shared it. But he said, "That's the way it's got to be. This SEAL team is not assigned to this ship. We have no specific duties during a damage control evolution."

"Slick went to sick bay," Buzz said.

"Slick's a medic," Marcus said unarguably. "He went where he could do some good." Again, he met each man's eyes. When general quarters sounded, all hands without assignments reported to the mess desk in the relative safety of the center of the ship. Marcus and his men sat at a table apart. Jimmy and Garcia, Jacobs and Buzz—they were all watching him, prepared to live or die or even sit one out on his orders. "But once we boarded this frigate, the rest of us are strictly along for the ride."

Some ride. Because at that moment the deck bucked up and the bottom fell out of the world.

The force of the blast slammed Marcus off his feet and hurtled him through the air.

Just like Superman, he thought in the instant before he came down hard. He twisted to take the impact on his shoulder, which might have worked if the ship wasn't still pitching under him.

His head thumped onto the metal deck. Flares went off inside his skull. His blood roared. His vision grayed.

But he was obviously alive and more or less whole. He spread his palms on the gritty deck and levered himself up to see how bad it was.

It was bad.

An officer's job was to think big picture, but it was difficult to see past the bodies and debris, difficult to think through the groans. If the mess deck was hit this bad, then the frigate had to be taking on water below. Which meant... Blood ran into Marcus's eyes. He blinked to clear his vision, but the air was thick with dust. Or smoke. He staggered to his feet on the pitching deck, looking for the rest of his team.

There. His chest squeezed. Lying there, under the twisted piece of steel that used to be the chow line. Wasn't that—

The lights below decks flickered and died. The square yellow battle lanterns mounted on the walls snapped to life.

"Lieutenant? Clark?" The voice came from around his feet.

"Here, Jimmy." He dropped to his knees. He had always had excellent night vision. But even without it, there was enough spill from the battle lanterns to see that Robinson wouldn't make it out on his own. "How are you doing?"

"Can't move my legs. Think I broke my back?" he inquired, like he was asking whether Marcus thought it would rain tonight or something.

Marcus drew a deep breath—*mistake*—and glanced again at the improbable angles of his best friend's body. "No. I think you broke both legs when you came down on the chow line. Let me get you looked at." He raised his voice. "Garcia!"

"Here, Lieutenant."

"Behind you, sir."

Garcia and Buzz materialized from the dark.

"Where's Jacobs?" Marcus asked.

"Jacobs busted his arm. Maybe some ribs. We took him to sick bay."

Marcus nodded. "We need a corpsman here. And a stretcher."

"Hoo yah, Lieutenant." Garcia melted away.

It took five minutes for the hospital corpsman, nicknamed Doc—they were always nicknamed Doc—to make his evaluation and get permission to move Robinson to the weather deck.

He got off the phone with the locker officer and handed Marcus a piece of paper with a string of scribbled numbers. "There's your route out of the fire. Can you read it?"

Marcus glanced at the tack numbers, each one denoting a different passageway, hatch or door. He smiled in reassurance. "Good to go."

The young man's face relaxed. He was probably relieved he didn't have to explain coordinates to a dipshit officer. "Yes, sir. And, uh, DC central could use four bodies on fire seven."

"We can give you three. Buzz."

His explosives man rose and went to find the damage control officer.

"Garcia and I will report as soon as we get Robinson to the weather deck," Marcus said.

Robinson was already cocooned in the flexible canvas stretcher designed to maneuver through the hatches.

Marcus wrapped the lead rope around his arm. "Time to roll, Jimmy."

"I'm gonna hate this, aren't I?" Robinson asked.

"Beats drowning," Marcus said lightly, and lifted him. Their route was planned to keep them out of the fire's way. But the metal passageways echoed with the groans of stricken sailors and tortured steel, the rush of the fire mains, the roar of fire, the shouts and rapped commands of men and women fighting for their ship. For their lives.

The emergency diesel engine shuddered and clanked as Marcus and Garcia navigated up a ladder and through the watertight doors, trying to keep the stretcher clear of the sides. They had to step over hoses snaked through the passageways. In every section, pumps with tubes and switches sucked water from the bowels of the ship and forced it up and over the side. Each small connection shot a spray of oil and water onto the decks, making their footing treacherous.

Marcus pulled the stretcher after him up a ladder and onto the flight deck. Bits of fiery debris rained down from the superstructure. For a second, he stood transfixed, pierced by a vision of burning and black water and the memory of someone—a little girl, her face white between streaks of black hair—depending on him.

Which was crap.

He didn't know any little girls.

His sister Honey was a blonde.

And the only people depending on him were his men and the sailors trapped below.

Garcia moved toward the hatch. Shaking the ghosts from his head, Marcus lowered Jimmy gently to the slanting deck. His former swim buddy had passed out sometime during the awkward passage. But now he groaned and grabbed Marcus's wrist.

"You going...back?"

"I have to," Marcus said simply.

Robinson nodded, accepting that. But as Marcus began his descent into the fiery, steaming guts of the ship, his buddy called softly, "Watch out for kryptonite."

One

Work was a good drug. It revived her better than NoDoz, muffled her moods more effectively than Prozac. There were no negative interactions; it never made her sleepy or jittery.

And it didn't wear off in twelve hours, either.

The Honorable Samantha Barnes, acting U.S. ambassador to the Republic of Delmonico, pulled another stack of reports toward her across the cherry wood desk. The one thing work couldn't do was guarantee her a good night's sleep, but everything came with a price. As long as her staff didn't have to pay for her sleepless nights, Samantha was satisfied with her bargain.

So she made a point of smiling at the maid who came in to clear her breakfast tray. She thanked her secretary, Philip Scott, when he set her Washington schedule and the daily news summary on top of her briefing from the deputy chief of mission.

Idly, she glanced at the excerpted headlines: President Seeks to Soothe Investors' Fears in Aftermath of World Bank Heist. Mideast Negotiations Stalled. Designer Babies Products of Government Project?

The last one made her raise her eyebrows. "Are we taking our news from the tabloids these days, Philip?"

"That's from the *Post*," he protested. He studied her face. "Have you been working all night?"

Almost. There was so much to do. So much to catch up on.

Samantha summoned another smile. "Hardly. I got up a little early, that's all. Hotel or not, I can't work in bed all morning like—" What was the name of that playwright, the one who'd served as Eisenhower's ambassador to Italy? "Clare Boothe Luce," she finished triumphantly.

Philip was not impressed by her feat of memory. He frowned after the departing breakfast tray. "You didn't eat."

Samantha didn't taste food anymore even when she tried it. Not since Stan— She cut the thought off and made another note in the margin of her schedule.

"I had coffee."

"You drink too much coffee."

"Philip." She kept her tone mild. Philip, brown haired, slim and organized, was as conscientious and inoffensive as the Latin Club president he must have been in high school. "Don't fuss."

He picked up the stack of letters she'd prepared to go out. "It's not fussing to suggest that you eat occasionally."

"I'm having lunch at one-thirty with Senators—" she consulted the list again "—Dobson and Twitchell, and a dinner party at the Ivesons' tonight. I promise I won't starve."

"You'll spend all your time explaining European economic integration and expounding on investment opportunities in Delmonico, and you'll forget to eat."

Samantha smiled ruefully. This had to be the first time in her life anyone was concerned about her losing weight. "I can afford to forget a few calories. I can't afford to waste an opportunity. It's bad enough that I'm a recess appointment. I don't want to give anyone any more reason to criticize the president's choice."

Philip frowned. "It's not as if there's a question of the Senate approving your appointment as ambassador."

"There are always questions in politics, Philip. And

while I'm deeply honored by the president's confidence, I must accept that naming an inexperienced woman to a sensitive diplomatic post makes certain members of the Foreign Relations Committee decidedly nervous.''

''What about Madeleine Albright? What about Condoleezza Rice? A Republican appointee, I might add.''

''Both full professors, both older than me and both better qualified.''

''Excuse me, ma'am, but concluding negotiations for the Delmonico Accord certainly makes you qualified.''

She shook her head. ''The key word there is *concluded.* There are many people who would argue that I simply furthered the work begun by my late husband.''

And they'd be right, she added to herself.

Wealthy industrialist Stanley J. Barnes had been the president's original appointee to Delmonico. Stan's death in a car accident a year ago had devastated Samantha. It had also derailed the effort by the United States to separate the coastal country of Delmonico from its hostile neighbor, Rebelia, and bring it one step closer to the European Union and NATO.

So while Washington sought an appropriate replacement for the late ambassador, Samantha had buried her grief in her husband's cause. With beauty pageant idealism and uncompromising courtesy—dished up with personal attention over lavish dinners—she'd brought the negotiators to the table and kept them there.

A triumph, trumpeted the newspapers.

A fluke, sniffed her detractors.

A miracle, Samantha thought. But it was her responsibility now to nurse the fragile accord to maturity.

It was her inheritance from Stan. And since the two of them had never been able to have any children, it was likely to be their only legacy.

"Ma'am?" Philip was watching her, his shrewd gray eyes concerned. Oh, God, had he asked her something?

"Sorry. I was—"

Sad, she thought.

"—thinking," she said.

"I said, Matt Tynan's office called to remind you of the dinner at the White House on Friday."

"Wonderful. Thank you." The prospect of seeing her old friend again actually brought her a moment's pleasure. But she didn't linger on it. She had work to do. Sliding the schedule to one side, she picked up the briefing again. But Philip still waited, his face and shoulders stiff. "Was there anything else?"

"A small security matter. Nothing to bother you about."

"If you didn't want to bother me, you wouldn't be standing here. What is it?"

"DS is concerned that you may be the target of Rebelian operatives during your visit to the United States."

The State Department's Bureau of Diplomatic Security was responsible for implementing security at U.S. diplomatic missions around the world. They provided intelligence information and protection at the embassy in Delmonico. And, in the person of Security Agent Thomas T. Walker, they were keeping Samantha safe in Washington, as well.

"This isn't news, Philip. Security Agent Walker has already made it very clear that I must cooperate with his bureau's security measures."

Her secretary pulled a face. "Yes, well, even Agent Walker wasn't prepared for the latest measure."

"Goodness, that sounds serious," she said mildly. It was difficult to make herself care. All the security measures in the world hadn't saved Stan. "What is it? Guard dogs?"

"Seals."

Samantha blinked, envisioning a sleek, whiskered face

and a bright circus ball.... No, that couldn't possibly be right. "Excuse me?"

"Some higher-up in DS has assigned a U.S. Navy SEAL to your security detail."

"Oh." She flushed slightly. She must be more tired than she thought. "Yes, of course. There's a marine detachment at our embassy in Delmonico. And the Navy Seabees—"

"This man is not a marine. Or part of a navy construction battalion. He's a lieutenant in one of the most elite fighting teams in the service, and Walker's nose is seriously out of joint."

Now she understood. If Philip put her in mind of president of the Latin club, Agent Walker was more like the hall monitor. He wouldn't take kindly to having his competence or his authority challenged.

"I see. And have they negotiated a reasonable division of labor?" she asked, only half joking.

Philip smiled wryly. "I'm not sure Agent Walker is trained to negotiate. He'll continue to provide your routine security, and Lieutenant Evans will accompany you as a, ah, visible deterrent."

A visible deterrent? Her stomach dropped in dismay. How was she supposed to circulate, how could she encourage others to talk freely, how could she do her *job,* with a uniformed Navy SEAL lurking at her elbow?

"I think perhaps I'd better see him," she said.

"Oh, you will," said Philip.

She arched her brows in question, and he smiled apologetically. "He's escorting you to lunch today."

This assignment was a bitch.

But the ambassador was a babe.

Marcus Evans stood, hot, itchy and at attention, as Samantha Barnes entered the silk-paneled meeting room. The ambassador's suite at the old Georgetown hotel included three such rooms, along with two offices, a formal dining area, a private study and four bedrooms. He'd scoped out the layout with the grudging cooperation of Security Agent Thomas T. Walker this morning.

The combination of his dress whites and the stuffy atmosphere of the Snobs R Us hotel should have been no sweat. But he was definitely feeling the heat.

Maybe it was because all that stiff, stuffed furniture, the baby grand piano and the silver bowls full of dead flower petals reminded him of his parents' home in Conover Pointe.

Maybe it was because Security Agent Walker was glaring at him from the other side of the room like he'd just taken a piss on the Oriental rug.

Or maybe it was because when Ambassador Barnes finally walked in, the temperature in the place shot up about twenty degrees.

Man, was she hot. Not young. There was nothing schoolgirl about those curves. And those were genuine laugh lines at the corners of her eyes.

But she was tall and stacked and—whoa, pretty mama—a redhead, too. And all of her was packaged in this neat, tight, short little suit, light gray and sort of boring, really, until you noticed the way it wrapped the body inside.

Which he did. Notice. Hell, he practically swallowed his tongue.

She smiled politely. "Hello, Lieutenant...Evans, isn't it?"

The voice matched the body. Deep. Fluid. Sexy. Enough to make a guy forget his own name.

But he answered, "Yes, ma'am."

"And you're a Navy SEAL."

He felt a pang of disappointment. Was she one of those? A SEAL groupie. He'd run into them before, but only in bars, not in embassies. Was that why he'd got dinged for this assignment? Because Miss Ambassador here wanted to get herself some of the biggest, the baddest, the best the Navy had to offer?

"Yes, ma'am," he said woodenly.

"And what were you doing before this assignment?" she asked.

Her big blue eyes were clear and direct. Up close, her concentrated interest hit him like a dose of pure oxygen.

Marcus wasn't sure what to say. The heroic battle of the *Stoker*'s crew to save its ship had made headlines. Fortunately, his small part in the incident had not. At least, he didn't think it had. So he didn't know if the ambassador was digging for details to feed an adrenaline addiction or just making small talk.

"Recon in the Gulf," he said.

She tilted her head. "This must be something of a change for you, then."

Hell, yeah.

"Yes, ma'am. It's a temporary assignment."

That was what his CO had said, looking almost as confused as Marcus felt. Just a temporary assignment, Commander Woods had promised. Three months, six months tops, while James Robinson recuperated at the naval hospital in Bethesda and the rest of the squad conducted training exercises at Little Creek.

Marcus had thought at first, resentfully, that his political appointment was the result of his old man pulling strings. But the commander had assured him it was nothing like that.

"Well." Samantha Barnes pressed her full lips together on whatever it was she was about to say, and then parted them to smile. She had great teeth. "I hope your time with us will pass quickly and pleasantly."

Okay. Was that quickly as in "I can't wait till you go?" Or pleasantly as in, "After lunch, let's get naked?"

Marcus had no idea. But at least Ambassador Babe didn't grill him about his qualifications in front of the hard-eyed, tight-assed security agent.

Walker knew his job. Marcus had to give him that. And he performed it with a conscientious attention to detail that a SEAL had to notice and appreciate. As they left the suite, the agent checked out the hotel exit, checked out the limo driver, checked out the gray Lincoln Towncar. Ambassador Barnes got into the back and immediately buried her pretty nose in some papers. So any fantasies Marcus might have had about getting it on in the back of a limousine were pretty much relegated to prom night.

Walker sat in front, where he had full visibility and a better shot at anything that needed shooting. Marcus watched—*Pay attention, Evans, there'll be a quiz*—as the security agent ordered a change in their route to the senator's house and arranged a place to park and a time for pickup.

And then, with all the real work done, Walker turned the game over to Marcus.

"Why don't you accompany the ambassador inside," Walker suggested, his tone smooth and his eyes hostile.

Obviously, he expected Marcus to fumble. But then, he didn't know who he was playing with.

Winners always wanted the ball. It was a concept drilled into Marcus since his first football season in seventh grade.

"Thanks," he said. "I will."

He got out of the car first and scanned the street as the driver handed the ambassador onto the curb. Even with his senses alert to possible signs of trouble—a half-open window, a line of parked cars, a bum resting in the shadow of a stairwell—he noticed her skirt ride up her thighs as she slid across the seat. Not a lot, but enough to get his blood pumping.

The game, he reminded himself. Focus.

He stepped back so she could go ahead of him up the shallow granite stairs. Nice rear action, too. Not that he was staring.

Walker was, though, the son of a bitch. Marcus shifted over on the steps so he blocked his view.

A foreign-looking maid admitted them and led the way back to a patio overlooking a private garden. Walker was clearly determined to demonstrate that Marcus didn't have the skills or the background for this job. But that was okay. He knew these surroundings. He'd grown up in a house a lot like this one.

Senators John Dobson and Dick Twitchell were waiting on the patio, posed under a rose trellis. Typical Mall rats, thought Marcus. His baby sister worked in the White House basement. He recognized the type. Even during the August recess, Washington was full of these office jocks, their waistlines maintained by visits to the congressional gym, their hairlines maintained by discreet stylists, their tans acquired on the golf course. On a ship, they would have been officers.

Or shark bait.

Marcus nodded politely as Ambassador Barnes introduced them. Dobson—it was his house—clearly wasn't expecting him. Neither man looked pleased. As they stepped forward to shake hands, Marcus saw the intimate round table behind them, set for three.

Well, hell. What was he supposed to do now? Eat in the kitchen with the maid? Or stand behind the ambassador's chair like a waiter or a damn footman?

Help came from an unexpected quarter.

"Lieutenant Evans is one of the heroes of the USS *Stoker*," Samantha Barnes said, threading her arm through his to draw him forward. He stiffened with surprise. But her breast was soft against his arm and she smelled good, better than the roses. "I was so pleased he could give me his escort today."

Okay, so she paid attention to the news. And either his part in the incident had received more media coverage than he'd thought, or she'd read some kind of dossier on him when he'd joined her security detail.

Either way, her explanation impressed the two Senators. They all stood around making patriotic noises while the maid hastily reset the table for four. Marcus felt like a bear at the zoo. Or a teenager at one of his parents' parties, forced into a rehash of Friday night's game.

It was better when they sat down. The government men pretty much concentrated on the ambassador and ignored him. Marcus took off his hat and set it on his knees. He wasn't going to wow anybody with his conversation. The best he could do was to keep his mouth shut and use the right fork.

It was hot, and his end of the table was out of the shade. The other men were in shirtsleeves. The ambassador slid out of her suit jacket, revealing white arms and pale cleavage showcased in some silky green top. Very hot. Marcus gulped his iced tea.

She kept talking as the maid cleared her full soup plate and replaced it with a cold lobster salad. Dobson and Twitchell paid close attention. That, or they were sneaking looks down the pretty green blouse.

"More than geographically, we need Delmonico as a bridge between the Balkans and the rest of Europe."

Twitchell swallowed noisily. "I don't like it. Any U.S. presence there is too damn close to that nutcase DeBruzkya in Rebelia."

Samantha leaned forward earnestly, giving Marcus an even better view of her breasts. "On the contrary. Not only would a close bilateral relationship between Delmonico and the United States help isolate Rebelia, but the country is strategically positioned to give us direct access from the Adriatic Sea to military targets. Delmonico could serve our interests in Eastern Europe as a platform for both diplomatic initiatives and military action.''

Twitchell stabbed a piece of lobster meat. ''We shouldn't be spending money and manpower propping up some two-bit former communist republic.''

Samantha Barnes pressed her lips together and then said, very pleasantly, ''We have to demonstrate our willingness to stand by our commitments.''

The senator shook his fork at her. ''Explain to me how sending American boys and girls into some foreign rat hole proves anything.''

Marcus put his napkin beside his plate. ''Maybe some of us like to put our money where our mouth is.''

The fork arrested in the air. ''What do you mean?''

Under the table, the ambassador pressed her foot down hard on Marcus's toe. ''I believe the lieutenant means the willingness of American men and women to stand in defense of democratic values ought to prove the importance of a politically neutral, professional military. Was that it, Lieutenant?''

Marcus grinned. Politically neutral, huh? ''Yeah.''

''Excellent point,'' said Dobson. ''Is anyone ready for dessert?''

Samantha slid the limo's privacy glass closed. Agent Walker in front would be annoyed, but it couldn't be helped. She had issues with the newest member of her security team, and she wouldn't embarrass him, or herself, by addressing them in front of an audience.

''We need to talk,'' she said.

Lieutenant Evans sat beside her, his long-fingered hands lightly balancing his hat on his knees, looking good enough to be on a navy recruiting poster. For the past year, she had closed herself off from everything but work, her feelings dulled, her senses deadened. But the lieutenant breached her safe, soft, stifling cocoon without even trying. The angles of his knees, the sheer size of his body, even the smell of him, hot male and uniform starch, encroached on her space.

"Yes, ma'am," he said politely.

She almost sighed. Did he have to be so gorgeous?

And so young. Practically young enough to be her— No, not her son, she decided in relief, studying the power of his chest and arms, the maturity in his eyes. But young and fit and healthy enough to make her feel old and tired.

"What you said today to Senator Twitchell..." She hesitated.

"He was the blowhard, right?"

She bit the inside of her cheek to keep from agreeing with him. "It was inappropriate. In future, I would prefer that you not express your opinions about the deployment of U.S. troops in Europe. You have no understanding of the intricacies involved."

He stiffened on the broad bench seat, but his tone was perfectly even. "With respect, ma'am, I may not know much about your job, but I do understand military service."

Of course he did.

"I'm not questioning your grasp of the military realities," Samantha said softly. "Only your grasp of the political ones."

He regarded her for a moment, his blue eyes bright in his tanned face. "Fair enough." He smiled. The impact knocked the air from her lungs. "Anything else?"

Samantha inhaled carefully. "There is one more thing. When we were saying farewell, why did you get between me and Senator Dobson?"

Marcus Evans shrugged. "He was too close. I didn't like the way he was crowding you."

Embarrassment washed her cheeks and flooded her stomach. She hadn't liked it, either. John Dobson had definitely taken advantage of the pretend intimacy of a political embrace to let his hands wander. But she hadn't thought anyone else had noticed. Much better, in her experience, for her not to notice, too.

"It was a little awkward," she admitted. "But it's less awkward if we simply ignore it. You need to be something of an invisible partner at these events, I'm afraid."

The lieutenant shook his head. "No."

She felt her jaw drop. "Excuse me?"

"You want me to keep my mouth shut, fine," he said. "But I'm supposed to be your bodyguard. And as long as I'm guarding your body, I'm not going to let some guy play grab ass with you."

He took her breath away. His blunt defense was completely unexpected. Totally unacceptable. Utterly disarming.

She firmed her lips. "I'm a diplomat, Lieutenant. I cover my own ass. Your job is to protect me from more serious threats."

He didn't even bother to answer her.

Two

The last person Marcus expected to see when he answered the door of his hotel room was Security Agent Thomas T. Walker.

Okay, the next-to-last person.

Dead last was Ambassador Babe, despite the fact that she'd shown up—naked and willing—in his dreams last night.

He wasn't even staying in her suite. The State Department had rented out the entire sixth floor of the hotel, and Marcus was quartered in a cramped and airless room by the service elevator and the ice machine. To guard access to the floor, Walker had told him.

Possible, Marcus thought. Or possibly Walker just wanted to stick him as far as he could get from the real work of protecting the ambassador.

Which was why he was so surprised when Walker banged on his door the next morning.

Marcus stood there, barefoot, in his skivvies, his hair sticking up from his head while the agent sneered.

"Interrupt your workout?" Walker drawled.

Actually, he'd been napping. But he figured that would only piss off Walker more.

A lot of people—even his fellow SEALs—assumed he must work out all the time. But he didn't have to. He'd always carried a lot of muscle. Good genes, he guessed, but since he was adopted it was only a guess.

He opened the door wider. "You want to come in?"

"No." Walker's dismissive gaze flicked over him again. "You need to change."

Marcus held on to his temper. "Okay."

"Aren't you going to ask why?" the agent prodded.

Marcus scooped up his shirt from the floor. "Because the ambassador's going out and needs an escort?"

"She's going shopping this morning, yes. But it will be the last time you go with her."

Son of a bitch. Walker knew something.

And he was looking forward to sharing it, or he would have just picked up the phone.

"Guess I'd better shave, then, too," Marcus said.

Walker scowled. "It won't help. Jerry Baxter from DS called. He wants to see you in his office this afternoon at three o'clock."

"Who's Jerry Baxter?"

"Special Agent in Charge Baxter is coordinating the effort to protect Ambassador Barnes."

The boss, in other words. Walker's CO.

Marcus threw his dress pants on the bed. "And he wants to see me because…?"

"Can't you guess?"

Well, yeah, he could. Obviously, his off-color comment had bothered Samantha Barnes more than she'd let on.

He was oddly disappointed. First, because he'd misjudged her. He'd thought she had the guts and the honesty to confront him herself. And second, because it seemed likely he wouldn't be seeing her after this morning.

There was a lot about this assignment Marcus wasn't crazy about. Samantha Barnes was so brainy she scared him. So determined, she was no picnic to protect. So out of his league in every way that his attraction to her made him uncomfortable. But he hated that he'd screwed up. And he really hated that he'd screwed up so badly he wasn't going to get another chance to prove himself.

Not to mention he was going to miss that body.

"Did she say anything to you? The ambassador?"

Walker snorted. "She didn't have to. It's obvious to all of us you don't belong here."

Obvious, huh? Well, what did he expect? Wasn't that the story of his life? He didn't belong much of anywhere.

Except in the Teams. Whatever else happened, he was a U.S. Navy SEAL.

He reached for his uniform pants and began to dress.

She really needed to get out more, Samantha thought, studying her reflection in the boutique's dressing room mirror. Her cheeks were pink. Her eyes were bright. It was embarrassing.

There was no way any thinking thirty-six-year-old professional should be as excited over a simple shopping trip as a fifth-grade girl buying her first lipstick. Since Stan's appointment, and even more since his death, the right clothes were simply part of her existence, as necessary to living as the food she put into her mouth, as essential to her work as multiple phone lines or the current tariff figures.

But there was no denying she was actually enjoying buying a dress for dinner at the White House on Friday night.

Well, it was the White House, she thought in excuse, turning to inspect her profile in the coffee-colored silk dress. Dinner with the president was a big deal. She would see her old school buddy Matt Tynan again, too—who, newly engaged or not, had always had an eye for a well-dressed woman.

She faced the mirror again. Maybe she could forgive herself a flutter of purely feminine excitement. She sucked in her breath and her stomach and stepped out of the dressing room.

Lieutenant Evans stood facing the racks of dresses, big

and solid and about as out of place among the ladies' after-five gowns as a tank in a tea shop. From this angle Samantha could look into the mirror behind him, one of those large three-fold mirrors that let you see how bad you really looked from all angles. The long silver panes captured his image and repeated it, throwing the light back on itself, throwing his reflection back on itself, the broad shoulders, the straight back duplicated a hundred hundred times until he made up an army, a one-man army all in white and pledged to her protection. *Magic*.

She must have made some sound, or maybe he saw her, too, because he turned. His gaze met hers. His eyes were hot.

The flutter of excitement she felt this time was almost certainly unforgivable.

Panic struck. The man was assigned to guard her, for goodness sake. She couldn't possibly be attracted to him. It was fraternization or sexual harassment or something.

Anyway, he was much too young. Stan—dear, perfect-for-her Stan—had been a healthy, vigorous fifty-two. This boy couldn't be thirty.

He grinned at her and her insides turned to mush.

"How come you always wear such dark colors?"

It was so different from what she expected, so unlike what anyone else would say to her, that she blinked.

"It's not dark," she protested.

"Brown?"

"Coffee," she said firmly.

He shrugged. "Looks brown to me. They're all dark."

She couldn't believe she was letting herself be drawn into a fashion argument with Captain America. "I tried on a green dress, too."

"*Dark* green."

He was right. Damn it. She raised her chin defensively. "Celeste told me I looked nice."

Celeste was the boutique manager, pencil thin, pencil straight, with improbably black hair and a face that looked as if she'd just stepped away from the Elizabeth Arden makeup counter.

"Was she the skinny one?" Evans asked. "In black?"

"She was the woman helping me, yes."

He shrugged. "Well, there you go. She's female. And she doesn't like colors."

Samantha was not, absolutely not, going to ask him what being female had to do with it. It was too much like flirting. But she said, "And what do you think I should wear? Red?"

"Why not?"

"Well, aside from the fact that it would be a disaster with my hair, the first lady is likely to be in red."

"Okay." He jerked his thumb toward the racks. "How about that?"

She looked and felt a purely acquisitive catch in her chest. "That" was a shimmering confection of ice-blue silk sewn all over with seed pearls and tiny crystals, bias cut, form fitting and strapless. A dress for a queen. A dress for a goddess. At the very least, a dress for a woman who spent her spare time doing toning exercises at the gym, not reading environmental impact studies on lead production along the Tangris River.

Samantha exhaled. "I don't think so."

"Why not?" he asked again, his blue eyes wide. "It's pretty."

Could he honestly be that complimentary? That clueless?

She sighed. Ultimately, she supposed, it was less humiliating to agree than to explain to her hunky young bodyguard that she could not possibly dine at the White House in a spangled sausage casing.

She unhooked it from the rack. "It won't fit."

But it did.

Alone in her dressing room, Samantha turned slowly in front of the mirror. The style was quite modest, really. Even flattering. As long as she didn't eat too much, which wasn't a problem these days. Or breathe too deeply. She was surprised to see her lips curve in the mirror.

Well, smiling or not, she wasn't going out there to model. Lieutenant Evans was a bodyguard, not a fashion consultant. She'd already involved him more than was appropriate. Worse, she'd enjoyed it.

She stripped off the dress with penitential roughness and went in search of Celeste.

"You didn't like it," Evans said as she approached.

Samantha was surprised he even saw her. While she conferred with Celeste, he had moved closer to the store's entrance, scanning the doors and aisles, watching for…what?

"No, I did like it,' she said honestly. "I bought it."

He turned his head, a question in his eyes. *Then why aren't you wearing it? Why not let me see you?*

But he didn't ask, and that was good, because she didn't have an answer for him.

It was simply too embarrassing to say, "I wanted you to see me in that dress. I wanted to see myself in your eyes, and that's why I didn't wear it out here."

He was too young for her.

Or she was too old. Too old and too aware of her position and still grieving for her husband.

But she'd bought the dress, anyway.

She held it out to him, a plastic bag on a padded hanger with the store name emblazoned in silver across the front. She wasn't sure if she was putting him in his place or offering him a kind of consolation prize.

"Would you mind carrying it for me?"

He shook his head briefly. "Not what I'm here for."

And that, she thought, put her in *her* place.

"Of course," she said stiffly. "I understand."

He grinned. "I don't think so. I mean, it's *really* not what I'm here for. I've been watching Walker. He always keeps both hands free when he's on duty. So he can react to protect you."

She blinked. "Oh. Well, that's very—"

Scary, she thought.

"—professional of you," she said.

He smiled again, but his blue eyes were watchful. "Thanks. Does that mean I'm not in trouble anymore?"

"In trouble? What kind of trouble?"

"With you. With DS." When she continued to stare at him blankly, he prompted her. "This afternoon's little visit to see Baxter?"

"I don't know what you're talking about."

He raised his dark eyebrows. "You didn't complain about the grab-ass comment?"

"I…" Her cheeks heated. "No, I told you, I can take care of that kind of thing myself."

"Interesting."

She frowned. "Is there a problem? Can I help?"

Marcus felt some of the stiffness leave his shoulders, some of the resentment leave his gut. She looked so cute, her full lips pouted and her eyes dark with concern.

Politicians made good liars, he reminded himself.

Still, he was inclined to believe her when she said she hadn't complained. Which made his summons to DS even more of a puzzle. What the hell was going on?

Special Agent in Charge Jerry Baxter was a sharp-eyed, middle-aged man in a dark suit with a white shirt and narrow tie, like one of the bad guys in *The Matrix*. He had a big office in the same block as the Federal Building and a wide smile. Maybe the office accounted for the smile. Maybe it was the other way around. Either way, he was pretty damn chummy for a guy who had called Marcus in to chew him out.

Baxter settled back in his chair. "I'm sure you've been wondering what's going on."

Hell, yeah.

"Yes, sir," Marcus said politely.

"You know, of course, that this administration credits Samantha Barnes with negotiating the Delmonico Accord after her husband's death."

She was a widow. He remembered that. He wondered how long ago her husband had died.

"Yes, sir."

"General DeBruzkya in Rebelia wants the accord set aside. He's been laundering money and running terrorist operations through Delmonico for years. And there are factions here and in Delmonico itself who have profited from his activities. They don't want pro-Europe, pro-U.S. policies in place any more than he does."

Marcus nodded.

Baxter leaned across his desk. "We've received reports that Ambassador Barnes is a target of both the Rebelian Secret Service and this criminal element within Delmonico."

"Why?" Marcus asked. "The accord has been ratified. Killing Barnes isn't going to change the Delmonican government's foreign policy."

"It could. Ambassador Barnes secured that treaty on the basis of her personal relationships with the president of Delmonico and his cabinet. Her death would certainly impact their commitment to the process. It could scare them into revisiting certain provisions in the treaty. And it would eliminate an effective symbol of U.S.-Delmonico cooperation."

Marcus sat very still. Baxter meant Samantha. She was

his "symbol." There were very real bad guys out there who wanted Samantha seriously dead.

"What's your office doing to stop them?" Marcus asked.

"We have, of course, stepped up embassy security in Delmonico. And we've assigned you and Agent Walker to the ambassador's protection while she's here in Washington. However…" Baxter paused significantly "…recent intelligence suggests those measures are not enough."

Marcus's gut cramped hard. "Why not?"

Why the hell weren't they doing everything they possibly could to protect her?

Baxter's eyes fell to his desk blotter. He moved a paper clip a fraction of an inch to the right. "Because along with those reports, we have received evidence of a security leak in our own office."

Marcus inhaled. "What kind of a leak? Sir," he added respectfully. He didn't want to risk pissing off the DS man and shutting him up.

"A big leak. A human leak." Baxter looked up, his gaze straight and his voice regretful. "A mole."

"Walker?"

If Walker was working for the other side, it would certainly explain his antagonism.

Baxter shook his head. "We don't know."

"Why not arrest him and find out?"

"Because we don't know," Baxter said. "We can't risk any moves until we understand the scope of their operation. We need to leave Walker in place while we investigate."

Anger flared, quick and hot. "Even if it means putting the ambassador's life at risk?"

"No. Plans are being made to safeguard the ambassador while we proceed with our investigation."

Okay. Just because Baxter buffed his nails and styled his hair was not a reason to mistrust him. But something about this didn't feel right.

"What kind of plans?"

"Samantha Barnes will be extracted to a safe house by a trusted operative. No one will know her location but the operative and myself until the agents involved in the plot against her have been identified and apprehended."

"Extracted?" Marcus repeated.

"For her own safety. Yes."

"And the operative?"

But Marcus already knew. He *knew*. Why else assign him to her detail in the first place? What else was he doing here?

"You," Baxter confirmed. "Your affiliation outside the bureau makes you the only one I can trust."

"You could say the same thing about any man on the Teams. Why not assign a squad to protect her? She'd be safer."

"Maybe. Maybe not. We don't know how widespread our problem is. Or how high up it goes."

"So how do you find out?"

"You don't need to know that. It's my job to coordinate the investigation, Lieutenant. It's yours to protect the ambassador." He smiled thinly. "We could say you are her Hector."

Who the hell was this Hector dude?

"Like the nursery rhyme," Baxter said, apparently responding to Marcus's blank face. "'Hector Protector.' Do you know it?"

"No."

Baxter cleared his throat and recited softly, "Hector Protector was dressed all in green. Hector Protector was sent to the queen. The queen did not like him, no more did the king; so Hector Protector was sent back again."

Whoa. Marcus had a brief moment of total disorientation. Was he nuts? Or was Baxter out of his mind? Somebody was trying to kill Samantha Barnes, and this guy was quoting Mother Goose. He was saying something else, too, about complete secrecy and utmost trust, yada yada, et cetera et cetera, the usual administrative bull.

Marcus tried to concentrate, but Baxter had momentarily lost him with that little side trip down Muffin Lane.

"—imperative that we maintain secure communication," Baxter said.

Okay. He was making sense again. Marcus straightened in his chair.

"So how will I get in touch with you?" he asked.

Baxter looked pleased. Why, Marcus had no idea.

"You don't," the security officer said. "It's too risky. We'll be using this." He set a slim laptop on the desk between them. "Each day you'll turn on this computer and log on to a secure Web site. Your user identity is *Hector*. *Protector* is your password. Quite simple."

Quite stupid, Marcus thought, but at least Baxter's Mother Goose moment made sense now. Sort of.

"And what will I do after I log on to this Web site?"

"Nothing. Watch. It will look like a children's game. If the activity on your screen hasn't changed from the previous day, that means there's no change, no progress, in the investigation. Once our perpetrators are caught, however, the children's game will vanish and you'll be directed to return with the ambassador to Washington."

"And she agreed to this?"

"She doesn't know about this. It will be your job to tell her." Baxter put his finger on the paper clip and slid it another inch to the right. "After the two of you are away."

Marcus's stomach sank. "Tell her. Tell her what?"

"Whatever you feel is necessary to ensure her cooperation."

Ah, hell. He'd rather crawl back into the steaming, sparking belly of the *Stoker* than face the ambassador with the news that she'd just been kidnapped for her own good.

But Baxter was counting on him.

Samantha Barnes, though she didn't know it, depended on him.

And Marcus had never in his life let his team down in the fourth quarter.

He looked from the computer lying flat on the desk to Baxter's watchful, waiting eyes. ''When do we do it?''

Three

Lieutenant Evans was upset.

Samantha stole another look at his hard profile in the back seat of the limo. At least, she thought he was upset. It was hard to tell beneath that stoic he-man front and the officer-and-a-gentleman polish. Maybe it was the tension around his usually smiling mouth. Maybe it was the strain in his clear blue eyes.

Frankly, she wasn't sure what she had noticed or why she should care. She'd spent the past year with her senses wrapped in cotton batting. She rather resented Evans's ability to poke through her absorption. He certainly wasn't letting it—whatever it was—get in the way of his doing his job.

She straightened against the Towncar's leather seat. And she wasn't about to let it get in the way of her doing hers.

Tonight she had an intimate dinner for forty at the embassy of Holzberg, Delmonico's eastern neighbor. The Holzberg ambassador was determined to impress upon her the pride and independence of his tiny coastal nation. Samantha was equally committed to communicating that unless Holzberg strengthened its ties to the U.S., it was vulnerable to General DeBruzkya's military buildup in Rebelia.

She had the peace of Eastern Europe to worry about. She couldn't waste time brooding over her hunky bodyguard's moods.

Barred light from the streetlamps slid over his large, square knee.

Anyway, she couldn't ask Evans what was bothering him. Agent Walker and the driver were listening from the front seat. She wouldn't slide the privacy glass closed again. Not in the intimacy created by the spangled night and the cool, dark interior of the car. Not with Walker watching in the rearview mirror.

The limo rolled to the curb of the Holzberg Embassy. The lit steps teemed with red-jacketed wait staff and dark-suited security personnel. Walker sprang to the sidewalk. Evans followed more slowly. He handed her out of the car, his touch firm and impersonal, his mouth a tight line.

She wondered if he'd been injured somehow in the attack on the *Stoker* and if his secret wound caused him pain. She wondered if his afternoon meeting at Diplomatic Security had gone badly. Or maybe he'd had a fight with his girl-friend. Did he have a girlfriend? Of course he did.

Mostly Samantha wondered if she were guilty of weav-ing a lot of silly, romantic fantasies around him because her social life was boring, her personal life empty and her sex life nonexistent.

Her heart shook. She closed her eyes.

"Ma'am?" Evans's voice broke into her thoughts.

Samantha opened her eyes and summoned a smile. "Thank you, Lieutenant Evans. Agent Walker."

Gathering her wrap around her, she went up the steps to the party alone.

She was getting away. He had to stop her. Now.

Marcus blinked, disoriented.

They were back at the hotel. It was late, and the ambas-sador was going to bed.

But he cleared his throat and said politely, "Ma'am, can I talk to you a minute?"

Samantha Barnes turned in the doorway of her sitting room, an expression of faint surprise on her face. Marcus figured she was searching for a nice way to tell him to buzz off.

Beside the ambassador, Walker scowled.

But Samantha, after that one, brief moment of hesitation, smiled at Marcus warmly and— Oh, wow. She had these deep, amazing dimples. Like a Kewpie doll.

"Of course," she said. "Would you like a cup of coffee?"

"Yes, ma'am. Thank you."

Walker looked ready to spit nails. Marcus gave him a smug look—yeah, you're not invited—as he sauntered past him and into the ambassador's private rooms.

She'd been living at the hotel for a little over a week, and except for some sheet music on the piano and the papers stacked everywhere, Marcus had seen sailors' bunks with more personality. There were none of the girlie touches his sister scattered around. No shoes kicked off under a chair. No bright magazines on a table. No snapshots on her desk.

Maybe the ambassador kept a photo of the dead husband in the bedroom.

Maybe she'd invite Marcus in for a look.

Yeah, and maybe he needed to have his head examined.

She sank onto the velvet couch, her back straight and her hands still like a good horsewoman's. His family raised Thoroughbreds, so he recognized the pose. On the froufrou table in front of the couch, somebody had left her a tray with a thermal pot and a doily-lined plate of pastries and a single cup.

The ambassador lifted the pot. "How do you take your coffee?"

"That's your cup," he protested.

"I've just come from a very long dinner. I'm not hungry

or thirsty or in need of caffeine." She finished pouring and offered him the coffee. "Black?"

"I can drink it black. But when I can get it, I take it blond and sweet. Milk," he explained in response to her startled look. "Two sugars."

She dimpled and added both before handing him the saucer. He waited politely for her to choose a pastry. When she didn't, he helped himself to two.

For a minute, he let himself relax and enjoy the soft chair and the beautiful woman sitting opposite, her red hair glowing against her white throat and the green pillows of the couch. Enjoy the smells of coffee and perfume, and the crisp buttery pastry on his tongue. It sure beat bolting MREs in the cold water off the coast of Iraq.

"What can I do for you, Lieutenant?" she asked in her husky voice.

Oh, man. His lower body tightened. He could think of a lot of things he'd like her to do for him and to him, all of them inappropriate and some of them illegal in certain states.

But he wasn't going to screw this up by mentioning them. Waiting for her outside the embassy this evening, he'd had time to figure how to play this. Enough time to realize he couldn't protect the ambassador on his own, whatever Baxter said.

He wanted—needed—Jimmy Robinson.

"Well, ma'am, you know about my squad being aboard the *Stoker* when it hit that mine."

She nodded. "There was a detailed article in the *Post.* And the AP wire service picked up a photo of you—I believe it was you—on the deck as one of your men was being life-flighted out."

Hell. "That explains it," Marcus said.

"Explains what?"

"Why I got a bunch of phone calls from my family. I

don't keep up much with the news." As a covert operative, he knew how often the media got things wrong. "I couldn't figure out why my brother would call."

Samantha Barnes arched her brows. "You're not close?"

Close? No. Two years apart in age, light-years away in temperament. Marcus couldn't remember a thing before the age of ten, when the Evanses had adopted him. But it sure felt like he'd spent his whole childhood trying to crawl out of the shadow cast by the shining example of the Evanses firstborn son.

"We each go our own way." He grinned. "And our sister, Honey, goes a little further. She sent me a singing telegram over the wireless Internet on board. The communications officer screened it and the next thing I knew everybody on the ship was ribbing me about it."

"A singing telegram sounds harmless."

"A naked singing telegram," he said, feeling his face get hot. "Some stripper in a nurse's uniform."

The ambassador's cheek indented like she was trying not to laugh. "Your sister must have been worried about you."

He shrugged. He never thought about it. It was his job to worry about Honey, not the other way around. "I guess. Anyway, that's not what I wanted to talk to you about."

Ambassador Barnes didn't try to prompt him with questions. She sat there, her hands clasped in her lap and her deep-blue eyes fixed on his face. Wow. Someone who was actually ready to let him talk in his own way and his own time.

"The thing is… That guy in the chopper pictures—the one being lifted out—is my XO. Executive officer," he added, in case she didn't know the lingo.

She nodded, still not interrupting.

"Both his legs got smashed in the explosion. He's in Bethesda now. I'd like to go see him."

"Of course," she said promptly. "Tomorrow? I can arrange—"

He took a deep breath. "Actually, ma'am, I was hoping you could come with me. To...to cheer him up."

Her eyes narrowed, but her voice was still warm and sympathetic. "You think a visit from me would cheer your friend up?"

Okay, he had to be careful here. Ambassador Barnes was no dummy. The only things that were going to make Jimmy feel better were class one narcotics or a clean bill of health, and Samantha Barnes looked like she knew it.

Marcus shrugged. "It might. Anyway, it would sure make me happier."

Her full lips curved. Her eyes were as warm as the seas off the coast of Venezuela. "Then I guess I'd better come."

Looking into those blue eyes made Marcus feel very good and really bad at the same time. Because she was being nice to him, and he was lying to her.

For her own good, he reminded himself. He couldn't leave her alone with Walker. He still didn't know if the DS agent could be trusted. The only way Marcus could guarantee Samantha Barnes's safety was to keep her with him. So in that sense, bringing her along would definitely make him happier.

Happy, and guilty as hell.

Philip looked at Samantha as if she'd just suggested "Do You Really Want to Hurt Me?" as the high school prom theme. "What's the point of visiting some laid-up sailor if you're not even going to let me arrange for a photographer to be present?"

"The point is this sailor was laid up in the service of our country." Samantha spoke gently, but she saw her secretary flush. "And for some reason he wants to see me. Or maybe it's just that his friend wants me to see him. In either case, his sacrifice is worth at least a little of my time."

"Your schedule is already packed."

Her schedule was always packed. It helped to fill the general emptiness she'd felt since Stan died. But for the first time in a long time, Samantha wanted to do something that wasn't on the schedule. Something unplanned. Something spontaneous.

"Philip, it's August in D.C. It's stinking hot. Everyone who can afford to be anywhere else has already left the city. Surely I can take an hour or two to make a sick call."

He raised both hands in surrender. "Fine. But let me send a photographer. He could take a really nice souvenir photo for the guy."

Samantha smiled and shook her head. "If he wants a souvenir, I'll sign his cast, all right? I'm not exploiting his injury."

"And if he's exploiting you?"

"How would he be doing that?"

"What if he wants special treatment or something?"

"He's in Bethesda, Philip. It's the national naval hospital. They treat the president. You don't get treatment more special than that."

"Not the patient. Evans. I think he wants something," Philip said.

Maybe he did. The shocking thing was, Samantha couldn't bring herself to mind.

"Then I'll find out what it is," she said.

"Ma'am, are you sure you're not..." Philip hesitated, but Samantha knew what he wanted to say.

Flirting with scandal?

Risking your objectivity?

Losing your mind?

Possibly, she admitted. Probably. She couldn't deny she was looking forward to a sunny afternoon spent with her young, hot escort. But it wasn't as if they were sneaking away for a few hours of sweaty sex. They were visiting his wounded friend in a military hospital. Perfectly commendable. Totally innocent.

"I'm fine, Philip," she assured her secretary. Assured herself. "Everything is fine."

Because anything improper between her and Lieutenant Hottie was completely out of the question.

Wasn't it?

Marcus knew the exact moment when the ambassador spotted him waiting by the car. She sucked in her breath. Her eyes widened. For one stupid second, he thought maybe she was actually glad to see him.

But then she blurted, "You're not in uniform."

Behind her, Walker smirked.

Bite me, Marcus thought.

He glanced down at his clean T-shirt and jeans and up into her pretty-as-a-princess face. "I figured I wasn't exactly on duty today," he drawled. "But I can go put on the ice cream suit if you don't want to be seen with me like this."

"Oh, no." Samantha Barnes's cheeks turned pink. "I only meant... I feel overdressed now."

She was wearing another of those blazers that didn't do a whole lot to hide her breasts, and a skirt that revealed her amazing legs to a couple of inches above the knee.

Overdressed? Oh, yeah. He'd like nothing better than to slip her out of that jacket. To peel her out of that skirt. To get his hands on all that white, smooth skin and—

Walker was still watching jealously from the hotel curb.

Marcus cleared his throat. "You look fine to me." He opened the door of the limo. "Better get in the car. You're a target standing here."

Obediently, she bent to get in the back seat, and all his fantasies twitched to life.

Walker pushed forward, rigid with irritation and importance. "The ambassador shouldn't leave the hotel without a full security detail."

Marcus raised both eyebrows, distracted from the ambassador's smooth, round rear end. "You're not coming?"

"I didn't think it was necessary," Samantha said from inside the limo. "Since 9/11, security at Bethesda is extremely tight."

Tight was good, Marcus thought, the vision of her lush rear still burning the back of his eyeballs.

"Assuming you get there," Walker said darkly.

Marcus leveled a look at him over the top of the open door. "She'll get there. Hell, it's not like the Rebelian Secret Service knows where she's going."

"Unless they're watching," Walker said.

Or you tell them, Marcus thought. Damn, damn, damn.

He opened the car door wider. "Fine. You want to join us?"

Walker stalked around the front of the limo. "Yeah. I do."

He got in beside the driver and slammed his door.

Marcus lowered himself to the seat next to the ambassador and slammed his door, too.

She waited until the limo was underway before she leaned forward and slid the privacy glass shut. "Do you mind telling me what that was about?"

Well, hell. Marcus couldn't exactly explain to her that the two men charged with her protection didn't trust each other to keep her safe, now, could he?

It will be your job to tell her, Baxter had said. *After the two of you are away.*

Marcus rubbed his face with his hand. "We're just pissing on trees. Marking our territory," he explained when she looked confused. "Walker resents me being pulled in on his job, and I don't like him horning in on my date."

She laughed. She had the greatest laugh, kind of throaty, very Kathleen Turner. "This is hardly a date."

"Well, no," he agreed, straight-faced. "Not *now*. Not with James and J. Edgar Hoover sitting in the front seat."

She dimpled. "The driver's name is Eric."

Marcus liked that she knew, that she cared enough to find out the driver's name. But then she stiffened up and said, "Anyway, we wouldn't be dating in any case."

So, okay, she wasn't flinging herself at him yet. Under the circumstances, that was probably a good thing. He couldn't be distracted from the business of protecting her. And if the two of them were going to be holed up alone together for days in a safe house, sharing meals and a bathroom and— Oh, man. He had to lose that thought.

But curiosity and ego drove him to ask anyway. "Why not?"

She blinked. "Well, I'm… For starters, I'm too old for you."

"How old?"

"I don't think—"

"Come on," he coaxed. His mother would have disapproved, but he really wanted to know. "How old?"

"Thirty-six," she said, as if it was sixty-three and she was Madeleine "Granny" Albright.

He would have guessed she was a couple of years younger. Still…

"I'm thirty-three," he said.

Her pretty mouth dropped open. "You can't be."

He didn't know whether to be flattered or insulted by her surprise. "Sure I can. I'm getting up there for active duty, but—"

"Why do you do it?"

He shifted, uncomfortable now that the conversation had

turned to him. He hated having to explain himself. He wasn't any good at it. The first day of school had always been hell.

Yes, ma'am, I'm adopted.

No, ma'am, I can't remember my teacher from kindergarten. Or my birth parents. Or my real name.

Only in the SEALs it didn't matter. In the Teams he was judged by what he could do and not where he came from.

He shrugged. "I'm still in good shape."

"Yes." Her gaze flicked over him and down. He could feel himself swell—his head, his chest, everywhere.

Down, boy.

"So I can get the job done."

She bit her lip. Was she smiling? "I'm sure. But I didn't ask how you could do it. I asked why."

"Somebody's got to. Protect the planet. Defend truth, justice and the American way." It was a joke he used to share with Jimmy.

This time Samantha Barnes definitely smiled. She also shook her head. "There has to be more to it than that. Was your father in the military?"

"Father and brother," he admitted. His adoptive father. His adoptive brother. The armchair warrior and the fly boy.

"Navy?" she guessed.

He looked at the car window. "Yeah."

"SEALs?"

Damn. When had they started playing twenty questions?

"No, that was my big idea. The SEALs—Sea, Air and Land Teams—are the elite. Only the best of the best even apply. You've got to survive six months of some of the toughest military training in the world to make it. Ninety percent of some classes drop out. And that's just the beginning. If you do make it, you've got to be prepared to go places nobody else will go, to tackle missions nobody else can do."

"And why do you?"

"Why does anybody do anything? Because I can. Because I'm good at it. Same reasons you're an ambassador, I bet."

"Actually, I inherited my position from my husband. I'm continuing his work."

It was a good line. He wondered if she'd repeated it so often she believed it. He didn't. He'd seen her in action.

He grinned. "Nope. You do it because you get a kick out of it. Same as me."

She lifted her chin and glared at him like there was something wrong with her enjoying her job. With loving it. With wanting it. Or maybe there was just something wrong with him commenting on it.

"It's not the same at all," she said crossly.

It was kind of cool he could make her mad like that.

"Truth, justice and the American way, baby."

"Yes, but I don't get shot at," she said.

And just like that, his enjoyment died.

I don't get shot at.

She had no idea.

Four

"It's not that I don't appreciate the view," James Robinson said from his wheelchair. "Because that much of me is working fine, thank you, Jesus. But why did you bring her with you?"

The two men were on the hospital terrace, watching Samantha wander the flat, grassy rectangle below—her round, tempting figure; her neat, dark suit; her red hair blazing in the sunlight. She'd slipped down the steps a few minutes ago. To explore the gardens, she'd said, but Marcus knew it was an excuse to let him talk with Jimmy.

He was grateful for her tact. And determined to take advantage of her absence.

"I can't leave her alone," he said.

Jimmy pursed his lips. "That's not like you."

Heat crept into Marcus's cheeks. He was glad he was standing behind the wheelchair so his buddy couldn't read his face. "No, I mean I *can't* leave her alone. I've got to protect her."

"Well, you brought her to the right place, then. There are enough deck apes around to hold off a full scale attack."

"Yeah." Marcus stared glumly out at the sunlit lawn. Samantha was inspecting a boring green bush like it was part of the White House rose garden. "The problem is after we leave."

"The hotel?"

"Hotel security's fine. But I may have to move her."

"Where?"

"I can't tell you."

"Okay. Why?"

Marcus's hands tightened on the back of the wheelchair. "I can't tell you that, either."

Jimmy didn't protest, as he had a right to, that Marcus could tell him anything. Could trust him with everything, including his life. "What do you need, Lieutenant?"

"Let's take a hypothetical situation," Marcus said.

"Hoo yah."

"Say you were guarding somebody. Hypothetically."

Jimmy gestured to the casts on both legs. "Have to be hypothetical."

Marcus grinned. "Yeah. So you're protecting her against assorted bad guys—spooks, T's—and the situation is complicated because there may be somebody higher up among the good guys who wants to see you fail. With me so far?"

"Spies, terrorists, traitors. Got it."

"Anyway, you get orders to extract her to a safe house. Only you're thinking, if there really is a security leak somewhere, how do you know this house is safe?"

"You don't," Jimmy said promptly. "You have to take her someplace they don't know about."

Marcus nodded. "That's what I thought. But if you were this hypothetical bodyguard and you had a real friend, someone you could trust, whose family used to have a place somewhere close by—"

"—like Virginia."

"But still out of the way—"

"—like a farm."

"And deserted—"

"—since his parents had retired, which you knew, since you helped the friend move them down to Florida a couple years ago."

Marcus smiled and a fraction of the tension left his

shoulders. "Yeah. Well, anyway, you might ask this friend if you could hole up there for a couple days or weeks or whatever."

"You need a key?" Jimmy asked simply.

Gratitude eased Marcus's grip on the wheelchair. "No. I don't want you implicated. Better for you if I break in. If they come after you—"

But Jimmy shook his head. "Not going to happen. Place has been empty for two years now. Nobody outside the family even remembers it. And it was in my mother's family, so my name isn't even connected with the place on the tax rolls."

"What about utilities?"

"There's a well. And if the wiring still works, there's a backup generator in the barn. But it's a dump. You've got water and electricity and not much else."

"How about a car on blocks in the front yard?"

"You need wheels?"

Marcus grinned. "Unless you think we should take a cab."

"Funny, Clark. Why don't you just tuck her under your arm and fly?"

The idea had real appeal. Except he didn't want her under his arm, exactly. He watched her cross the grass in her tight navy skirt and two-inch heels, and he just wanted her. Under him. Moving with him, stretching, soaring. Flying.

Jimmy cleared his throat. "Earth to Superman."

Marcus flushed. Oh, man. What was he thinking? What was he saying?

"Actually, I, uh, bought a car. Through the paper. Paid cash, haven't registered the title. But I need somebody to pick it up."

"And leave it where?"

Marcus felt the usual appreciation for his swim buddy's

quick understanding. ''Dunn Loring Metro Station. The far back corner of the commuter parking lot.''

''When?''

''Friday. This Friday.''

Jimmy rubbed his jaw. ''I can't drive. But Garcia would do it. Or Buzz.''

Marcus weighed both possibilities. The squad was currently stationed at the Naval Amphibious Base in Little Creek, Virginia, about three hours away. Buzz would throw himself into action without thought or hesitation. But Garcia was the squad's weapons specialist. And he'd keep his mouth shut.

''Garcia,'' Marcus decided. He slid a blank envelope from his back pocket and held it folded against his palm. ''Here's the key. Tell him to leave it under the mat. And I've got a list here of some things I'll need that I can't get myself.''

Jimmy raised his brows. ''Are we talking the kind of things that money can't buy?''

''There's money in there, too,'' Marcus said. ''If he needs it.''

''Hoo yah, Lieutenant.'' Jimmy extended his hand.

Marcus took it. And when he released his grip, Jimmy closed his fingers carefully over the envelope.

Samantha's eyes misted as she watched them clasp hands, the tall, muscled warrior and the slight black man in the wheelchair. There was something so sweet about that simple gesture.

No, *sweet* was the wrong word. Moving, maybe. In the cloaked and compromised world she lived in, where a handshake could hide or disguise a man's true intent, there was something deeply moving about the honest affection and absolute trust that flowed between Marcus and his wounded comrade.

She started up the steps toward them. Marcus looked over and saw her. Just for a second, some subtle alteration in him—a shift of gaze? a change in posture?—made her hesitate.

But then he smiled, and her quick discomfort evaporated. "All set?" he asked.

"Only if you are," she said, smiling back.

"What do you think, Jimmy? Are we set?"

The two men exchanged glances. Once again, Samantha had the oddest sense of…something. She was being excluded.

And what in heaven's name was wrong with that? They were shipmates, after all. Friends.

"Yeah, we're set," the skinny XO said. He turned his head toward Samantha. "Appreciate your coming by, ma'am."

"My pleasure," she said, and meant it. "Can we take you back to your room?"

"No, I think I'll stay out here a while and enjoy the sun."

Marcus touched his shoulder briefly. "Take it easy, Jimmy."

"Take care, Clark."

Samantha waited until they were walking down the blue-and-white hallway before she asked, "Clark?"

Did she imagine it, or did Marcus color under his tan?

"It's a nickname. A lot of guys get handles in BUD/S training—that's Basic Underwater Demolition/SEALs."

"Your friend didn't," she pointed out.

"Yeah, he did."

"'Jimmy'? That's not a handle."

Marcus cleared his throat. Definitely embarrassed. She was charmed. "Jimmy for Jimmy Olsen. The little reporter guy who hung with Lois Lane and Clark Kent?"

"And you're Clark. Oh!" She got it now. "Superman."

Black hair, blue eyes, chiseled jaw, muscled body...
Mischief crept into her voice. "It suits you."

"Don't start with me," he warned.

Oh, she was enjoying this. "Are you faster than a speeding bullet, too?"

He slanted a look down at her. "Are you asking to see
my moves, Ambassador?"

Now she was the one whose cheeks got hot. Hurriedly,
she asked, "So you've been friends since training?"

His eyes gleamed, but he allowed her retreat. "More than
friends. Swim buddies. The instructors at Coronado paired
us together our third week of BUD/S."

They made an unlikely couple, she thought. Almost as
unlikely as— But she didn't allow herself to finish that
thought.

"Why so late? Or wasn't that late?"

He shrugged. "Halfway through the course. Normally
boat teams are created by height to equalize the weight of
the boat. You get a couple of tall trainees, they can end up
carrying the whole thing while the short guys slack off.
Anyway, when we started BUD/S, Jimmy was on the Smurf
team, and I was leading boat team two."

He opened a glass door for her, and she thanked him and
walked through.

"Our class had a lot of DORs—trainees Dropped On
Request," he explained. "Usually a third will make it all
the way. We were down to half that. All the Smurfs were
gone. The instructors had to shuffle the teams, and Jimmy
was assigned to my boat."

She smiled. "And you pulled him through."

"No. We pulled each other through. I dragged him
through some of the physical rotations, but he saved my
sorry butt a bunch of times."

It was hard to imagine this comic-book-hero-brought-to-life in need of rescue. And yet he had no reason to lie to her.

"Really," she said. "How?"

"Being a SEAL isn't all about being the fastest or the strongest. It's mental toughness, too." He looked right at her and admitted frankly, "I wouldn't have survived the classroom training without Jimmy. I wouldn't have been a SEAL."

Samantha met those clear blue eyes and got lost.

Marcus Evans wasn't anything like the cocksure career officer she was expecting: arrogant, aggressive, gung ho.

He wasn't like the cautious politicians she knew: educated, opinionated, pretentious.

He wasn't like her.

Samantha had graduated summa cum laude from Stanford University and earned her master's degree at the Harvard School of Diplomacy. She couldn't begin to relate to his problems in the classroom.

On the other hand, she understood lonely. And it was loneliness she saw in his eyes now. Saw and responded to.

She found her breath. Found her voice. "You must miss working with him very much," she said gently.

He broke eye contact. His jaw tightened. "More than you know," he said. "More than you can ever know."

She didn't look like a widow tonight.

Samantha drew a deep breath, making the beads sewn onto the ice-blue bodice of her Donatella Versace gown shimmer. She looked good. She felt good. She felt *alive*.

And when she swept into the outer room of her hotel suite to find Marcus Evans on his feet and waiting for her, her heart beat harder. Her breath came faster. The crystals on her dress twinkled a little more.

"I hope I didn't keep you waiting."

"That's okay. I'm—" He broke off and stared at her, heat in his eyes.

Warmth flooded her cheeks and pooled in her belly.

"You're what?" she prompted, hoping he would say "stunned" or "dazzled" or at least "impressed."

"—early." He grinned. "And I left the corsage at home, too."

"Oh." She smiled wryly at his prom reference. And at herself for thinking... For hoping... Well, anyway, what a good thing he'd made his little joke before she made a fool of herself.

"My corsage and your tuxedo," she said.

He wasn't in uniform tonight. He wore a dark suit with a dark T-shirt under it. *Miami Vice* noire. He must be hot, she thought, under that jacket.

"Yeah, since I'm filling in for Walker, I figured I should try to look the part."

For the first time she noticed they were alone. "Where *is* Agent Walker?"

"In his room. He got sick after lunch. He's either got a bug or he ate something that disagreed with him."

Her awkwardness dissolved in concern. "Is he all right?"

Marcus lifted one shoulder. "He feels like crap now, but he ought to be better by morning. If it's food poisoning, that is. You want me to contact DS, ask for a replacement?"

"Is that necessary?"

His eyes were bright blue and very intent. "Well, you've got me. But it's your call."

"I'm sure you're all I need." She bit her tongue. That hadn't come out at all the way she intended. "For tonight."

Oh, dear. Worse and worse.

But Marcus smiled at her. Her insides jittered. "I hope so," he said.

She cleared her throat delicately. "There's no point in embarrassing Agent Walker by requesting another agent."

"Nope." Marcus held the door for her.

"And we're going to the White House. I'll be surrounded by Secret Service all night."

Her shoulder brushed his arm. It was warm and very hard. He didn't say anything.

"It's not as if I'm in any real danger," she said.

His smile faded. "Yeah. You are."

His softly spoken warning shivered through her.

Samantha knew she was a target of both DeBruzkya and the criminal faction that profited from his regime. The Coalition, they called themselves. But it was hard to concentrate on the foreign general and his shadowy coconspirators when her mouth was dry and her heart was pounding from a very different threat.

Marcus Evans threatened her. He compromised her dignity. He jeopardized her composure. He assaulted her senses.

He followed her onto the elevator and she felt almost faint at how warm he was. How close. She was five foot eight and wearing heels, and he still dwarfed her. He was only an inch or two over six feet, but there was a lot of him packed onto those long, strong bones. A lot of strength. A lot of power. She was dizzy with his nearness, drunk on the scent of shaving cream and starch and skin. He smelled wonderful.

She wanted to turn her face into his jacket and inhale him.

Oh, dear Lord.

The mirrored elevator doors rolled shut. She closed her eyes so she wouldn't have to meet her own gaze in their reflection.

She couldn't possibly be developing a crush on her navy bodyguard. Yes, he was sweet and funny and conscientious and had a body to die for. Now that she knew his real age, he wasn't even too young for her. Three years wasn't that much.

But he was so not her type.

She moved among Washington's elite. She had always been attracted to men who were older. Educated, sophisticated, knowledgeable men. Powerful men. Men like Stan.

Maybe that was her problem. She was thirty-six years old and her husband had been dead for thirteen months. Maybe she simply missed being married, the intimacies of shaving lotion in the bathroom and please-pass-the-paper over the breakfast table, the warm body breathing in the bed beside her. She missed Stan.

Missed sex.

She opened her eyes, startled by the truth.

Oh, dear. Well, at least now that she'd admitted it to herself, she could begin dealing with it. And the way to deal with it was not to start sniffing men in elevators. No matter how good they—he—smelled.

She inhaled carefully and held her breath the rest of the way down.

But when they reached the lobby, Marcus was all-business. He didn't offer her his arm. He didn't guide her with a warm hand on her back. He walked five paces ahead of her, his head turning to scan the scattered couches, the uniformed attendants behind the registration desk and the guests in evening dress waiting on the hotel curb.

She appreciated his professionalism. Of course she did.

But when he shut her into the back of the limo and slid into the driver's seat, she frowned and leaned forward.

"Where's Eric tonight?"

Marcus turned his head. His face was shadowed by the roof of the car. All she could really see was the angle of his jaw and the jut of his nose. "He never showed. Maybe he caught the same bug as Walker."

She relaxed. Of course. "And how do *you* feel?" she asked, teasing.

His shoulder lifted. "I never get sick. Is it okay if I drive you?"

"Do you know the way?"

"I think I can find the White House. But if you want me to arrange for another driver—"

"No," she decided. "I don't want to be late."

"What time do you have to be there?"

"Dinner is at nine." It was only seven now. "But there are people, friends, I'd like to talk to."

"They expecting you?"

She wasn't used to having to account for herself. But it made sense, since Marcus was responsible for her security, that he would need to know her schedule.

"I'm sure I'll be seated with Matt at dinner." White House advisor Matt Tynan was an old friend and political ally. They'd attended the same high school, and Samantha had been delighted to renew the acquaintance years later. As two of the youngest movers and shakers on the D.C. scene, they tended to stick together. "But I'd like to arrive early. Once these things get started, it's too easy to miss friends in the crowd."

Marcus's dark profile went very still against the bright windshield. Her heart hitched foolishly. And then his teeth gleamed over his shoulder.

"Better roll, then."

He pulled the limo along the curving drive and edged into the street. She settled back against the soft leather.

She certainly had enough room tonight. Room and privacy. She felt as if her silk-clad, beaded butt would slide right off the seat next time they rounded a corner.

Amazing how accustomed she'd grown to Marcus's presence in just a few days. She rather missed his solid, reassuring bulk beside her. She felt…alone.

Which had to be the stupidest claim made in Washington since "I didn't inhale." She wasn't alone. She was never alone. She was surrounded by people all the time. Wait staff, secretarial staff, diplomatic staff, security staff, people who wanted recognition or recommendations, direction and advances.

She took a deep breath and let it out slowly. Okay, so those were all people who worked for her. It was natural for them to want a piece of her. But she knew plenty of other people, she thought bracingly. Other diplomats. Colleagues who valued her opinion, who wanted her help, her influence or her consent.

The thought made her tired.

But she had friends. Not women friends. For some reason she'd never had the knack of making women friends. She had no confidantes. No sisters.

But she had lots of male friends. Good friends, not just escorts. There was Ethan Williams, whom she'd dated briefly when she first arrived on the Washington scene. He'd likely be at the dinner tonight with his beautiful bride, Kelly. Samantha smiled. His beautiful, *younger* bride, Kelly.

And there was always Matt, unmarried Matt, her oldest and closest friend.

Who, now that Samantha thought about it, had just gotten himself engaged to *his* sweet, wholesome and much younger secretary, Carey. Which left his old, dear friend Samantha widowed and alone in the back of a limo, without a date for dinner at the White House.

Samantha bit her lip. Oh, dear. Now she was leaving stupid and moving rapidly into pathetic.

And while she was on the subject of the White House and moving, shouldn't they be there by now?

She glanced out the window. She never drove herself in the city, but...

"I don't think we should have gotten on the freeway," she said.

Marcus didn't turn his head. "It's okay. I wanted to use an alternate route. You know, in case anybody's going to make some kind of attempt on the way."

She sat back, only partially reassured. "Well, this is certainly an alternate. Didn't we pass the turnoff for the Kennedy Center?"

"Did we?"

"You know we—" She broke off as a new suspicion struck her. "Are you lost?"

"Hey. Don't you trust me?"

She smiled. "I'm not sure. Do you have a map up there?"

"Give me a minute. I can get us where we need to go."

Possibly.

Except it looked like they were entering Virginia. She squinted through the dark. She was sure that was... Yes, there was a sign for I-66. Even if they turned around right now, she wouldn't reach the White House until almost eight o'clock.

She regarded the line of his military-style haircut across his broad neck and the backs of his perfectly shaped ears. He was a warrior trained in infiltrating enemy lines and making his way through hostile territory. Could he really not negotiate traffic in the capital?

Samantha smiled to herself in the back seat. Apparently not.

After five more minutes spent watching the lights of the city fade away and the occasional streetlamp take their place, she spoke up. "Should we stop for directions?"

As if he would. Stan would never ask for directions.

But Marcus surprised her. He turned the limo into a public lot—she thought she glimpsed a Metro sign—and slowed.

"We'll stop here."

She peered doubtfully at the dim, deserted lot. Most of the commuters had already collected their cars and gone home. There was a line of vehicles pulled close to the platform and a few cars scattered at a distance. Maybe he intended to go up on the platform to ask for directions?

But he drove past the stairs and over the empty white lines to the far end of the lot. He parked beside a plain dark sedan.

Samantha looked for the driver, but there was no one in the front seat. No one in back. The first faint prickle of unease ran up her spine.

Marcus turned and addressed her over his shoulder. "We need to get out of the car."

To get directions?

"Why?" she asked.

"I can't leave you here alone," he explained patiently.

Well, no. And she trusted him. She ought to trust him. But...

"Maybe we should try someplace else," she said.

"We're here now." He took off his jacket, struggling a little in the confines of the front seat, and passed it through the open privacy window. "Put this on."

"I'm warm already."

"It'll help hide your dress in the dark. Put it on."

Why did that matter? Although he did keep insisting she was a target, she reminded herself.

Wordlessly, she slipped her arms into the sleeves. The silk lining was warm against her skin. The jacket smelled like him, like hot male and clean starch. She shivered in reaction.

"Okay." He sort of flowed out of the car. Samantha blinked. For a big man, he certainly could move quickly. He opened her door. "Let's go."

She swung her legs out and stood slowly. "Go where?"

"Listen— Oh, hell."

She flinched. "What?"

He turned his head, and she saw what he saw: a well-dressed, middle-aged couple strolling across the nearly empty lot to their Lexus parked a few rows away.

Samantha opened her mouth, still unsure what she would say. Hello, I'm Ambassador Barnes, can you give me a ride to the White House?

Marcus grabbed the lapels of his jacket and dragged her against him. Off balance in her heels, she stumbled into his chest. His broad, solid chest. His hard arms wrapped around her.

"Make this look good," he whispered hotly against her lips, and crushed his mouth to hers.

Five

She couldn't breathe.

She couldn't think.

Response was out of the question.

Samantha Barnes was simply not the sort of girl—*woman*—men grabbed. "Intimidating" was how one high school boy had described her. The description had stung at the time. Intimidating did not get you a date to the prom; who wanted to be intimidating when cute and sweet and pretty were so much more popular? But by the time she'd graduated from Stanford she'd prided herself it was true.

So it was surprise that hurtled her heart to her throat when Marcus grabbed her. It was shock that paralyzed her when he hauled her against him—he was huge and hard and hot—and ground his lips on hers. It was outrage—wasn't it?—that made her hands ball into fists and her blood roar along her veins like a train going into a tunnel.

She was almost positive it was outrage. It certainly wasn't fear. And she couldn't allow it to be anything else.

His mouth cruised from her lips to her cheek to the sensitive underside of her jaw, robbing her mind, stealing her breath, plundering her control. He filled her senses. His hair smelled clean. His skin smelled hot. His beard prickled the side of her face. His lips were warm.

Oh my goodness, oh my goodness, oh my.

She opened her mouth. To gasp? Or to protest? Marcus's finger touched her upper lip, rubbed her bottom one. His finger tasted like salt.

"Shh," he said against her throat, making the nerve ends there vibrate. "You could *try* helping."

It was so not what she was expecting that her jaw dropped.

"Why would I want to help?"

He raised his head and smiled. In the shadows cast by the security lights, his normally blue eyes were deep and dark.

"Because we want those nice people over there to get in their car and drive away. As long as we look like a couple necking in the parking lot, they won't come over. If we're lucky, they won't even stare too much."

"But—"

His arms hardened around her. "I think they need convincing," he said huskily, and her whole body tightened in response. "Let's try it again, okay?"

It was not okay. She was sure something was wrong, that he was wrong, that she should not be kissing her bodyguard. Kissing Marcus.

Her heart pounded. She was going to object. She was going to demand an explanation. She was going to insist he drive her to dinner at the White House.

He bent to her and the shape of his head blotted out the night sky behind him. Samantha felt dizzy. Yes, she was going to do all of those things.

Later.

She parted her lips again and he moved his mouth over hers, molding, tasting, possessing. Her tongue touched his shyly. His tongue thrust into her mouth. He was breathing faster. So was she.

She hadn't kissed a man like this since Stan died.

She had never kissed a man like this.

Dear Stan had been average: average build and average weight, middling tall and middle aged.

Marcus was distractingly large, disconcertingly hard, demandingly intent. He felt solid. Strong. Alive. His kisses were deep and fierce. He devoured her. And she locked her arms around his neck and held on, held tight, as if she could inhale him, as if she could consume him, as if she could absorb him through her skin, all his vitality and strength, and keep it to warm the cold and empty places inside her.

He made a sound low in his throat, crowding her against the car, and she moaned because he felt so good, real and hot against her.

Oh. Oh, my goodness.

How embarrassing.

She tried to stiffen, to pull away, but he only slid his big, warm hands down her back and grasped her behind, fitting her more firmly against him.

"That's good," he said encouragingly. His breath stirred her hair. "Very convincing."

Convincing?

Her face flooded with heat. She could feel him, thick and insistent, against her belly.

She needed control. If not of him, if not of the situation, then of herself. She couldn't just stand here throbbing like one big gland.

"Yeah…" She cleared her throat and tried again. "You can let go of me now."

He turned his head. She followed his gaze toward the departing car, the sweep of its headlights on the black asphalt lot, its beady red taillights as it pulled onto the road.

His hands lingered on her butt, weighing, caressing. She sucked in her breath. "Sure?"

No.

"Now," she said.

"Right." He gave her a final squeeze before his hands slid away. "Better get a move on."

Her thoughts struggled against the warm tide of desire. "Move on…to the White House?"

He hesitated.

She fought an eddy of apprehension. "I'm not going anywhere with you until you tell me what this is about."

There. That sounded firm. In control.

He shook his head. "No time. We've got maybe an hour before somebody notices you haven't shown up for that fancy dinner of yours, and after that I'm going to have a hell of a time getting you away."

An hour. Matt would notice if she didn't show up in an hour. And the president....

"Away where?" she asked.

"Can't you trust me?"

Yesterday—this afternoon—forty minutes ago she would have said yes. Now she couldn't even trust herself. She crossed her arms against the beaded bodice of her gown. "Give me one good reason why I should."

He rubbed the back of his neck. "Well…"

Her toes curled in embarrassment. If he mentioned that kiss…

"You don't really have any choice," he said.

She lifted her chin. "Of course I have a choice."

He met her gaze directly. His eyes were dark. His mouth was a flat line. "No," he said quietly. "You don't."

She believed him. Despite the warmth of the night and the weight of his jacket, she shivered.

Marcus reached into his pocket and pulled out a key. Grasping her elbow, he tugged her around the hood of the dark sedan parked beside her limo.

He unlocked the passenger door. In front. To make her feel more equal? Or to keep a better eye on her? "Get in."

She stared at the dark, uninviting interior of the car. A horrible thought emerged from the flood in her brain like a corpse on the tide. She didn't want to know. She had to know.

"Where is Eric?"

Eric, her driver. If Marcus had done anything to her innocent driver, no power on earth could persuade her to get in that car.

"He's fine."

"I don't believe you," she said, proud that her voice didn't tremble.

Marcus frowned. "Okay, not fine exactly. He's locked in a utilities closet by the men's room on the lower level of the hotel parking garage. But he didn't see me. When the night janitor lets him out, he'll think he's just another D.C. mugging victim. *Now* will you get in the car?"

Her mouth dropped open. "A mugging victim? You hit him?"

"No. I popped a bag over his head and took his wallet. Damn it, you're a target out here. Get in the car."

His exasperation was more reassuring than any soothing response could have been. Her gaze swept the broad, flat expanse of empty crosswalks, empty sidewalks, empty parking lots. Trees cast shadows in the moonlight. Deserted passenger shelters glowed, islands in the dark.

"Do you have a gun?"

He sighed. "Of course I have a gun. I'm supposed to be protecting you."

"Nice of you to remember," Samantha muttered. But she got in the car.

He slammed her door and stalked to the other side of the car.

Samantha took a deep breath. She should be terrified. And on some deep-down level she was. But at the same time there was a surreal quality to the whole incident, not quite on the level of one of those tabloid stories. "Ambassador Abducted by Aliens" or "I Gave Birth to Mutant's Baby."

Only this was more like some campy movie. "I Was Kidnapped by Brendan Fraser." The man was a good actor, you could half believe in the danger, and then you'd get that trademark twinkle, look into that utterly good-guy face and think, *Brendan Fraser? Get real.* It was like being abducted by the Jolly Green Giant.

Surreptitiously, Samantha tried her door handle. It didn't budge.

Marcus slid his bulk into the driver's seat. "Driver's side locks," he explained.

She pressed her lips together.

"Hey, they're for your own safety," he said defensively. "I don't want you to do anything stupid."

"Like trust you?"

"Cheap shot, Ambassador." He started the car.

"I think now that you've stuck your tongue down my throat and kidnapped me, you could call me Samantha."

She watched in satisfaction as a muscle jumped in his jaw. "This is not a kidnapping," he said through his teeth.

She craned her neck to read the Dunn Loring–Merrifield Metro sign in case she was ever called to take the stand or write a rescue note. "No? What would you call it?"

"Protective custody."

"And who do you imagine you're protecting me from?"

"The Rebelians."

"You're expecting trouble from the Rebelians? In D.C.?"

"Big trouble."

His grim tone slid into her like a knife, sharp and chilling. She told herself she understood the consequences and accepted the dangers of her position. But she didn't really believe she was being threatened on U.S. soil.

"You think I'm an assassination target."

"It doesn't matter what I think. What matters is what I've been ordered to do."

"By whom? Agent Walker?"

He was silent. Which could only mean…

"Walker doesn't know where I am, does he?" The realization hollowed her chest.

"That was the plan." Marcus turned his head to look at her. "You're safer that way."

Was she? Safe? Alone with him?

Oh my goodness, no.

She peered out her window, trying to memorize their route. Tall, slender trees stood sentinel along the street. Gallows Road. How appropriate, she thought, and tried to ignore her jumping pulse.

"You know, DeBruzkya's opposition to the accord is nothing new," she said, choosing her words carefully. "I appreciate the need for security, but there's no reason to act precipitously here."

"DeBruzkya's not our only worry." She was only a little reassured by his use of the word *our*. "You've got that crime family, the whatchamacallit, after you, too."

"The Coalition. Rebelia is a base for their arms traffic and money laundering."

"Whatever. The point is, you're a target."

She drew herself up. She had herself together now. "I am willing to assume the risks of my job. Just as you are willing to assume the risks of yours."

"Uh-huh." He didn't sound convinced. "Only I can take care of myself. You can't."

"Obviously, or I wouldn't have gotten in this car with you."

His hands tightened on the steering wheel, but he didn't say anything. At least he wasn't going to strangle her.

Not yet.

"Anyway," she said, striving for reason, reaching for calm, "if I'm not in D.C. to be confirmed in my appointment by the president, if I don't go back to Delmonico next week, what do you think will happen to the treaty then?"

"What are you talking about?"

"You're correct in assuming that General DeBruzkya and the Coalition leadership would like me removed from negotiations with Delmonico. But they don't have to kill me to achieve their objectives."

Marcus frowned. "Can you say that again using really little words?"

"My disappearance will have the same effect on the future of the Delmonico Accord as my death." She waited a moment for him to absorb her argument, and then risked a touch on his bare arm. She was still wearing his jacket. His skin was warm. His muscles were knotted with tension. Or else he was always as hard as a rock. "You have to take me back. You must see that you have to take me back."

He didn't answer her. The white lane markings flashed by and faded as the odometer numbers crept upward.

How long would it be, Samantha wondered, before her absence was noticed from the White House? How long before Matt or somebody phoned the hotel? Before the police were alerted? Or the FBI?

"You have to call," Marcus said suddenly.

She blinked. "Call who?"

"Your secretary. Philip. Tell him you're okay, you're taking a vacation or something."

"Are you stupid?"

He cut her a dark look. Hurt, almost. She half opened her mouth to apologize. She was never rude.

But he said evenly, "No. It's a good idea."

Forget apologizing. The man of steel had the stubbornness of a mule and the sensitivity of a rock.

She set her mouth. "I won't do it."

"Yeah, you will. All that stuff you said? About the treaty? You can't risk the Delmonican government backing out because they believe you're not a player anymore. If they link your disappearance to the attack on your driver, you lose. Everybody loses. You tell them you're on vacation and everybody's still in the game.''

Frustrated, she stared at his hard, dark profile. He was right.

"How can you do this?'' she appealed. "You've pledged to protect the interests of the United States.''

"At the moment, I'm pledged to protect you. I'm doing my job. And you'll do yours.''

"How?'' she demanded.

"From a pay phone,'' he said, deliberately misunderstanding her. "There's a rest area up ahead. You know what you want to say?''

"I can think of numerous things I'd like to say.'' Four letter things, most of them. "And I'd say them, if I thought it would do any good.''

His full lips quirked. "You're not exactly keeping quiet over there.''

"If you wanted quiet, you should have kidnapped somebody else.''

His smile faded. "This is not a kidnapping.''

"Will you drive me back to D.C.?''

"No.''

"Well, then…'' She let her voice trail off suggestively.

The bright blue rest area sign stood square against the darkness. Marcus turned the car off the highway.

Samantha peered through the windshield. It wasn't much of a rest area: picnic tables and trash cans, a pump with a water fountain on top set in a block of concrete, a phone. No rest room. No other cars, no sharp-eyed highway patrol officer or friendly truckers. She bit her lip in disappointment.

Marcus cruised to a stop beside the phone, a dimpled metal box on a pole. He lifted his hips to reach the wallet in his back pocket. He was very…big. She looked away. It was one thing to admire his body when he was escorting her through her world; quite another to cope with his massive presence now that they were on their way to… Where, exactly?

"I've got a phone card you can use," he said.

"Aren't you afraid they'll trace the call?" Even to her own ears, she sounded bitter.

"It's prepaid. Cash," he explained, as if her question were perfectly reasonable. "The phones at the hotel aren't set up for a trace. Besides, if we do this right, your secretary won't know anything's going on."

"Philip is very capable. He's going to know something is going on."

"Then it's up to you to convince him otherwise."

If she did what Marcus wanted, she would become an accomplice in her own abduction. If she didn't, if she alerted Philip to initiate a search for her, if her disappearance became public knowledge, she could undo everything she had worked so hard to accomplish.

Under his giant jacket, her fingers worried a bead sewn into the design of her dress.

"What should I tell him?" she asked.

"Whatever you want. No," Marcus corrected. "Whatever you think won't make him suspicious."

She twisted the bead. "What exactly do you imagine I could say about my disappearing on an evening when I was invited to the White House that he would not find suspicious?"

To her surprise, Marcus appeared to give her question serious thought.

"Tell him you're sorry," he said finally. "Tell him you've met someone and he asked you to go away with him for the weekend."

Twist, twist. Tug, tug. She almost had it. "Philip knows I am not the kind of woman who goes away for a weekend with a man I've just met."

She could feel Marcus's gaze, warm and speculative. "No?"

Her face got hot. She had opened her mouth for this man. She had clutched his shoulders and moaned. Whatever she said to him now, whatever she did, he had cracked her open and eaten her up like an oyster in its shell. She felt exposed. Slimy.

"No," she said firmly.

"Okay. Then tell him you needed a break. It's true, so he ought to believe it. Tell him you were in the car, headed for the White House, and all of a sudden you couldn't take the prospect of talking and laughing and making nice to a bunch of self-absorbed politicians who don't care that you're strung out and sick of holding it in and tired of holding it together. Holding the treaty together. Holding yourself together. Tell him that."

She was shaking. The kiss had already laid her open. This was salt on the wound. "I don't—"

"Tell him one more damn night of being cool and perfect Ambassador Barnes was just too much for you." There was an actual edge to his voice that cut through her fear and embarrassment and lanced her heart. "Tell him you need a couple of days for yourself."

Her head reeled. Her fingers twisted and twisted the bead under the concealing folds of his jacket until it fell into her hand. But she managed to ask calmly, "Only a couple of days?"

One shoulder lifted. "We can hope."

She got out of the car to make her phone call.

It amazed her how simple it was, how easily Philip accepted her explanations and excuses.

"I told you you weren't taking care of yourself," Philip scolded. "Maybe now you'll get some rest and eat occasionally."

She had to hold the receiver away from her ear so that

Marcus, looming over her, could hear both ends of the conversation. "Yes. About dinner—"

"I'll call the White House and make your excuses," Philip said with kindly efficiency. "I'll say you weren't feeling well."

She was a little put out by how readily he dealt with the repercussions of her supposed breakdown. "Thank you. Philip—"

"Will you be using Eric?" her secretary continued.

"No, I want to be alone. Anyway, he didn't show up tonight."

"Really?" Philip's voice sharpened.

"I'm sure he's—" *just another D.C. mugging victim* "—fine," Samantha said. "Unless he's sick, like Agent Walker."

"Oh, right. Stomach virus, wasn't it?"

"Something like that."

"Is there a number where I can reach you in an emergency?"

Marcus stiffened.

"I don't really know yet where I'll be staying," Samantha said, thinking dryly that that much at least was true. "But I'll call you as soon as I get the chance."

Marcus's eyes narrowed. She met his gaze steadily, hoping her expression didn't reveal her racing heart.

"And you're sure you're all right?" Philip asked.

No, I'm being kidnapped by a large, pigheaded Navy SEAL who tastes like honey and kisses like sin.

"I'm fine. Tell Matt I'm sorry to have missed the chance to meet his Carey."

"Will do," Philip said cheerfully.

They said goodbye. Samantha hung up, clutching the receiver to hide her hand's trembling.

"All set?" Marcus rumbled.

She inhaled slowly and released her breath, released the grip of her hands. Both hands.

"Yes," she said clearly. "I'm ready to go now."

She hurried the few steps back to the car, not turning to see if he followed. She couldn't see him behind her. Or hear him, either. It struck her again how silently he moved for such a big man.

He closed the passenger side door and walked around the hood of the car. He folded himself behind the wheel, his knees, thighs and shoulders crowding her space.

"You dropped this. Back there." His face was blank. His voice was flat.

He tossed something small and sparkling into her lap. It caught the light as it fell. Her heart hitched as she recognized it—the tiny, glittering bead she had twisted from the stitching of her gown and left in the tall grass by the phone as a clue.

"Sucks for you that I was watching," he said, and started the car.

Six

It felt like frigging Amateur Night, the day after payday, when nothing on board went right.

Marcus clenched his jaw and concentrated on the dark road ahead. He'd almost missed that bead.

The realization made him sweat. It was a mistake, and he never made mistakes. He was trained not to make mistakes. Only the fact that his eyesight was better than the average bear's had saved him from this one.

Of course, one bead in the grass might not have been a problem. Not as long as nobody was looking for a missing ambassador in an evening gown covered in designer doo-dads.

But suppose somebody was? Suppose her secretary got suspicious, after all, or her White House buddy tipped off the feds, or the cops made a connection between her driver's getting shoved into a utility closet and the ambassador's sudden desire for a vacation?

There was no getting away from the fact that Eric the chauffeur was a loose end. And that business about how her disappearance would affect the treaty... He so hadn't seen that one coming. Why hadn't he? Hell, why hadn't Baxter?

There were too many loose ends. Too many damn variables. How could Marcus be expected to anticipate them all?

But until Baxter dug up the mole in his department, this mission depended on Marcus.

His career could depend on this mission.

And Samantha's life depended on both.

His hands tightened on the wheel. Okay. He could handle this. No more screwups. No more distractions. No more looking at her lush, full body in that tight, shiny dress and dreaming about ripping it off like this was Christmas morning and she was his present.

Definitely, definitely no more kissing.

Unless, of course, she started it.

He glanced across at her pale, perfect profile. She'd turned her face to the darkness outside as if she couldn't stand the sight of him. He felt an unfamiliar pang in his chest.

Okay, so kissing was out of the question. Probably. Although he might have the chance to change her mind. They'd be stuck together for at least the next several days. And nights.

His body surged at the thought. Days and *nights*.

Except, you know, that was exactly the kind of distraction he didn't need. The kind of distraction that could get her killed.

Better for both of them if she was pissed off. Safer for both of them if she retreated from that wild, hot, passionate woman who had exploded in his arms, and went back to playing Madeleine Albright.

He shot another wary glance her way. Except Ambassador Albright never had hair that red or a mouth that soft. Ambassador Albright had never kissed him and clung to him and made him feel... Made him want...

Nope, he was never going to be able to think of Sam as Madeleine Albright.

She had the pose down fine, though. She sat like a good girl in the front pew of the church with her back straight and her hands folded in her lap.

Yeah, and if he took his eye off her for one second she'd

go tiptoeing through the woods, scattering a trail of bread-crumbs.

Gutsy, he thought. But strain had tightened the muscles around that lush mouth. Her face was white above his dark jacket. She looked tired.

"Almost there," he offered.

She straightened against the vinyl seat. "Where?"

"This farm I know about. It's not the Ritz or anything, but it's safe. Nobody will find you there."

She arched her brows. "Am I supposed to find that re-assuring?"

"If I had Rebelian spies and Coalition hit men gunning for me, I'd find it reassuring."

"You actually believe that, don't you?" she asked slowly.

"Believe what?"

"That I'm in some kind of danger."

"I wouldn't be chiseling you out of dinner with the pres-ident if I didn't."

"Hasn't it occurred to you that I could be in more danger stuck out here alone with you?"

He didn't like her question. But there was a lot about this assignment he did not like. He watched the sagging rail fence along the road for the turnoff to the farm and wondered what the hell he should say to her.

Baxter told him and his gut told him that she had to get out of D.C. She couldn't remain the visible target of an unknown assassin and an unidentified mole. She had to be safer with him.

And yet if anything went down, if he went down, she'd be left alone and defenseless.

"It's not my call," he said finally. "But if it was, I'd say you're only safe if you can trust the people entrusted with your protection."

Samantha sniffed. "Well, you just made that difficult, didn't you?"

He winced. Okay, so *defenseless* was the wrong word. But a guy with an AR-15 and a rifle scope could still blow her brains out and never come close enough to get flayed by that tongue of hers.

"Get over it," he said tersely. "As of tonight, I'm all you've got."

Samantha blinked. "Get over it?"

He barely spared her a glance. "Yeah."

Samantha was ambushed by the anger that flared in her. The car lurched off the road and up a narrow, rutted track lined with trees, but she hardly noticed. Did he have any idea what he was talking about? Any idea who he was talking to?

In the past year she had accepted the end of her dreams for a family. She had endured the loss of her husband. She had embraced the challenge of his career and buried her life and her heart in his work. In the past few hours, she'd been deprived of dinner at the White House. She had been kidnapped and kissed within an inch of her life. And she hadn't once broken down or fallen apart. Not once.

"I do not need Navy Rambo telling me how to cope," she said coldly. "I cope. I cope beautifully." Everybody said so, didn't they? "*I* do not have to be told to get over *anything*."

The glow from the dashboard gave an odd cast to Marcus's face. Or else he was looking at her strangely.

"Good," he said. The car stopped. He pulled the keys from the ignition. "We're here."

"What?"

"We're here. At the farm."

"Oh."

Disconcerted, cheated, she peered through the windshield. In the shelter of the trees stood a tall plank house with a long front porch. Slivers of white paint gleamed in the moonlight.

Marcus got out of the car and lifted the hood, blocking her view.

"What are you doing?" she called.

"Making sure you can't hot-wire the car," he replied.

She tried not to feel flattered. "Actually," she said dryly, "I missed the course on car theft at Harvard."

"Lucky for me," Marcus said, and put something in his pocket.

She raised her eyebrows. "Isn't this trust thing supposed to go both ways?"

He opened her car door for her. "You told me a minute ago not to underestimate you. I'm taking you at your word."

"What if we need to leave in a hurry?"

He nodded once, acknowledging her fear. "It's a risk. But, ma'am—Samantha…" His hand cupped her elbow. His gaze, dark with purpose, sought hers. "You're not in danger here. I won't let anything happen to you. I swear. Besides…" His smile glimmered. "I can get this or any other vehicle operational in under sixty seconds."

Her heart drummed in her ears. She swallowed with effort. "I take it you did not skip the class in car theft?"

He merely grinned, and her pulse raced.

Oh, she was in danger, all right. Terrible danger. Of losing her distance. Of losing her focus.

Of losing her— But she wouldn't let herself finish that sentence, even in thought.

Marcus parked the green sea bag at the foot of the ratty couch. He set the lantern on an end table, where its light pooled on the braided rug and sparkled on the hem of Samantha's gown.

"I've turned on the water pump. In the morning I'll go

out to the barn, see if I can get the generator working. Make yourself at home. I want to check out the upstairs.''

Samantha raised her eyebrows. ''Aren't you afraid I'll run away?''

''Nope. Car's out of commission. You can't run in those heels, and the nearest neighbor is over a mile away through empty fields and dark woods. I figure you'd rather take your chances with me tonight than the bears.''

Her blue eyes widened. ''Bears?''

He grinned to himself as he slipped up the stairs. She wasn't as tough as she liked to pretend. But when he came down a few minutes later, after checking the windows and mapping the layout in his head, the laughter stuck in his chest.

Samantha had taken off his jacket. She stood unmoving in the shabby living room, tall and straight as a candle lighting up the darkness. Her hair was a banked and coiled fire on top of her head. Her dress shimmered over her bodice as she breathed. She looked too beautiful to be real and too remote to be touched.

He cleared his throat instead. ''The bedrooms are in pretty good shape. Dry. I found some sheets in a closet. You're the second door on the left. You want to go ahead and get changed now?''

She turned her head and looked at him, a goddess contemplating destruction. ''Get changed into what? I don't have any clothes.''

''Actually, you do.'' He came down the last few steps and hefted his bag. ''My sister stays at our family's place in Georgetown. I borrowed some of her things.''

''That was kind of her,'' Samantha said politely.

''Not really. I let myself in while she was at work. Honey works in the White House basement,'' he explained. ''I doubt she'll even notice these are gone. And I picked you up some other stuff.''

"Thank you," Samantha said. But she made no move to take the bag from him.

Marcus tried again. "You have time to get changed before dinner."

"I don't need dinner."

"You should eat."

Her beautiful eyes narrowed. "I should have eaten at the White House."

He felt guilty. Damn it. "Next time I kidnap you, I'll do it after dessert, okay? You want soup?"

"I'm not hungry."

"Got to keep your strength up."

"Are we arm wrestling later?"

Wrestling was good. Naked body wrestling. With oils.

He had an instant vision of Samantha, her pale skin glistening with oil, her full breasts and smooth thighs gliding, sliding over and around—

Bad idea. No wrestling. No distractions.

He wrenched his mind back to the job, to the immediate objectives of food and survival.

"I'll heat some soup. It'll be ready when you come down."

She looked annoyed. Good. Annoyed was better than frozen. Annoyed wasn't scared. Annoyed wasn't depressed.

"I told you I'm not hungry," she said.

"So you're just going to starve yourself until you faint or something and I've got to take you to the hospital? Which, I have to point out, does not exactly fit my plan of not drawing attention to ourselves."

"Oh, I'm so sorry," she said. "I guess being kidnapped spoiled my appetite."

He snorted. "Honey, I've been watching you for a week. I sat in on your lunch with Senators Dumb and Dumber, remember? You have no appetite. Ever. You're making yourself sick."

"It won't hurt me to lose a pound or two."

"How many?"

"Excuse me?"

"How many pounds have you lost since your husband died?"

She frowned. "I don't know. A few."

"Three? Five?"

"More than— I fail to see how this is any of your business."

"More than five? Because that could be a sign of something. Anorexia, maybe. Depression."

Samantha sighed. "I am not anorexic. For heaven's sake, would you look at me?"

"I am," he said, eyeing her frankly. "And you look great. But more than five pounds—"

"What do I have to do to convince you?"

"You could eat some soup."

"Fine." She blinked. "You set me up," she said, a note of discovery in her voice.

He grinned at her. "Yeah."

The corners of her mouth indented like she was trying not to smile. "I'm really not very hungry."

"That's okay," he said. "I am. You can keep me company."

The smile escaped. She had the greatest smile, wide and full, with deep, amazing dimples. He felt the pull of it low in his gut.

"I can do that," she agreed. "After I change. Where am I sleeping again?"

With me.

He picked up the bag and the lantern, glad to have something to do with his hands. "Second door on the left. I'll show you."

"Thank you," she said politely, like he hadn't kidnapped, bullied and insulted her.

He followed her up the stairs, directing the light at her feet and trying not to notice how really, really great her butt looked flexing and swaying under her sparkly dress.

It was a good thing she was taking it off.

And maybe, you know, her zipper would get stuck or something and she would ask him to help her. Maybe she'd raise her hands to her warm, red hair, so that her breasts lifted with the movement, and turn her head a little, so she could see him over her shoulder, and ask him in that rich, incredible voice…

"Could I have a candle?"

"What? Oh." He felt the heat crawl into his face, but maybe she couldn't see him blush. He set the lantern on the dusty dresser and stepped back quickly, out of the light. "I'll leave you this."

"What about you?"

"I've got another lantern in the car."

She tilted her head. "And how does a lantern in the car help you going downstairs now?"

"I have pretty good night vision."

He could see like a cat in the dark. It made him a natural for night ops. And it meant he didn't miss one detail of her appearance now: the fatigue that lay like bruises under her eyes, the tired pout of her lips, the gentle pull of fabric against her softly curved belly and generous thighs….

He looked away. "You should get changed," he said hoarsely.

That would help.

That had to help. There was no way they could survive the next couple of days alone together with her looking like the queen of the night and him with a raging hard-on.

He clomped down the stairs, making no attempt at all to move silently, and escaped outside to unload the car.

Samantha made her way down the staircase by feel, gripping the banister while the lantern's light bounced and swayed at her feet. She found her way to the kitchen by smell, guided by the comforting aroma of chicken soup and the promise of fresh coffee.

Marcus stood with his broad back to the door, stirring a saucepan on an old gas range. Blue points of light danced under the pan and the bubbling coffeepot. A lantern cast a yellow glow over the old wood cabinets, the scuffed and faded linoleum floor and the scarred oak table set with thick white china. Limp curtains stirred at the window over the sink. The breeze carried with it the scent of grass and a chorus of insects.

The scene was heartbreakingly homey, reassuringly domestic. Until Samantha noticed the dirt deep in the corners and the gun tucked into the holster at the small of Marcus's back.

Her heart jolted.

"Soup's ready," he announced, turning from the stove. "Why don't you— Whoa."

His gaze hit her chest and riveted there.

She was wearing stiff, dark jeans so new she'd cut the tags off and a tiny red T-shirt with the words *Kiss Kiss* blazoned in silver glitter across the front.

She raised her chin. "One of your sister's, I presume?"

"Oh, God." Marcus managed to drag his gaze to her face. Appalled humor filled his eyes. "I'm sorry. I just reached into the drawer and grabbed. I never thought they'd be so—so…"

His attention drifted back to her breasts. Her nipples puckered.

"Short?" Samantha inquired helpfully, praying he wouldn't notice her body's reaction to his continuing scrutiny. "Tight?"

He shook his head. "Suggestive."

She glanced down at her front. "Kiss" sparkled from her left breast. "Kiss" twinkled on her right.

"I had a choice," she informed him wryly. "The black one says *Sexy Chick* and the blue one says *I'm Yours.*"

"I'm going to kill my sister," Marcus said. "That, or lock her up until she's, like, ninety or so and no longer a danger to herself or others."

Samantha laughed. "How old is she now?"

"Honey?" His gaze was still fixed on Samantha's breasts. "Twenty-three."

She shrugged, both uncomfortable with and flattered by his regard. "Young enough to wear racy slogans."

"Old enough to know better," he said grimly. "I, uh... Oh, God, I'm staring." He focused on her eyes. "You must think I'm a jerk. A jerk and a hypocrite."

"I think you're protective," she said, biting the inside of her cheek to keep her smile in check. "And honest."

And sweet, she thought but did not say. There was a limit—wasn't there?—to the amount of positive reinforcement you were supposed to give a man who had recently kidnapped you.

"I'm sure your sister appreciates having her big brother critique her moves and her wardrobe."

If possible, he turned even redder under his tan. "Oh, my sister thinks I'm a caveman. And I think she's a loon. But you know, we mostly get along okay."

His embarrassment and his affection were plain. And very, very endearing. "I'm sure you do."

"She's not a bad kid, really. She's a lot brighter than our parents give her credit for. Brighter than me."

"Why do you say that?"

He shrugged and removed the hot soup from the stove. "Because it's true. Sit down."

She sat. "But—"

"It's okay," he assured her. "I got used to the idea that

I wasn't the sharpest tool in the family shed a long time ago."

"I don't see that at all," she said.

He slanted her a look as he spooned soup into her bowl. "You got brothers and sisters?"

"No."

"There you go, then," he said obscurely, and served himself some soup.

"I always wanted brothers and sisters," she said, oddly defensive.

"Uh-huh." He sat opposite her. "Eat."

She picked up her spoon. "I like large families."

He reached for the peanut butter jar in the middle of the table. "Yeah? You got kids?"

Practice had made her experienced at hiding the pain. Stan had given her so much. But not the children she longed for. She swallowed a mouthful of broth. "We weren't blessed with children."

"You ever think about adopting?"

Stan hadn't wanted to adopt. Think of the risks, he used to urge. How can we disrupt our lives for a child of unknown parents and unreliable genetic makeup?

Her spoon clanked against the side of her bowl "Adoption was not an option."

Marcus tilted his chair back on two legs and regarded her through slitted eyes. "You got a problem with adoption?"

"No." But that seemed disloyal to Stan, so she added, "It's such a gamble. An adopted infant may have unidentified health problems or special needs. And with an older child, there's no memory of you as his parents to help you through the teen years."

"Or no memories at all," Marcus muttered.

"Pardon?"

He dropped the legs of his chair. "It doesn't matter. More soup?"

She looked down, surprised to discover her bowl was half-empty. "No, thank you," she said politely. "What about you?"

"Guess I will. Thanks." He reached for the pot.

Samantha bit her lip. "No, I meant do you have children?"

His blue eyes gleamed. "Are you asking me about my personal life, Ambassador?"

"I…" Oh, dear. "It seems reasonable. Given that we're going to be spending a certain amount of time together."

Not to mention that you stuck your tongue in my mouth, she thought.

He shook his head. "No kids. No dependents of any kind. Is that what you wanted to know?"

She felt herself blush and grabbed a cracker in self-defense. "I was simply wondering how it's possible for you to disappear for days on end without anyone objecting."

"I got called," he said, as if that explained everything. And maybe for him it did. "When you're on the Teams, you've got to give it one hundred and ten percent. There's nothing left over for a relationship."

"You have a problem with marriage?"

Let him see how he liked the question. Although, would she like the answer?

Not that she cared. She wasn't supposed to care.

He spread peanut butter on a cracker and handed it to her. "I like marriage fine. I like it so much I'm not doing it until I can do it right."

Her heart beat faster. "Which means what, exactly?"

"Another hundred and ten percent."

She licked crumbs from her lips. "Which is what? A total of two hundred and twenty percent?"

He shrugged. "So math's not my strong suit. You missed some."

"Excuse me?"

"You missed some. Peanut butter." He leaned forward across the table. His big, strong hand approached her face.

She pulled back.

"Easy," he murmured.

His eyes were focused on her mouth. She noticed little rings of gold deep in the blue, haloing the wide, dark pupils.

This time as his hand approached, Samantha held very still to prove to him, to prove to both of them, that she was in control. His thumb rubbed slowly at the corner and then across her lower lip. His skin was warm and slightly rough and tasted of salt.

"There," he said quietly. "That did it."

Oh, goodness. Oh, yes. It did.

She exhaled. "I should go upstairs. I have—"

"Work to do?" he finished for her. "I don't think so."

"Reading," she said. "I can catch up on my reading."

"You could. If I'd brought any with us."

Her sensual fog evaporated, burned away by something like panic. She could accept—barely—that Marcus had kidnapped her as part of some misguided stratagem to keep her safe. But to deprive her of her work, her reports, her buffer... "You didn't bring *anything?*"

He stood to clear the table. "Groceries."

Groceries, fine. But— "Nothing to read?"

"Not unless you count Honey's T-shirts."

Samantha narrowed her eyes. He was joking and she wanted to throw things—the soup plate, the peanut butter jar. But of course she didn't. She never did. "This is very inconvenient. What am I supposed to do for the next few days?"

"I don't know. Eat. Sleep. Play the piano."

His gaze collided with hers, the rim of gold around the black, the burning blue. She felt the impact in her stomach. *Have sex with me.*

She retreated from the very idea, the unspoken invitation. The temptation.

She cleared her throat. "There's a piano?"

"Yeah. You play, don't you?"

She was surprised he'd noticed. "A little. Enough to know this one must be out of tune. How long has the house been empty?"

But he didn't answer her question. "You should give it a shot," he said. "Maybe it's not so bad."

A kidnapping and a private piano recital in one evening? She shook her head. "I think my time would be better spent putting sheets on the bed."

He rinsed their bowls in the sink. "Wait till I get the dishes done and I'll help you."

"No. Given the T-shirts you picked out, I think I'll choose my sheets myself. I really don't want to wake up between Scooby-Doo and GI Joe."

His mouth quirked. "That would be kind of kinky."

Marcus enjoyed the little huff that escaped her then, half laughter and half exasperation. Her chest rose and fell with it. The silver letters winked and twinkled on her shirt. *Kiss Kiss.*

"I think I'll say good-night now," she said.

He watched the yellow light bob away with her down the hall, listened to her footsteps climb the stairs and tried real hard not to think about clean sheets and Samantha bending over the bed.

At least he had work to do.

He retrieved his laptop and opened it on the kitchen table. Maybe once he got the generator going and didn't have to depend on the battery, he could let Samantha go online to get her news fix. This computer had one of those wireless Internet hookups.

Only the best for our boys at the State Department.

He typed the URL Jerry Baxter had provided, waited for the lock sign to appear and then tapped in his ID and password: Hector Protector.

Almost immediately, a jerky, goofy animation glowed on his screen. Some funny little game. Some funny little guy, dressed all in green.

Marcus watched a moment, amused by the tiny character's antics. *Hector Protector was dressed all in green, Hector Protector was sent to the queen.*

The queen did not like him....

A noise yanked his attention from the screen. He frowned. What was—

Scraping wood. Upstairs.

The window was being forced.

Samantha!

Marcus slipped the Glock from the holster at his back and moved smoothly and silently toward the stairs.

Seven

The target was alone.

The man in the shadows watched, his heart racing, as she bent over the mattress.

The open window was a break he hadn't counted on. It was an easy shot.

Sweat prickled under his arms and at the small of his back. Nice and easy. He flexed his fingers, savoring the reassuring weight of the gun.

Ready. Aim.

Eliminate the target.

The crack was loud enough to make her jump. The painted trim around the open window splintered. The glass shattered.

Samantha screamed.

Marcus burst through the open door like a one-man SWAT team, his face grim and his gun at the ready.

"Damn it, get down!"

She dropped behind the bed and lay with her cheek against the dusty carpet and her heart threatening to pound its way out of her chest. She watched Marcus's feet cross the room in long angry strides, his boots crunching on broken glass.

"What happened?" she asked. "Did you get him?"

"No."

He was standing by the shattered window, a darker

shadow against the night outside. She could see his feet surrounded by shards of glass.

"For goodness' sake, be careful!" she said sharply.

"Stay down. Did you get a look at him?"

She raised her head from the carpet. "At who?"

"The guy trying to get into your room."

She squinted, not sure she'd heard him correctly. Maybe she'd hit her head on the way to the floor. Or inhaled too much carpet dust. "No one was trying to get into my room."

"Samantha." Marcus's voice was tight with patience. "Somebody tried to force your window. I heard him."

Her window… She levered herself cautiously to her knees. The broken edges sparkled, framing the black, soft night. She bit her lip. "I think… It's possible you heard *me*."

Marcus went as still as a bronze soldier on the Mall. "Explain."

Of course she could explain. She had a perfectly reasonable explanation. "It was very stuffy up here. Hot. And I thought—" Her rationale stumbled under his stony regard. "I thought— You had a window open in the kitchen. I thought it would be all right."

"You opened the window," he said without expression.

She nodded.

He jammed the gun into the holster at his back with so much force she was surprised it didn't go off. "Do you have any idea how much danger you were in?"

"Well, obviously. Since somebody shot at me."

"Not exactly." His voice was grim.

She blinked. "I don't understand."

"Damn it, Samantha, look at the window."

"It's broken."

"Yes. Because my bullet hit the frame and the impact shattered the glass."

Her stomach did a slow roll. "Are you saying *you* shot at me?"

He scowled. "No, I shot at— There was somebody there."

"But you said no one knew where to find me."

"They don't. They shouldn't."

"Then…"

"Christ, Samantha!" The words burst out of him. "I could have killed you."

The bronze soldier on a monument was just an act, a hard shell over Marcus's real, live, anguished concern. He believed what he was saying. He actually believed he could have shot her. The possibility shook his voice and made his hands tremble.

And somehow his doubts, his fears, stilled hers. His very uncertainty made her sure of one thing. He would not hurt her. He would never hurt her.

"No, you couldn't," she said. "You're too experienced. You wouldn't make a mistake like that."

"I almost did!"

"But you didn't." She got to her feet and came around the bed toward him. "I'm fine."

His mouth set. "For now. You can't sleep here."

She tilted her head. "Does that mean you'll take me back to D.C.?"

"I can't." His hands curled into fists at his sides. "Until I have orders—unless I know DS has caught whoever is behind this breach in security—I can't take you back."

He believed that, too. Was he wrong on both counts?

"All right," Samantha said. "Then how many bedrooms does this house have?"

"You…aren't you going to argue with me?"

She smiled slightly. "Maybe in the morning. But right now I just want to go to bed."

The words hung in the air between them, sparkling and dangerous as the broken glass around their feet.

Marcus exhaled. "Four bedrooms. One's downstairs, but I don't want to be that far away from you. There's this one. I could sweep up the glass and board up the window, but—"

"It's too late and we're both too tired," she finished for him. "That leaves two other rooms."

"Yeah. Only…" He stooped to brush up a large shard of glass.

"Don't do that with your hands. You'll cut yourself. Only what?"

He straightened, oddly reluctant to meet her gaze. "After their daughter, Luanne, moved out, the Robinsons turned her old room into a sewing room. So there are still two other bedrooms upstairs. Just not…"

Her heart thumped. "Just not two beds."

He nodded once. "It's not a problem. I can sleep on the floor."

Of course he could. It was a good idea. A fine solution. A safe, workable—

"Or we could share the bed," she suggested.

His face went blank. "You want to share the bed."

She *wanted*… She wasn't admitting what she wanted. Not even to herself.

"To sleep," she said, as if this was a practical suggestion. "Like a sleepover."

"Honey…" His voice was edged with amusement and something else. "We're grown-ups. We don't do sleepovers."

"Precisely. We are grown-ups. Not hormone-crazed teenagers. If I were another SEAL—"

"There are no women on the Teams."

"All right. If I were a man—"

"If you were a man, we would be *so* not having this discussion."

She stuck out her chin. "You mean it's only women you object to sleeping with?"

He gave her this funny look, as if he couldn't believe what he was hearing. She didn't blame him. She hardly believed it herself. It must be the adrenaline talking.

"No," he said patiently. "I like sleeping with women fine."

Her face flamed. "So it's me you have a problem with."

"Let's see. Do I have a problem with a beautiful, intelligent woman—a woman I consider totally hot, by the way—inviting me to share her bed? To sleep next to her and smell her skin and touch her hair? Maybe to roll over and feel her all warm and soft next to me?" He pretended to consider. "Nope. Nope, that's not it."

She felt warm and soft, all right. All over. Just from his description. "Then why…?"

"I'm the problem. Me. I don't know that I trust myself to lie next to you all night and not, you know, act like a guy. Or react like a guy. If you get my drift."

Oh, goodness. She jerked her gaze away from the front of his dark slacks. Pleated, to hide— "I get it."

"Yeah, well, that might not be all you get if we cuddle up for the night," he said frankly. "You really want to risk that?"

She understood risk. Every diplomat did. She knew how to weigh her options and calculate her chances. It wasn't like her to gamble on the unknown. It definitely wasn't like her to lie down with a man she'd known less than a week. And yet…

Her heart beat faster. "I trust you," she said.

Marcus stared at her, his usually open face inscrutable in the darkness.

"Let's hope that's not your first mistake."

Mistake, hell.

This whole mission was a disaster.

Lying on the lumpy mattress, Marcus drew in a shallow breath and let it out slowly through his mouth so that Samantha wouldn't hear him pant. Combat breathing. Only the enemy he fought this time was his own unruly body.

He could do a four-mile run wearing boots in under twenty-six minutes; he could do a two-mile ocean swim in less than an hour. He was trained to subdue hunger, to control thirst, to ignore pain and fatigue.

But pretending to sleep beside Samantha in the dark, he couldn't do a damn thing about the fact that he was painfully, completely aroused.

If he lay on his back, the covers stuck up like a tent around a tent pole. If he lay facing her… No, she didn't need him poking at her all night. He twisted onto his right side, toward the door, away from her.

"I'm sorry," Samantha said softly. "Am I keeping you up?"

He almost groaned. If he weren't so damn uncomfortable, this would be funny.

"No, I'm good," he said.

Anyway, he was trying to be.

"Sometimes when I have trouble falling asleep, I take a warm bath," Samantha offered.

Okay, there was an image he didn't need. Samantha wet. Samantha naked. Samantha with her round breasts floating on the surface of the water like a couple of lilies.

He shifted and the mattress creaked.

"No baths," he said. "The hot water tank seems to be working, but we're on a well here. Tomorrow, after I get the generator going, I've got to prime the pump and test for water contamination."

"How do you know that?" Samantha asked.

Talking was good. Talking was better than thinking what he was thinking.

"I grew up on a farm."

"Your parents are farmers?"

"My father is a former navy doc who made a pile of money as a hotshot brain specialist in Baltimore. My mother is Conover Pointe country club and DAR all the way. But they raise horses."

"And children." She sounded wistful.

"Yeah, but the horses never let them down."

His joke—if it was a joke—fell flat in the darkness. He could hear Samantha breathing. He could feel her waiting. He could keep talking into that warm, receptive silence or he could roll over and—

Talk, lunkhead.

"I'm sure no brain surgeon," he said.

"Is that what they wanted?" she asked quietly.

He'd never known and he didn't have a clue how to ask. He'd been ten years old when he went to live with the Evanses: a too big, too quiet kid who struggled in school, a freak with nightmares and no memories.

He used to wonder when he was growing up if he'd done something so horrible his brain had blotted it out. Something so bad no one from his life before wanted him after his parents died. Right after the Evanses adopted him he used to torture himself with the idea that maybe his birth parents hadn't died, that they didn't want him either.

Mostly now he didn't think about it.

"They never told me," he said. "I think my dad was disappointed when I turned down the football scholarships, though. I could have gone to Maryland."

Marcus wasn't sure why he told her that.

"Why didn't you?"

"I wanted to be a SEAL."

"Navy, like your father?"

"And brother," he admitted. "Drew was a search and rescue pilot."

"You didn't want to fly planes?"

"I didn't have the scores to get into Annapolis."

"But with your father's service record—"

"I didn't want to be accepted to the academy because my family pulled strings. Anyway, I went to Coronado as an enlisted and got my degree at night."

"I can respect that. I know my appointment was only a courtesy thing after Stan died. But I'd like to be confirmed on my own merits."

It was understanding on a level Marcus hadn't expected and was grateful for. So he gave back to her what he could. "You negotiated that treaty on your own."

"And you went through— What did you call it? BUD/S?"

"Yeah. Six months of the toughest military training in the world."

"Six months? That long?"

"How long were you in graduate school?"

"Point taken." He couldn't see her smile, but he could hear it in her voice. He felt the mattress dip as she shifted, smelled the trace of her perfume.

He was dying and going to hell for what he was thinking now.

He was already burning.

To distract himself, to distract her, he said, "The training never ends, really. You've got five weeks' indoctrination before the physical screening test. Basic conditioning is eight weeks—that includes Hell Week." Four hours sleep in five and a half days of continuous training. He wondered if he'd get that much sleep this week. She smelled really good.

Talk, he told himself.

He cleared his throat. "Second phase is diving, another

eight weeks. Then nine weeks of land warfare, three weeks basic parachute training at Army Airborne in Georgia, fifteen more weeks at the Naval Special Warfare Center. At which point—if you haven't dropped dead or dropped out—you get your Budweiser and assignment to a SEAL Team.''

''You do all that and they give you a beer?''

He shook with silent laughter. ''No, that's what we call the pin. The Naval Special Warfare trident insignia. A budweiser. For BUD/S, you know?''

''You didn't do all that for a pin, either,'' she observed softly.

He had to be honest with her. ''In a way I did. Because that pin marks you as part of the toughest, most elite fighting force on sea, air or land. Once you've got that budweiser, you can walk onto any base, into any bar in any port all over the world, and every man there knows it. You know it. I wanted that.''

''To know what you were made of.''

''Yeah.'' And then, because that sounded so touchy-feely and he felt dangerously close to her in the dark, he added, ''Plus, I really dig swimming around blowing things up.''

Now she laughed, a warm, throaty chuckle that made him think of Kathleen Turner and full penetration sex.

''I can sympathize. I certainly had days—with the Rebelian delegation in particular—when I would have loved the option of blowing things up.''

''Yeah, well, we do it so you don't have to.''

''Keeping the world safe for truth, justice and the American way?'' she asked wryly.

He was used to the Superman gibes. But Samantha didn't sound as if she was making fun of him. ''I don't know so much about truth and justice. I'm not the one with the Harvard degree in government. But I do believe in my country.''

"'America, right or wrong'?"

He shook his head, forgetting she couldn't see him in the dark. "More like, 'America, right more often than not.'"

"And you would die for that." She sounded serious.

He didn't want her serious. He didn't want to know that in addition to being tall and stacked and incredibly hot, she was also kind and perceptive.

And so he tried to make light of both his danger and his dedication. "I'd fight for it. I'm pretty hard to kill."

"I'm glad," she said softly.

She touched him then, just her hand, warm and light between his shoulder blades.

At her gentle touch, his heart swelled. He swelled—damn, he swelled everywhere.

He stuffed one arm under his head, squashing his pillow flat, and closed his eyes.

He was going to sleep now. He could do it. He was trained to grab power naps when he could, to drop off quickly, to wake up instantly.

He concentrated on relaxing his muscles, on emptying his mind, on steadying his breathing, in and out, and tried not to notice how his weight depressed his side of the mattress and rolled her toward him. How her body warmed the air at his back. How her scent crept to him in the dark.

He was a navy SEAL. He could control his sleep.

But not his dreams...

In the water, no one could catch him. He was sleek as a seal, quick as a dolphin.

"Mark, come in," his mother called, ankle deep in the blue water. Her figure wavered against the dazzling white sand. One arm shaded her eyes.

He laughed and dived.

He dived.

He dived…and the water was cold and deep, and the current was fast and strong.

He pulled against it, unafraid. He heard the boat explode behind him. So soon? Too soon. But he was expecting it, their mother had warned them, so when the water surged around him, he relaxed and tumbled with it, over and over.

Dark. It was so dark.

Particles stung his arms and legs. Blood roared in his ears. Fear drifted at the edge of his mind, but he pushed it away.

He was the strong one, and the water was his home.

He floated, orienting himself, opening his eyes against the grit and the saltwater, seeking the light. Up. There.

He kicked. The light grew. The water rushed around him. His head broke the surface, and he gulped great, glad gasps of air. He'd made it! He was strong.

He turned his head, laughing—We made it!—and counted other dark, wet heads in the water. One, two, three…

The fear this time struck cold and sharp as a cramp.

Where was his sister?

His heart pounded into his throat. He opened his mouth to call, to scream, and a wave reared up and slapped him in the face.

He choked. Spat. Gasped.

He gasped.

"Marcus?"

Her small hand tugged at him. Her words rippled over him, warm as the sea at low tide.

"Marcus, wake up."

He bolted upright. His heart pounded. His skin was clammy. Disoriented, he blinked at the pale, concerned face in the dark.

Samantha.

He dragged a shuddering breath into his lungs.

"It was only a dream," she said soothingly. "You were dreaming. Everything is all right."

He scrubbed his face with his hand, as if he could wipe the images away. "Sorry."

"You have nightmares?" Her voice was gentle.

"No. Yes. Hell. I thought I was over them."

"Is it the explosion? The *Stoker?*"

"Yes. No." He didn't want to talk about it. He never talked about it. *Freak.* But he had woken her up. She deserved some sort of explanation. "I mean, there's some sort of explosion, but I don't think... It's all mixed up with my sister."

"Honey."

"No. The other one."

"You have another sister?"

The loss cut like a combat knife, jagged and deep. Pain flowed in to fill the wound. He took another deep breath.

"*No.* Sorry," he said again. "I just..."

"It's all right." Samantha didn't press him. He was embarrassingly grateful that she didn't demand answers he didn't have. Had never had. Not since...

Her fingers spread on his chest against his damp T-shirt. Her touch seared him through the thin cotton. His heart thudded against her palm.

"Let's take off this shirt," she said. "And then you can lie down and go back to sleep. It's all right."

Obedient as a child, he helped her pull the wet shirt over his head before he lay back against the pillows and closed his eyes. He felt her shift beside him, felt her knee brush his thigh and her hair tickle his shoulder. Her breath was warm. Her hand was steady on his chest.

His lips were stiff, but he had to tell her. He had to thank her.

"Sam—"

''Shh,'' she soothed. ''Sleep.''

This time he slept without dreams.

And woke in the morning with his body heavy and throbbing with need, and Samantha draped over him like a blanket.

Eight

Samantha woke with her fingers splayed on Marcus's hard chest and her nose pressed to his hard shoulder. Her smooth thigh rode his hairy one. Her elbow rested on his warm, ridged stomach.

She stared at the tight brown nipple inches from her face and thought, Goodness. This was certainly different.

"Good" different, but strange.

For over a year, she had missed sleeping with a man. In the lonely stretches of the night, she missed the warmth and the sound of breathing. She missed the simple human contact of flesh touching flesh. Now she inhaled slowly, stealing air, luxuriating in the morning closeness of male heat and male weight and male scent. It was wonderful. Reassuring. Familiar.

Different.

Marcus Evans was not her husband.

His skin was darker and firm. His hair was thick and springy. He smelled different—musky—his skin and his hair and his breath. She sniffed again, cautiously, and felt her insides soften and loosen.

He was bigger than Stan, too. His chest was massive. His abdomen was solid with muscle. Legs, arms, hands, feet—he was big all over. She slid her leg exploringly.

Goodness, yes. All over.

I don't know that I trust myself to lie next to you all night and not, you know, act like a guy. Or react like a guy. If you get my drift.

Samantha smiled. He certainly was reacting like a guy now. She was touched, flattered and aroused by the way Marcus responded to her even in his sleep.

Last night she'd soothed him the way she would have comforted the children she longed for. Maybe she could have fooled herself into believing the tenderness she felt was maternal.

Only... She looked at the sheet tenting his erection. It was quite clear this morning he was no child.

Okay. She wouldn't pretend, even to herself, to be shocked or surprised. What did surprise her was that she was reacting to his morning arousal like a...well, like a woman. The woman she hadn't allowed herself to be since before Stan died. The woman she'd denied.

His breathing was slow and even. Curious, tempted, she let her hand drift down over his hard, furred abdomen to the band of his boxers. He didn't move.

Heart thumping in anticipation, she eased her hand under the soft elastic barrier. Her fingers combed the coarser hair at his groin before she stopped. Should she...? No, of course she shouldn't. But his long limbs were still relaxed in sleep. Only the heat of his arousal strained just out of reach beyond her fingertips.

He was less than inches away. So warm. So close. She flexed her hand and touched him, her fingers barely brushing his hot, firm, smooth flesh. She sucked in her breath. Oh, goodness. Oh, yes.

She stole a look at his face.

And found him watching her from under lowered lashes, his eyes as warm and brilliant as the sea off the coast of Italy.

"Gotcha," he said.

Her cheeks flooded with embarrassment. But there was no accusation in his eyes, only a lazy appreciation that made her heart beat faster.

She moistened her lips and did her best to sound easy and sophisticated instead of nervous and needy. ''It seems to me that I'm the one who's got you.''

''Not yet,'' he said frankly. ''But you will if you don't move your hand.''

''Oh.'' Flustered, she started to withdraw her hand from his boxers.

He gripped her wrist to hold her right where she was. ''Sure? Because in case you haven't noticed, I am more than willing.''

She had to laugh. ''Oh, I noticed. Thank you. But I think… That is, I don't…''

''Too soon?'' he asked.

She nodded gratefully. ''I'm sorry. I realize when you woke up you must have thought—''

''That I'd died and gone to heaven?''

''That I was taking terrible advantage of you.''

''Nope. Didn't think that. Mostly when a guy wakes up and finds a beautiful woman with, you know, her hand down his shorts, he doesn't think much of anything. Especially not that she's taking advantage.''

''I'm sorry,'' she said again.

''For what?''

''This is so unfair to you.''

''We could make it fair.''

She blinked. ''How?''

His warm blue eyes caressed her. ''You could let me touch you.''

Her breath clogged her lungs. ''Let you…''

''Let me touch you. To make things even,'' he explained.

He had to be out of his mind to suggest such a thing. She had to be out of hers to consider it.

''Make things even,'' she repeated.

''Yeah.'' He sounded serious.

''You're joking.''

"Not really." He held her gaze a moment longer and then shrugged, making her arm move against his stomach. "Okay. Bad idea. But you did ask."

It *was* a bad idea. A terrible idea.

A dangerous idea.

"You just want to touch me?" she asked uncertainly.

His eyes flashed. "Actually, I'd like to do a lot more than that. But touching you would even things up."

Her pulse raced. Her body hummed. The sunshine edged the blind with gold and painted a bar of light across the foot of the bed.

"All right," she whispered.

Marcus looked as stunned as she felt. "Yes?"

"Yes. It's only fair."

He smiled the wide, bright smile she loved. "Hot damn."

She laughed.

He raised himself on one elbow and eased her onto her back. His gaze skimmed her face, dropped to consider her breasts. She was wearing one of his T-shirts—Property of the U.S. Navy was stamped across the front—and a pair of her own panties. No bra.

He met her eyes again, and the heat in his melted her bones.

"Do I get to take off your shirt, too?"

Oh, goodness. She swallowed and pressed her knees together. "I don't think—"

"You took off mine last night."

It was like a game. A silly, delicious, dangerous game. I will if you will. Simon says. Mother, may I?

She knew better than to play. She did.

"Well…in the interest of fairness," she said. She sat up to pull her shirt off, but her elbow caught in her sleeve. Her hip pinned the hem in back. By the time she struggled free, she was feeling more awkward than seductive.

Until she dragged the darn thing over her head and saw his face.

He was breathing hard, as if he'd just come in from a fourteen-mile training run. He looked at her breasts. They puckered. He looked in her eyes.

"Wow," he said with perfect sincerity.

Her awkwardness disappeared. She smiled.

"Thank you," she said, equally sincere.

"You're beautiful." He shook his head. "Pretty lame, huh?"

His honesty pleased her more than any pretty words could have.

"No," she said quickly. "That's very nice."

He lifted one big, tanned hand toward her pale breast. "Do you mind if I...?"

She was almost dizzy with anticipation. "No."

He stopped. "No?"

"No, I mean..." She wet her lips. "I don't mind."

He gave her another of those mind-blowing, heart-stopping smiles. "Hoo yah."

His knuckles grazed the soft, full underside, bringing her nipple to aching, full attention. So he touched it, too, opening his hand on her breast, running his fingers over the erect tip, stroking, squeezing, teasing.

Her blood pounded in her head. Pleasure coursed through her veins.

And then he took his hand away and clenched it in the sheets.

"There." His voice was tight. "Now we're even."

She opened her mouth to breathe. "No, we're not. I touched more than your chest."

His mouth opened, too. He shut it with a snap. Despite his expressed willingness, she'd managed to surprise him.

That was okay. She'd surprised herself.

"Close enough," he said.

But it wasn't.

"It's all right. I don't mind." Oh, now, there was an invitation likely to drive a man wild with desire. "I want you too," she said. Better.

His throat moved as he swallowed. His voice was raw. "I touch you anyplace else, babe, and I'm not going to stop. Is that what you want?"

Was that what she wanted?

Warm and tingly feelings aside, was she actually contemplating sex with a man-not-her-husband whom she had known less than a week? A professional soldier who'd locked her driver in a utility closet and forced her to lie to her secretary?

"Well..."

"No point overthinking things," Marcus said. The mattress lurched as he moved closer. "Forget I asked."

He was very large and very near. Nerves jumped in her stomach. "No. You're right. It's not like we have a relationship. We don't even know each other very well."

He spread his palms wide. "What do you want to know? Just ask me."

She smiled. It was like a continuation of their game. "All right. Where were you born?"

He gave her an odd look, as if she'd demanded something difficult or deeply personal. "How about instead I tell you I'm up to date on all my shots and you tell me how you like it?"

She arranged the sheet over her legs. "That's certainly to the point, but much less effective in creating an atmosphere of trust. Tell me about your childhood."

He got out of bed. "I can't tell you anything."

Hurt and confused, she watched him pull a pair of jeans from his duffel. "Why not?"

"I can't, that's all."

She stuck out her chin. "And I can't be intimate with a man who refuses to share himself with me."

He stopped in the act of zipping up his fly. "That didn't seem to be a problem for you five minutes ago."

She winced.

He swore. "God, I'm sorry. Look, I've got to check on the generator. Will you be all right?"

She held the T-shirt to her breasts. "What is this, emotional hit and run?"

"We call it tactical retreat in the navy. Will you be all right?" he repeated.

She wanted to tell him no. She wanted to demand he stay until she had what she wanted. Answers. An orgasm.

Only, of course, she didn't. She was too much the diplomat and too big a coward.

"I'm fine."

"Okay. Good." He put his keys in his pocket and holstered his gun at his back.

He was leaving? He was leaving.

"What am I supposed to do while you're off playing with tools?"

He yanked on his bootlaces. "Want to come hold my flashlight?"

She shivered between annoyance, laughter and lust. "You wouldn't let me."

"I changed my mind."

She tossed her hair. "I changed mine first."

He paused in the doorway, his eyes shadowed. "So you win. Go back to sleep."

At least he didn't suggest she cook them breakfast.

Although alone in bed with the still-warm sheets and her cooling desire, Samantha thought it might have been better if he had. At least then she'd feel more like a partner. At least then she'd have something to do.

She could have had a partner. She could be doing something right now.

With him.

She took a deep, frustrated breath and scrambled out of bed.

The blind at the window was the old-fashioned roll kind, tattered at the edges and gray with dust. She raised it and sneezed.

Marcus was crossing the yard, tall, dark and competent in boots and jeans. Her heart bumped at the sight of him.

I grew up on a farm, he'd told her last night.

So why wouldn't he talk to her this morning?

She didn't understand him, this warrior with his haunted eyes and blindingly bright smile. That more than anything had stopped her from making love with him. She was a woman who prided herself on her understanding.

And yet there had been raw need in his eyes and real frustration in his voice when he'd jumped from their bed. *I can't tell you anything.*

Why not?

What other secrets was he hiding?

Samantha frowned, staring out the window at the sunlit yard. She would have to show him that he could trust her, that was all. She would make him breakfast and they would sit down and talk calmly and openly. For goodness sake, she'd just brokered bilateral peace in Eastern Europe. She ought to be able to negotiate an understanding with her bodyguard.

With new confidence, she went to open the window. It raised two inches and stuck. Wiping her palms on her shirt, she tried again. It didn't budge.

Bending, she inspected the frame. Two nails were driven into the window sash, blocking the track. Sometime last night, while she had been changing the bed and getting her things from the other room, Marcus had nailed the window shut.

Her stomach clutched.

Was he trying to keep intruders out? Or keep her in?

Marcus stared at the tangle of power cords connected to the generator. That one fed the well pump and that one led to the refrigerator. The cable there should hook up with the house's wiring. If he could find the transfer switch, he might be able to swing real lights tonight.

Or he could backfeed electricity into the power lines and blow up the house.

He jerked the wrench against the rusty lug nuts that held the cover panel.

Tell me about your childhood.

Sure thing, honey. Which one? You want to hear what it was like to grow up big, fast and dumb in Conover Pointe or do you want the details of my life before that? The one I can't remember?

The metal panel slipped and sliced his hand. He stared at the bright welling blood and, unbidden, the memory came.

"Hold out your hand," the dark-haired girl ordered.

He shoved it behind his back. "It's just a scratch."

"Any wound that breaks the skin is prone to infection," she lectured, and then favored him with her small smile, the one he never could resist. *"Besides, I want to practice applying an adhesive dressing. Please?"*

"You mean, a Band-Aid?" he teased. But he held out his hand to her.

He held out his hand. It trembled.

God, he really was losing his mind.

And if he needed further proof of that, look at the way he'd just blown things with Samantha.

She'd been sitting half-naked in his bed, practically offering herself to him, her beautiful eyes shining, her beautiful body begging for his touch, and he'd said...

He closed his eyes in pain, remembering. He'd said, "Close enough."

Mrs. Crane, his eleventh-grade English teacher, was right. He really was an idiot. Because he hadn't been anywhere near close enough. Close enough, on top of. Close enough, inside of. All the way close, as deep, as hard, as often as he could go.

He drew an unsteady breath and propped the panel against the generator box. He had to stop thinking about it. Because it would never happen now. What had she said? *I can't be intimate with a man who refuses to share himself with me.*

And he didn't do sharing. He couldn't. Because where other guys had family stories and childhood anecdotes, he had nightmares and great big memory blanks.

He flipped the transfer switch and unscrewed the fuel intake, nodding in satisfaction when he found the tank full. James Robinson, Senior, was a practical man who prepared for emergencies. Just like Jimmy, his son.

Marcus's satisfaction faded. He had no clue what he might have inherited from his own father. No idea what he might pass on to his own son. No memories at all.

He secured the fuel cap and checked the vents for blockage and the power cords for fraying. There was no way he could give Samantha what she asked for.

But he would keep her safe. He would provide for her basic needs—her *other* basic needs—and maybe that would be enough.

It had to be enough. For both of them.

Marcus frowned in concern. "You're not eating. Is everything all right?"

Samantha set her coffee mug precisely on her flowered

place mat. Her red hair was confined in a neat ponytail at the back of her head. Her eyes were guarded and cool. Her T-shirt might read *Sexy Chick,* but her attitude said, *Ambassador Barnes to you, fella.*

"Are you inquiring how I feel about my enforced absence from Washington, or—"

"I was asking about your breakfast. Is it okay?"

"It's fine."

"Because I know powdered eggs and milk take a little getting used to. Now that the refrigerator's up and running—"

She arched her eyebrows. "You'll take me grocery shopping?"

"Well, no."

She sipped her coffee in silence.

"If you're bored, you can play the piano," he offered.

"I've played the piano. It's out of tune."

"It sounded fine to me."

She sniffed. "The D sharp sticks."

"What?"

"The D sharp above middle C. The key sticks."

"Is that bad?"

"It makes it difficult to play anything." She met his gaze and a little of her bad humor slid away. She smiled ruefully. "Particularly if the player is as out of practice as I am."

"It's only for a couple of days," he said. He hoped. "Just until they catch whoever's after you."

"There will always be someone after me. As long as the Coalition's in existence and DeBruzkya is in power."

She was right. Marcus had said pretty much the same thing to Jerry Baxter. The thought didn't make him feel any better about what he was doing here. "Until they plug the leak in DS, then."

She leaned forward, passionately earnest. "I have to be back in Delmonico next week to discuss the implications of the accord with the Euro-Atlantic Partnership Council. I don't have that long."

He met her eyes regretfully. "You don't have a choice."

Her gaze dropped. She toyed with her scrambled eggs, neither agreeing nor arguing with him.

Hell.

"You want toast?" he offered.

"No, thank you."

"You got a problem with toast?"

"The toast is fine."

"Okay, so it's not the food. Are you sick or are you just in a mood?"

She put down her fork in annoyance. "Has it occurred to you that a person might choose not to eat simply because he or she is not hungry?"

"No," he said frankly. "I'm always hungry."

For the first time that morning, she smiled. Relief loosened the knots in his shoulders.

"I imagine you are. But you're much more active than I am."

He shrugged. "So after breakfast we'll take a walk."

Interest gleamed in her eyes. "Walk where?"

He drizzled honey on a piece of bread and handed it to her. "To the well house."

She took the bread, but said, "I hardly need to bulk up to walk across the yard."

"It's farther than you think. A well has to be located away from potential sources of contamination. Animals, machinery, waste..."

She licked honey from her fingers and looked at him.

He felt his face redden. "Okay, it's not that far. We'll go to the farm pond after."

"The farm pond," she murmured. "Won't *that* be exciting."

He grinned. "Yeah. Maybe you'll fall in and I'll get to practice my highly developed lifesaving skills."

Mouth-to-mouth. His body on top of hers, pressed to the warm grassy bank...

She narrowed her eyes. "In your dreams, farm boy."

Nine

"Watch your step," Marcus warned from inside the dim well house.

"Easy for you to say," Samantha muttered.

Compared to the brightness outside, the well house seemed dark and cramped and creepy. Gaps between the wooden walls and tin roof admitted just enough light to reveal the encroaching wilderness. Spiderwebs festooned the eaves. Honeysuckle poked pale fingers over the sill to creep along the dirt floor. Something unseen rustled in a corner.

Samantha shuddered. There was too much here she could not see and did not trust. Spiders. Snakes.

Marcus?

No, she trusted him. She had to trust him. Didn't she?

She took a deep breath and one step forward. A plank wobbled beneath her feet.

"Stay by the door," Marcus ordered from inside.

She stopped. "Why?"

"These old hand-dug wells can be treacherous. This one's almost three feet across. Once I lift the cap off, there's nothing to keep you from falling in."

Her heart beat faster. "What about you?"

"Well, sure, I'd do my best, but—"

"No, I meant, what's to keep you from falling in?"

"I have room. The farmer who built this place didn't waste any wood on it, but he left some space to work in. Besides, I can see."

She could see, too, now that her eyes were adjusting. Beyond the plank on which she stood, a round concrete slab covered most of the floor. A plastic bucket, its bright orange diminished to gray by dirt and darkness, occupied one corner. Leaves occupied another. Marcus knelt next to a metal tank that looked like R2-D2. A short, low cylinder connected to a pipe that ran under the slab.

As Samantha watched, he stooped and wrapped his arms around the concrete slab. His muscles shifted under his T-shirt. As easily as a maid lifting a tea tray, he hefted the well cap, exposing a deep, dark hole in the ground.

Samantha gasped.

He flashed her a quick grin and set the slab beside the tank. "It's okay. I know what I'm doing."

Obviously. She wasn't about to admit she was weak-kneed and breathless because he was strong and competent and could lift concrete. He took a bottle and a coil of string from his pack on the floor.

"What *are* you doing?" she asked.

"A well should be disinfected once a year."

She really hated the casual way he was bending over that hole. There was some kind of pipe on one side she supposed he could use as a handhold, but… "So you're disinfecting the water?" she asked, to distract herself from his precarious position.

He leaned his big body farther over the gaping hole. Her heart hitched. "That, and I want to take a sample. Make sure it's safe to drink."

She couldn't watch. She couldn't look away. "If it's not safe to drink, then what have we been—"

"Bottled water." He straightened and she breathed again in relief. "I brought drinking water with us, but groundwater is more convenient. And we want an unlimited supply in case…" He stopped and capped the bottle in his hand.

"In case you have to keep me here," she finished for him.

"Until it's safe for me to take you back. Yeah."

Standing, he tucked the bottle away and pried the lid from the orange bucket. He threw something into the well. The plops drifting up from the water's surface sounded very far down. She took a step back.

"Not that I doubt for a minute that you are highly capable," she said carefully, "but don't you think if I were really in imminent danger, someone would have come up with a better plan than sending us alone into rural Virginia? If there's a problem within DS, I could have been assigned protection from another agency, FBI or Secret Service or something, that would have allowed me to continue to function."

Marcus thumped the lid back down on the bucket. "You were assigned other protection," he said. "Me."

"Yes, and then they sent us miles away from Washington to an abandoned farmhouse with no electricity, no water, no food, no phone and no security."

"We've got electricity and water now. And I'll feed you. Don't worry."

She flapped her hand. "Forget food. Food is not the point. Don't you find the whole setup a little odd?"

He gripped the edges of the concrete well cap. His fingers tightened. His shoulders bunched as he lifted the slab. "I would. Except the setup is my fault."

Samantha's jaw sagged. "What are you talking about?"

"I figured if there was a leak at DS, their safe house might not be so safe." He set the well cap squarely over the hole. "So I brought you here."

"You brought me."

He straightened, shrugging his pack onto one shoulder. "Yeah."

"Without telling anyone."

"Telling would have kind of defeated the purpose, now, wouldn't it?"

She pressed her lips together. She was not going to overreact. She was not going to cry or scream or lose her temper or do anything inappropriate for an ambassador of the United States of America. "So it's not just Agent Walker who doesn't know where I am. No one knows where I am."

Marcus nodded and sauntered toward her. "That's what I'm counting on."

No crying. No screaming. No—

"Are you out of your mind?" she snapped.

He met her gaze. "I sure hope not."

There was a shadow in his eyes that fell on her heart. She caught her breath. He was only joking. He had to be.

And then he smiled his warm, wide smile, and she felt as though she were the one losing her mind.

"Maybe I just don't want to question a mission that involves me spending time alone with you," he suggested.

She relaxed. Now she knew he was joking. And yet he tempted her more than she would have believed or could ever admit. "Take me back, and when all this is over, perhaps we can—"

"Write to each other? You from Delmonico and me from the latest hot spot outside CONUS?" Continental United States, he meant. He shook his head. "Hell, maybe we will. Maybe we'll have to. But for now, maybe we should take what we've got and be grateful."

"I can't do that," she said automatically.

He raised an eyebrow. "What, you think the world's going to end if you neglect it for a few days?"

She had been so focused for so long it was hard to see beyond her political agenda. "The accord might."

"It's been ratified, hasn't it? By the Delmonican government? And signed by our president?"

"Well, yes, but—"

"And you've got until next week before you have to schmooze it through the—what did you call it?—the Euro-Atlantic Partnership Council."

He listened, she thought. He listened and remembered. "Oh, the council doesn't have to approve the treaty. But the implications for the larger European community—"

He tugged the plank door firmly shut behind them. "So what you're saying is, the treaty's not going to fall apart if you disappear for a few days."

Frustrated, she followed him along the sunlit path. "Not for a few days, no. But—"

"But you might?"

His insight silenced her. She was appalled to feel tears burn the back of her throat.

He turned. "Hey." His voice was gentle.

Her vision blurred, but she saw his face soften and change. His hands were warm on her shoulders as he tugged her closer. She thought about resisting. But what was the point? He was too strong for her. And she was tired, weary of fighting the world and sick of denying her feelings.

With a sigh, she relaxed and rested her forehead against his broad chest. His arms came around her, but the rest of him didn't budge. There was no softness, no give to him at all. He was solid and calm and hard as the side of a hill, and he smelled like grass and summer sun.

It was tempting simply to lean on him, to absorb his strength and his comfort, to imagine he could take care of her, to hold on and believe that everything would be all right.

She knew better. She'd believed in Stan, and Stan was dead.

Still, she held on, her throat tight, her hands fisted in Marcus's shirt.

He brushed a kiss against her hair. "Poor baby."

"I am not a poor baby," she said, the words muffled against his chest. "I just need something to do."

Work helped. The past year had taught her that. Activity kept her mind occupied and her grief at bay better than any pills the doctor had prescribed. She needed to work.

"Okay," Marcus said slowly. "Want to help me catch dinner?"

She lifted her head. His blue eyes were warm and close and dazzling. "What?"

"The farm pond used to be stocked with catfish. Still is, I bet. We could have fresh fish for dinner."

"You're inviting me to go fishing?"

"Why not?"

"Because I don't know how. I won't catch anything."

"Honey, we're not fly-fishing for trout. We're dropping a couple of lines for catfish. You'll do fine."

Samantha was without a doubt the thinking-est woman Marcus had ever met. It could have been annoying. Or even intimidating. But he liked watching that first-class brain kick into high gear over something as simple as an invitation to go fishing. And there was that little pleat that formed between her eyebrows. He liked that. And the way she pursed her lips while she puzzled things over made him hot.

She pursed them now, and he grinned in pure appreciation.

"What?" she asked suspiciously.

"Nothing." When she continued to glare at him, he said, "You look cute, that's all."

She took a step back, away from him. "I do not."

He shrugged. He wasn't going to argue with her.

But apparently after yielding in his arms, Ambassador Barnes was more than willing to argue with him. "I have never been cute."

"Sure you were. When you were a little girl? I bet you were really cute then. Red hair, right? And dimples? All the little boys were probably crazy for you."

She blushed, but he couldn't tell if she was pissed at him or pleased.

"You'd lose your bet," she said. "Little boys didn't like me. I beat them in dodgeball and I talked too much in class."

It figured she was one of the smart kids. Marcus had been one of the dumb ones. It created a bond, of sorts, though she might not see it that way.

"I don't mind you talking," he said. "Fact is, I kind of like it."

"Maybe you don't mind it now. You would have thought I was a geek in high school."

"And you would have thought I was a dumb jock."

"You're not dumb."

"And you're not a geek." He caught one of her hands and drew lazy circles on the back of it with his thumb. "No geek ever had skin like yours. Or hair like yours. Or a body like yours."

She tugged. He didn't let go.

"You don't have to say that. I'm not fishing for compliments. I don't need them."

"Maybe not. Maybe I need to say them anyway." He brought her hand to his lips, watching her eyes darken when he kissed her knuckles. "Maybe I want to offer you all kinds of things you haven't asked for and don't need from me."

Her tongue touched her lower lip. "What kind of things?"

Help. Protection. Comfort.

Oh, yeah, like she wanted any of that stuff from him.

"Naked back rubs?" he suggested instead, and was relieved and rewarded when she laughed.

But she pulled her hand away. "I don't think I'm ready for that level of distraction yet."

Yet?

Did that mean...? No. Probably not. But even the possibility was enough to electrify his body and fog his mind.

He curled his hands into fists so he wouldn't do something colossally stupid like grab for her. "Okay," he said easily. "Guess we're stuck with fishing, then."

"I told you I wouldn't be any good at this," Samantha complained an hour later.

Marcus studied her from under the bill of his baseball cap. Cool, composed Ambassador Barnes was gone. The young woman parked next to him on the bank, the sun striking fire from her dark red hair and mud decorating the hip pockets of her new jeans, looked every bit the "Sexy Chick" her T-shirt proclaimed her to be.

"We don't know that yet. We've only been out here an hour."

She sniffed. "I should have caught something by now."

He grinned. "You know, for a woman who can stand around an embassy party in high heels and make small talk for five hours, you're pretty impatient."

She jiggled her line in the water. "I thought the purpose of fishing was to catch fish."

"Catching fish is good." He tilted his cap so it shaded his eyes again, leaned back and folded his arms beneath his head. "Some folks also like to relax."

"I'm relaxed," she insisted.

"You're bouncing like a buoy in rough water. You're as bad as my baby sister."

She flipped back her hair, the way a woman did when she wanted a man's attention.

She had his. He looked at the line of her throat and the

sunburn beginning to prickle her nose and thought she could have anything she wanted.

"I would probably like your sister," she said. "In fact, at the moment, she has my sympathies. Do you pull this tall-dark-and-stolid routine with her, or is it something I do that brings it out in you?"

Marcus switched his attention from her pink nose to the challenging lift of her chin. "It's just you," he said cheerfully. "You talk too much."

She practically sputtered. "You said you didn't mind."

"I don't." He raised himself on his elbows, enjoying the quick glance she stole at his body. "It's the fish. You're scaring them away."

"You're making that up," she accused.

"No. See, fish are creatures of instinct. They detect low-frequency vibrations. They can sense when you're agitated or impatient, and they stay away."

"Baloney," she said.

Amusement shook him. "I can prove it."

"You cannot."

"Yeah, I can. You relax, and I bet you catch something."

She rolled her eyes. "How can you tell if I'm relaxed or not?"

"I'm going to help you."

"Oh, that will work."

He folded himself to a sitting position. "Why don't we try it and see?"

She did not protest as he took the fishing rod and jammed it between a rock and a rotten log on the bank. But when he turned her gently by her shoulders, she said, "This really isn't necessary."

"Shh." He exerted pressure with his thumbs, finding the knots in her muscles.

"I'm prepared to take your word about the fish," she said over her shoulder. "I'll even be quiet."

"Good." He brushed her slippery hair off her shoulders before beginning to knead her *latissimi dorsi*. She was really tight.

"Honestly, you can..." She moaned as his thumbs found a particularly sensitive spot.

"Stop?"

Her head fell forward. "No. Oh, no. If you stop now, I'll have to kill you."

He chuckled and stroked her back, rotated her shoulders, massaged her arms. Her flesh was firm and smooth under his hands. Her skin—the soft skin at her nape and her pink upper arms—was warm and damp.

She stretched like a cat, bowing her back toward him so he could see the tiny bumps of vertebrae through her T-shirt and the pale sliver of waist above her jeans. She made another sound, a hum of pleasure deep in her throat that vibrated through them both.

He wanted to taste the back of her neck, wanted to suck and lick. He wanted to slide his hands around and squeeze her full breasts, wanted to press her down on the warm, grassy bank and push himself inside her, hard, fast, now, while she moaned.

He closed his mouth and tried breathing out his nose so he wouldn't drool. Damn.

Okay, so he wasn't going to win any points for finesse. That didn't mean he had to react like a nineteen-year-old sailor on his first shore leave in a Philippine whorehouse. Marcus concentrated on keeping his breathing steady, his touch gentle and his libido lashed to the mast.

And while he didn't fool himself into thinking he wouldn't crawl, kill or die for a chance to rip the jeans off that lush, incredible body and drive himself inside...well, maybe he fooled her. Because instead of jumping up and

GET 2 BOOKS FREE!

MIRA

MIRA® Books, The Brightest Stars in Fiction, presents

The Best of the Best™

Superb collector's editions of the very best books by some of today's best-known authors!

★ **FREE BOOKS!** To introduce you to "The Best of the Best" we'll send you 2 books ABSOLUTELY FREE!

★ **FREE GIFT!** Get an exciting surprise gift FREE!

★ **BEST BOOKS!** "The Best of the Best" brings you the best books by some of today's most popular authors!

GET 2

HOW TO GET YOUR
2 FREE BOOKS AND FREE GIFT!

1. Peel off the MIRA® sticker on the front cover. Place it in the space provided at right. This automatically entitles you to receive two free books and an exciting surprise gift.

2. Send back this card and you'll get 2 "The Best of the Best™" books. These books have a combined cover price of $11.98 or more in the U.S. and $13.98 or more in Canada, but they are yours to keep absolutely FREE!

3. There's <u>no</u> catch. You're under <u>no</u> obligation to buy anything. We charge nothing – ZERO – for your first shipment. And you don't have to make any minimum number of purchases – not even one!

4. We call this line "The Best of the Best" because each month you'll receive the best books by some of today's most popular authors. These authors show up time and time again on all the major bestseller lists and their books sell out as soon as they hit the stores. You'll like the convenience of getting them delivered to your home at our special discount prices . . . and you'll love your *Heart to Heart* subscriber newsletter featuring author news, horoscopes, recipes, book reviews and much more!

5. We hope that after receiving your free books you'll want to remain a subscriber. But the choice is yours – to continue or cancel, anytime at all! So why not take us up on our invitation, wlth no risk of any kind. You'll be glad you did!

6. And remember...we'll send you a surprise gift ABSOLUTELY FREE just for giving THE BEST OF THE BEST a try.

SPECIAL FREE GIFT

We'll send you a fabulous surprise gift, absolutely FREE, simply for accepting our no-risk offer!

Visit us online at
www.mirabooks.com

® and TM are registered trademark of Harlequin Enterprises Limited.

BOOKS FREE!

Hurry!

Return this card promptly to GET 2 FREE BOOKS & A FREE GIFT!

The Best of the Best ™

Affix peel-off MIRA sticker here

YES! Please send me the 2 FREE "The Best of the Best" books and FREE gift for which I qualify. I understand that I am under no obligation to purchase anything further, as explained on the back and on the opposite page.

385 MDL DRTA   185 MDL DR59

FIRST NAME   LAST NAME

ADDRESS

APT.#   CITY

STATE/PROV.   ZIP/POSTAL CODE

▼ DETACH AND MAIL CARD TODAY! ▼

(P-BB3-03) ©1998 MIRA BOOKS

THE BEST OF THE BEST™ — Here's How it Works:

Accepting your 2 free books and gift places you under no obligation to buy anything. You may keep the books and gift and return the shipping statement marked "cancel." If you do not cancel, about a month later we will send you 4 additional books and bill you just $4.74 each in the U.S., or $5.24 each in Canada, plus 25¢ shipping & handling per book and applicable taxes if any.* That's the complete price and — compared to cover prices starting from $5.99 each in the U.S. and $6.99 each in Canada — it's quite a bargain! You may cancel at any time, but if you choose to continue, every month we'll send you 4 more books, which you may either purchase at the discount price or return to us and cancel your subscription.

*Terms and prices subject to change without notice. Sales tax applicable in N.Y. Canadian residents will be charged applicable provincial taxes and GST. Credit or Debit balances in a customer's account(s) may be offset by any other outstanding balance owed by or to the customer.

If offer card is missing write to: The Best of the Best; 3010 Walden Ave., P.O. Box 1867, Buffalo, NY 14240-1867

BUSINESS REPLY MAIL
FIRST-CLASS MAIL   PERMIT NO. 717-003   BUFFALO, NY

POSTAGE WILL BE PAID BY ADDRESSEE

THE BEST OF THE BEST
PO BOX 1867
3010 WALDEN AVE
BUFFALO NY 14240-9952

NO POSTAGE
NECESSARY
IF MAILED
IN THE
UNITED STATES

yelling at him to take his hands off her, she gave this little sigh and let her chin drop to her chest. Pleased, he rubbed and dug and coaxed the tension from her shoulders.

He gave them a final squeeze and released her. "There. Now you're relaxed."

The fishing pole snapped forward. The reel rattled as the line spun out.

Marcus made a lunge for the pole before it followed the fish into the water.

"Nice reflexes," Samantha said.

He grinned and tested the resistance on the line. She'd hooked a pond monster, three, four pounds easy. "Good teamwork. See, I told you the fish could sense your mood."

She stood, brushing grass from her back pockets. "Well, the fish were wrong."

He played out line and pulled it in. "What are you talking about?"

"You said the fish would come if I wasn't impatient. I'm still impatient."

He mocked himself for his disappointment. He'd thought a back rub would change her mind? He took up more slack on the line. "Okay. After I clean the fish, I'll check in with DS. Maybe—"

Samantha shook her head, smiling. Her dark lashes lowered, then lifted as she met his gaze. Her red hair slipped over one shoulder and curled around her breast. Sexy Chick. "That's not what I'm impatient for."

When he gaped at her, she stood on tiptoe and brushed soft lips against his cheek. "I'll see you back at the house," she said, and sauntered away in her tight, dark jeans, leaving him to wrestle a big, fat, flopping fish and his own lust.

Ten

It was a good thing she was a diplomat and not a spy, Samantha thought, studying the back of Marcus's head. Because if her life or her job ever depended on her ability to seduce a man, she was obviously sunk.

She had thought—hoped—that after her little come-on by the farm pond he would follow her back to the house hot and urgent and hungry for more than fried fish.

It hadn't happened.

Oh, Marcus had followed her. And he'd been hot. The first thing he did when he came into the kitchen was break out a bottle of water from the fridge.

He'd been urgent. It seemed he couldn't wait to get that big ugly fish gutted and scaled. And after that he'd boarded up the broken window, and after that he'd tinkered with the plumbing and wiring in the house, and after that he'd encouraged her to take a walk with him along what he explained was the old riding trail. He was inventing activities for her like a reluctant baby-sitter with a bored toddler.

There was no denying their easy, sunlit ramble had restored her spirits and awakened her appetite. All her appetites, darn it. She felt awake and aware, relaxed and alive. But after dinner Marcus had pushed her off to play by herself while he did his homework.

She spent some time at the old upright piano, working to restore some flexibility to her fingers as she attempted her old favorites, "Fur Elise," "Clair de Lune," some Joplin tunes. But she was out of practice and one of the keys stuck. After an hour or so she gave it up and wandered back into the kitchen.

She stood in the doorway, watching Marcus's tanned, long-fingered hands play over the computer keyboard. She might still question his actions in abducting and holding her here. But any doubts she had about his motives or his character had been laid to rest. His restraint in their bed, his attention to her safety and his concern for her comfort had convinced her of the strength of his honor and the goodness of his heart.

Samantha nibbled her lower lip. Maybe he was a little too honorable? A tad too restrained?

Marcus glanced around. The glare from the computer screen lit half his face with a weird, greenish glow.

"Sounded good," he said.

She smiled. "Obviously you don't play. I had to really pound the E above middle C."

He raised one shoulder in a half shrug. "Did you want something?"

Yes. You.

She blinked. "No, I... Did you check in with DS?"

"Yeah. No change in the status of your case. We can't go back."

In more ways than one, she thought. She missed her work, missed the challenge, purpose and importance it brought to her life. She didn't miss the stress and emotional isolation. She wasn't ready to go back to what she'd had and to who she'd been before Marcus barged into her life. Not now. Not yet.

"Then we'll have to move forward," she said.

Marcus looked at her in alarm. "We can't go anywhere. It's not safe."

She raised her eyebrows. "Scared, Lieutenant?"

He pressed a few keys and shut down the computer. "Maybe. Are you flirting with me, Ambassador?"

She smiled wryly. "Not very well, apparently, since you have to ask."

He tilted the kitchen chair back on two legs. "You're doing just fine. Assuming, of course, you want me walking around hot and horny for the next couple of days."

Her body shivered in response to his words, but her face bloomed with heat. "I didn't mean... I don't want to be a tease."

"Hey." He set the chair straight. "Take it easy. A little frustration never killed anybody, no matter what the guys in high school used to tell you."

She remembered Matt Tynan's earnest, inexperienced attempts to talk her into the back seat of his stepmother's Porsche, and laughed.

Marcus's eyes narrowed. "Tell me his name," he ordered. "So when I meet him I can kill him."

She didn't approve of territorial male violence. But there was something darkly thrilling and mildly amusing about Marcus's reaction. "You don't have to. I said no. Anyway, we're still friends."

"Tell me his name anyway."

She considered. She was old enough to know a wise woman didn't kiss and tell. But after twenty years, she was pretty sure there had to be some kind of sexual statute of limitations. "Matt Tynan."

"The White House guy?"

"The president's political advisor, yes."

"Does he have Secret Service protection?"

A smile twitched the corner of her mouth. "No. And be nice. He just got engaged to a very sweet girl."

"Okay," Marcus decided. "Then he can live."

"The president will be relieved," she said dryly. "Please notice I'm not threatening your high school girlfriends."

"Girlfriend, singular. Kimberly Williams. And yeah, I noticed. Actually, my feelings are kind of hurt."

Samantha was amused. And yet... "Only one? You must have been serious."

"I was."

She heard his slight stress on the first syllable. "And she wasn't?"

Marcus shrugged. "Kim wasn't too happy I turned down a football scholarship to join the SEALs. She went to the University of Maryland. She was really smart," he added, as if that excused or explained something.

"Not that smart," Samantha said.

He frowned in question.

"Well, she let you go, didn't she?"

His frown cleared like the summer sky after a rain, leaving her breathless. "You bolstering my ego, babe?"

"Your ego seems to be in fine shape." Greatly daring, she let her gaze skim his muscular torso. "Along with the rest of you."

His hands clenched on the table's edge. "What do you want from me? Because whatever it is, you can have it."

Her whole body tingled and tightened. "I want..." She didn't know. "I guess I want to be in high school again. Remember? I want long kisses and long talks and long make-out sessions that don't go anywhere."

A muscle jumped in his jaw, but his eyes were kind. "You sound like one of the good girls. Were you a good girl, Samantha?"

She nodded, embarrassed.

His chair scraped back from the table. "Come here," he said huskily. "We'll only be a little bit bad."

She stared at his lap, transfixed by his invitation. His thighs looked strong and solid. His jeans did little to hide his straining arousal. A smart woman would march herself right out of this kitchen and upstairs to safety. A smart woman—

Her own words confronted her. *Not that smart…. She let you go, didn't she?*

Samantha sucked in her breath and sat on his lap quickly before she changed her mind.

His hands steadied her at the waist. He pulled her outside thigh more firmly onto his lap. His other arm cradled her back. He kissed her temple and then her ear.

"So is this, like, our third date yet? Because I've got to know the rules. Since you're such a good girl and all." His warm voice caressed her. His warm hand stroked lightly up and down her arm, his thumb brushing close to her breast.

He was very good at this.

"I'm beginning to think I dated the wrong boys back in high school," she said, trying to seem amused and sophisticated and sounding wistful instead.

"Don't you believe it, honey," said Marcus. "I've learned a lot since then."

Oh, goodness.

His voice was husky. "Of course, if I had known you in high school, I still would have made a play for you. By the third date, I'd have tried something. This." His long fingers traced her nipple through her shirt, making it pucker and push against the soft fabric.

"And this." He kissed her softly and then not softly at all. Warm, wet kisses. Hot, urgent kisses that made her melt. He teased and licked, sucked and rubbed, until they were breathing into each other's mouths and she squirmed on his lap.

The hot, hard ridge of his arousal pressed against her bottom. But they still had all their clothes on, so it felt wonderfully wicked and innocent at the same time. Safe. She snuggled and wiggled against him.

"And if you do that," he whispered against her lips, "I'll do this."

His mouth glided down her throat and closed over her

breast. He suckled her through the soft cotton, blew against the tingling tip and kissed her when she moaned.

He lifted his head a fraction. ''Are you going to let me touch you again? Because I really want to.''

She wanted him to, too. It had been a long time, but she still remembered the rules of conduct formulated at slumber parties and tested in the back seats of cars. Good girls could pet above the waist.

So she didn't object when his warm hand found its way beneath her short shirt. And when he pushed shirt and bra up under her armpits and bent his head to her breasts and licked and laved, she forgot all about being good. Her heart pounded. Her body pulsed. Drenched in pleasure, she closed her eyes and…started to slide off his lap.

Marcus hauled her back with a strong hand on her thigh. He kept his hand there, between her legs, moving it up and down, rubbing and stroking her through her jeans. His touch was firm and sure. He kissed her mouth. He kissed her throat. He bent her back over his arm and plundered her breast, and she clutched his shoulder and his short, smooth hair and came apart in a series of little explosions like hiccups.

His hot mouth stilled on her breast. He raised his head, his eyes gleaming.

''Wow,'' he said. ''That never happened in high school.''

She was nearly bursting out of her skin with satisfaction. She was flooded with it, filled, relaxed, replete.

''It certainly didn't,'' she agreed.

And darn few times since then. She stretched, feeling every muscle ease in celebration, and felt his arousal rock solid against her hip.

Oh, goodness.

She lowered her arms, guilt seeping in to replace her satisfaction. ''Are you— What about you?''

His face was flushed. His eyes were dark. "I'm fine. Frustrated, but happy."

Could she believe him? She reached for the elastic of her bra. "I don't want to be a tease."

"You're not. You're a good girl, remember?"

She stopped tugging and looked at him uncertainly. "Am I?"

He smiled into her eyes, and the sweetness of it warmed her through and through. "The best."

She bit her lip. "Can I ask you something?"

"Anything."

"Will you sleep with me again tonight?"

His arms tightened around her. "You want to sleep?"

She knew what he was asking. She wished she knew what her response should be.

"I…" She hesitated. "Never mind. It's not fair."

"Forget fair. Is that what you want?"

She buried her face against his shoulder. He smelled clean and warm and male.

"This is completely insane," she muttered. "Why don't I just have sex with you?"

"Because you're not ready?" His voice was amused and just a little bit strained.

"It's not that I don't want you," she said. "Because I do."

"Yeah, well, the feeling is entirely mutual. Which you probably noticed."

She'd noticed. The hard evidence, as it were, was right there under her hip.

Guilt prompted her to say, "It's only a year since Stan died."

Marcus was silent. He didn't hold her closer, but he didn't let her go, either. "You loved him a lot, huh?"

"I did. We had our problems." They had argued bitterly in the last year about her desire to adopt. "But I couldn't imagine my life without Stan. We were closer than many couples. Maybe it was because we didn't have children. Maybe it was because my life revolved around his career. He used to say I was all the family he needed.''

Okay, well, that sounded fairly pathetic. No wonder she never talked about her marriage. She drew a deep breath so she could get it over with. ''And then one morning Stan left to address the Delmonican board of trade, and a driver coming the other way lost control of his truck, and Stan wasn't there anymore.'' To her horror, she felt her eyes flood with tears. ''He'll never be there again.''

She stared at her knees and Marcus's arm, heavy across her lap, and thought if he had any sense at all he would drive her back to Washington tonight. Right now.

''I'm here,'' he said into her hair. ''I'm here all night if you want me. Even if it's only to sleep.''

And even though she told herself she had no right to ask and lots of good reasons to say no, she whispered, ''Thank you.''

But sleep was a long time coming that night for both of them.

Samantha lay awake in bed, listening to every creak and sigh, conscious of every twist and touch: his foot, his hand, his arm. The room was warm, and Marcus's body radiated heat. It was ridiculous, being this close to him, knowing all she had to do was roll over and ask, and she could have…

What do you want from me? Because whatever it is you can have it.

She dozed in fits and woke in starts. Once she thought Marcus had given up, gotten up and gone downstairs. But then his weight depressed the mattress and his arm came around her waist and he pulled her into the curve of his body. His legs brushed hers. His hand closed possessively on her hip. His breath stirred the hair at the back of her neck.

She felt the rhythm of her own breath slowing and deepening to match the rhythm of his until, nestled like two spoons, they slept.

It was a shame she had to die.

But the man moving silently through the shadows did not have the luxury of mercy or of choice.

She was an enemy. The Enemy, although a part of him was dimly aware there had to be worse threats to his cause, and another part insisted there were better ways for her to die.

If he met her in these woods he could slit her pretty white throat or drill a bullet between her wide clear eyes in seconds. He had a black Ka-Bar combat knife strapped in a sheath to his leg and a .40 caliber Glock 22 pistol in a holster at his waist.

He was familiar with killing. He was good at it.

But he could not touch her in her bed.

He glided through the barred moonlight toward his objective. Maybe he would not touch her at all. This was an old farm. They were surrounded by old things: broken, rotten, derelict, dangerous. It was extremely likely his target would simply meet with an accident.

He stopped by the moon-silvered door. Particularly if he arranged it.

When Samantha woke, she was alone.

Nothing new there, she told herself, fighting disappointment. For the past thirteen months, she'd awakened alone. Correction: for thirteen months minus one day. Because yesterday when she'd opened her eyes she'd been up close and personal with Marcus Evans's naked chest.

She missed his chest.

She missed Marcus. Simply looking at his powerfully muscled body and chiseled chin made her as breathless and dizzy as Lois Lane flying over Metropolis in the arms of Superman.

Samantha winced. It was like some embarrassing revelation on a tacky television talk show: "Sex-starved widow lusts for U.S. Navy SEAL."

Except her feelings went deeper than that. She admired Marcus's competence and dedication to duty. She liked his undemanding company and occasionally corny humor. She loved his uncomplicated loyalty and his gentleness and understanding.

She frowned at the dented pillow beside her. So if he was so loyal and uncomplicated and understanding, why wasn't he here?

A prickle ran over her skin, two parts frustration and one part unease. Where was he? If she really was in danger, then he was in danger, too.

The memory of his words came back to her. "I can take care of myself. You can't."

The farmhouse was very quiet.

He could be making breakfast. He could be in the barn. He could be buying fresh milk and eggs for their up-and-running refrigerator.

But she didn't smell coffee. The farm didn't have animals—not livestock that required tending, anyway. And when Samantha shook out yesterday's jeans and wandered to the bedroom window, she saw the car, minus whatever vital part he'd removed the night of their arrival, still sitting in the yard.

She pressed her lips together. This was not a problem. Marcus could be lots of other places. He could be…lying under a bush somewhere, the victim of a Rebelian sniper.

She fought a shiver. No, that was silly. No one even knew where they were.

She borrowed another one of Marcus's T-shirts—if they

stayed, she was going to ask him to hook up the washer and dryer—and shoved her feet into her new sneakers.

The door to the bathroom across the hall was open. No Marcus. Her heart thumping, she went downstairs.

He wasn't in the shabby living room or in the kitchen. No note propped against the sugar bowl told her where he had gone or when to expect him. Samantha smiled wryly. Should she be glad Marcus wasn't in the habit of leaving morning farewells for his lovers? Or should she be discouraged by his lack of domesticity?

Glad, she decided. He was domesticated enough. All around her, the scarred countertops and battered appliances gleamed. He'd even managed to scrape a layer of grime from the floor. All the kitchen needed to appear completely homey were flowers on the table and children's artwork on the refrigerator door.

A familiar pang sliced through her. She couldn't do anything about the farmhouse's lack of children. But she could certainly supply flowers.

She could take a short walk. They were safe here. No one knew where she was. Marcus certainly hadn't hesitated to leave her alone. Still, she dithered over her note. The text was easy enough. "Don't worry. Taking a walk. Back soon." Informative and to the point. And not spineless or sappy or besotted or any of the things she felt inside.

But then she had to sign the darn thing, and all her diplomatic training failed her. "Sincerely yours" was the correct social closing for everyone from the president of the United States to a Methodist bishop. "Yours sincerely" covered most of the peerage. But how did you sign a note to the Navy SEAL you'd spent the previous night with?

"Sincerely?" Hardly.

"Cordially?" She nibbled her pen. She did feel cordial—the dictionary defined the word as "warm, sincere, friendly, fervent''—but it still sounded far too formal for a morning-after note.

"Love?" Her stomach flipped. Her hand smoothing the paper trembled.

In the end, she simply signed her name in neat, elegant script and hoped he wouldn't read too much between the lines.

The farmyard was studded with the fuzzy heads of clover and dandelions, but Samantha was looking for more than a jam jar arrangement. There were daylilies blooming in a ditch. Daisies and Queen Anne's lace bordered the meadow. And didn't she remember honeysuckle growing near the well house door?

The well house. She hesitated at the top of the narrow dirt track. Was Marcus there? Testing the water or something?

She started down the path, drawn by the memory of flowers and the hope of finding him. She was no country girl, but she recognized the cardinal that flashed under the trees, noted the pair of gray squirrels chasing each other through last year's leaves. The air was rich with flora and drifting pollen. She was smiling when she reached the well house.

And stopped. The door was ajar.

Samantha shook her head, amused at herself. Of course the door would be open if Marcus was down here working on something.

She took a few steps forward. "Marcus?"

No reply. The pump clanked and chugged. He probably couldn't hear.

She put her hand on the weathered door and pushed. It didn't budge. The bottom was stuck tight. Shifting her flowers to the crook of her arm—the Queen Anne's lace tickled her jaw—she laid both palms flat against the door and pushed hard.

It flew open. She flew in. Her foot reached for the solid

plank at the entrance, but it was gone. She flung out her arms to catch herself before she smacked her face on the concrete slab that covered the well hole.

Nothing.

Her hands encountered nothing. The well cap was gone.

She pitched forward helplessly before her outstretched arms smacked the opposite side and her body slammed into the edge. The impact shuddered through her. Her bent legs slid into the hole. Her knees knocked the side where she clung. She hung suspended. Disbelieving. Winded.

Her mind whirled. Her heart went cold. Because she knew, as her fingers clawed at the slick, packed surface, as her nails broke and her body began its slow, inevitable slide, that she couldn't stop it. She didn't have the strength to hold on. She didn't have a thing to hold on to.

"Marcus!"

Pebbles and dirt loosened by her scrabbling fingers rained over her face. Her body slid another inch before gravity pulled her into the well. Like a roller coaster car plunging into a tunnel, she jarred and rattled down in the dark. Thump. Thud. Bounce. Crash.

She cried out. And then the freezing water closed over her head, and a shattering pain in her ankles ended her fall.

Above her in the open doorway, the fallen flowers lay scattered in the sunshine like an offering from Persephone.

Eleven

The back door was unlocked.

Marcus stared stupidly at the key sticking from the lock. He'd just locked it. Which meant the door was unlocked before. Which meant that when he'd left this morning, when he thought he'd locked the door, he hadn't. He could have sworn he did, but with all the mistakes he'd been making lately, who knew?

Or Samantha could have unlocked it after he left.

Or somebody else did.

His blood ran cold. Panic time.

Don't panic.

He unholstered his gun and let himself into the house. She wasn't in the kitchen. He inhaled. Okay. Then she was upstairs. She was sleeping safely upstairs in their bed.

He took the steps two at a time, jerked to a halt before he barged into the bedroom.

Easy, moron. Don't scare her.

His heart pounding, he eased around the door frame, hoping, praying, he'd find her still in bed, her round shoulders rising above the sheets, her dark red hair spread over the faded pillowcase.

But the bed was empty. She wasn't in the room. She wasn't in the bathroom, either.

His gut knotted. He wanted to hit something. He wanted to swear. He checked the window for signs of forced entry and the room for signs of struggle. Nothing. Nada. Zip.

He went back downstairs.

He had four ripe peaches tied into the bottom of his shirt. He'd gone out this morning to the old orchard behind the barn, hoping to find something to tempt Samantha's appetite. A smoother man would have picked her flowers. A smarter man would never have left her alone.

Marcus paused in the kitchen to unload the fruit. He couldn't hunt a potential kidnapper with peaches bouncing at his waist. He set them on the kitchen table, four red-and-yellow fuzzy peaches, only slightly squashed, and that's when he saw it. The note. Propped against the sugarbowl.

Don't worry. Taking a walk. Back soon.
Samantha

His breath exploded in relief. Don't worry? He'd just lost ten years off his life.

Taking a walk where? Along the trail? Down to the farm pond? Where was she, damn it?

And how soon was soon?

Samantha gasped from shock and cold. She was lucky. She wasn't dead. She hadn't drowned.

But she just might freeze to death.

She'd been too stunned and disoriented to brace herself agaist the sides as she fell. But her very ineffectiveness had probably saved her from breaking a bone. The few feet of icy water at the bottom of the well had saved her life.

But, oh, it was cold. She was cold. She was shaking with it, with cold and reaction and fear. She wrapped her arms around her own body, trying to trap in heat. Think positively, she ordered herself.

At least she wouldn't need ice packs for the bruises she was sure were forming under the water. It came to her armpits, deep enough to cushion her fall and shallow enough that she could stand. Two more positives.

Now all she needed was a way out.

Her chest constricted, making breathing difficult.

"Hello? Help! Hello?"

Her voice echoed from the walls. It sounded loud to her ears, but she was dismally aware that there was no one near to hear her.

It was black at the bottom of the well. But she could see the lip of the well, a dim circle of beaten earth, shadowed by the displaced slab and the squat metal pump. A pipe ran down the side.

A pipe. Hope trickled through her. Could she climb up?

She unfolded her arms. The cold pierced her chest. Her fingers were numb. Her hands were shaking. But she made herself fumble blindly along the slippery, dank walls until she brushed and siezed on cold, hard metal.

Her fingers explored it in the dark. It wasn't very thick, less than an inch in diameter. Could it possibly hold her weight if she climbed? Did she even have the strength to try? She tugged, testing it. No.

She looked up again. The opening was several times her height above her head. Twenty feet? Thirty? Her heart quailed.

"Hello?" she called again, her voice quavering in the dark. "Help me!"

But there was no reply.

Where was Marcus?

Where the hell was she?

Marcus had waited five full frustrating minutes already. "Soon," she'd said, and there was no point in launching a thorough recon of forty-eight acres if at any moment she was going to stroll through the door.

But she didn't. Five more minutes spent pacing the linoleum like a neurotic Doberman and he'd had enough.

He grabbed her note and scrawled at the bottom, "Out

looking for you. Stay put." And then, because that sounded as terse and pissed off as he felt, and she hadn't really done anything more boneheaded than go for a walk—without protection, God, what was she thinking—he signed it. "Love, M."

He slammed the door and went to find her.

She had to keep moving.

Pain stabbed her ankles. She couldn't feel her feet at all. But Samantha knew she had to keep the blood flowing to her fingers and toes, had to keep her body temperature up.

She tried bobbing up and down. That was bad. Her knees protested and her breath escaped in little sobs. So she walked in tiny circles and flapped her arms, like a chicken trying to fly. And she yelled for help. For Marcus.

But no help came.

Marcus never answered.

Tears burned her eyes and escaped down her cheeks—a stupid waste of body heat. Don't be a baby, she told herself, and cleared her sore throat and called again.

She imagined her breath hanging over the icy water in a vaporous cloud like a ghost. Which was ridiculous. She didn't believe in ghosts, and anyway, it wasn't that cold.

But, oh, it felt it. Pinchingly cold. Crampingly cold. Achingly cold. She found herself drawing in her body, pulling in her stomach, as if she could hold herself away from the water.

To distract herself, she looked up at the circle of light and the jutting curve of the concrete well cover. She pressed her trembling lips together. She was lucky she hadn't cracked her head when she'd slipped.

She rubbed her arms briskly, which didn't do any good, and attempted to wiggle her frozen toes. Although if she were really lucky she would never have fallen in the first place. The concrete slab would have been over the well where it belonged, and she would be back at the farmhouse with Marcus, where *she* belonged.

A thought disturbed her mind like a dropped pebble, sending out ripples of disquiet.

Why wasn't the cover over the well?

She'd watched Marcus move it into place herself, his well-defined muscles flexing under his plain white T-shirt. She'd never known, couldn't imagine, another man who could lift that solid slab by himself so easily.

No other man...

The phrase shivered through her, chilling as the water, disturbing as the thought of what might lie beneath the surface.

No *other* man. Who besides Marcus had the strength to remove the well cap? Who else had the opportunity?

"Samantha? Sam! Where are you?"

It was Marcus. And her suspicions evaporated. Even with the distortion of the well shaft and the water, he sounded scared. And really annoyed. He sounded as if he cared.

But it wasn't his emotions that convinced her. It was her own. It was the way her heart turned to the sound of his voice like a sunflower to the sun.

"D-down here!" she yelled.

She heard muffled swearing, which for some reason made her want to giggle. And then the dark outline of his head appeared in the circle of light.

"Are you all right?"

"All right" was a relative term. She was certainly better. Marcus had come for her. And the internal glow produced by his presence, while it didn't actually warm her, certainly cheered her up.

"F-fine," she called.

More of his body blocked the opening. Even though she was really, really glad to see him, Samantha shuddered, her own body instinctively protesting the loss of light.

"How the hell did you get down there?"

"F-fell," she said, her teeth chattering. She wrapped her arms more closely around her chest to hold in the last of her body heat.

"No, I meant…" His legs swung around. His big booted feet dropped down. Her heart jumped in her throat. What did he think he was doing? "How'd you get the cover off?"

"I d-didn't," she protested. "It was off. Shouldn't you g-get a rope?"

"And leave you alone?" She saw him shake his head before he lowered himself into the mouth of the shaft. "Naw. I don't think so."

He was climbing down. Unsupported, unprotected, bracing his hands and feet against the slick earthen sides of the shaft.

Fear made her tone sharp. "Better me alone than you with a b-broken neck and b-both of us at the bottom."

"Babe, relax." His muffled voice was perfectly calm. "I know what I'm doing."

"It's too f-far."

"Thirty-two feet," he told her cheerfully. "Piece of cake."

He was spread-eagled, his body spanning the width of the well. She flinched as something dislodged from the wall and struck the surface of the water.

Marcus stopped instantly, suspended in the darkness over her head. "You okay?"

She nodded, forgetting he couldn't see. But a moment later she heard the scrape of his boots as he resumed his climb down the shaft.

I have pretty good night vision, he'd told her their first night at the farmhouse, and apparently he hadn't lied.

Not about that.

She heard him above her, breathing. Another stone plopped into the water.

She shrank back, her shoulder blades brushing the icy wall behind her.

"That's good," he said. "Hold still."

Something swung in the dank air before her face. The cold water surged around her breasts. She heard his boots crunch on the pebbled bottom, and then he was there, real and warm and solid, wedged into the well beside her.

He pulled her close. She leaned on him, absorbing the heat and reassurance that rolled off him in waves. For a minute he held her, held her tight, his chin pressed to her hair.

"Nothing broken?" he asked.

She shook her head against his chest. She was shaking all over.

"Okay, here's what we're going to do," he said conversationally. "You're going to put your arms around my neck, and I'm going to climb out of here."

Her heart plummeted. He couldn't possibly neogiate these wet, hazardous walls twice. Maybe he had made it down. But to go up this slippery, verticle pit, pulling his own weight, carrying hers... He couldn't do it. No man could.

"T-too risky," she said. "You're not S—"

"No Superman cracks," he warned.

She clenched her jaw enough to answer. "Spider-Man."

He laughed, and even though she was scared and sore and freezing, his laughter made her feel fractionally better. Hopeful. "Guess we'll see. Come on, honey, hold on."

She was almost too cold to lift her arms. But she got them around his neck and lifted a leg to straddle his thigh.

She was numb below the waist. But the awkwardness of the position made her ask, "Shouldn't I be on your back?"

"Nope." He managed to unbuckle his belt underwater. He looped it through hers and fastened it again in a makeshift safety harness. "I might brace my back against the wall. I don't want to scrape you off."

She shuddered. Definitely not.

"I'm going to need both arms," he said, sounding apologetic, as if she might actually expect him to climb a 32-foot well shaft one-handed. "So you have to hold on tight, okay?"

Hold on? Her heart lurched. All the way up?

"What if I let g-go?"

"Then I'll catch you," he said patiently. "I'll be under you in the shaft. You won't fall."

How could he be sure?

"Trust me?" he asked.

The remarkable thing was that she did. She was a diplomat. She was trained not to trust anyone. And yet even after she'd been kidnapped and shot at and trapped down a well, she trusted Marcus. After he got them both out of here, she was going to have to ask herself why.

She nodded once in answer.

"That's my girl."

He hauled her closer with one arm until the knot he'd made of their belts poked her stomach. And then he released her and began to climb. Her hands tightened convulsively. She felt the muscles in his thigh bunch and shift, felt the play and flex of his powerful shoulders lift and lurch, pull and rest, in a peculiarly even rhythm. One of her feet brushed the wall. His breathing rasped. Her heart thundered. Up and up.

Dizzy, she clutched his neck and hid her face against his throat.

Marcus set Samantha on the edge of their mattress. Her knee was bleeding. Her nails were broken. Bruises were already forming on her arms. At least the icy water had helped to keep the swelling down. But she was too damn pale and shivering like a SEAL candidate in the surf at Coronado.

Shivering was good, he reminded himself.Shivering meant her body was still fighting hypothermia. But he hated that her face was so white and her lips nearly blue.

"We've got to get you out of these wet clothes," he said, starting to peel her shirt from her clammy back.

She lifted her head, nearly clipping him on the chin. "That is one of the lamest excuses for getting naked I have ever heard."

Despite his worry, he grinned. "You are so tough. Like some of the guys I went through BUD/S with—little skinny guys, not much to them. You'd swear they'd ring out the first week, you know? But they just wouldn't quit."

Samantha held up her arms so he could wrestle her wet shirt over her head. "Like your friend Jimmy," she said.

His smile faded. He pitched her shirt into a corner and reached blindly for a towel, trying not to notice that her wet bra was totally transparent and her nipples were tight with cold. The king of smooth.

"Marcus?"

"What?" He shoved the towel at her and started digging in the duffel for a dry shirt and underwear.

"Does Jimmy know you brought me here?"

Hell. Marcus set his jaw. "Why'd you ask?"

"That first night, you mentioned something about the Robinsons' daughter, Luanne. Putting two and two together…"

Fear and suspicion churned his gut and made him miserable. "You got five." He threw the shirt at her. "You think *Jimmy* had something to do with uncovering the well?"

She blinked at him. "Well, no, actually, I don't."

Relief staggered him. "You don't?"

"No." She pulled on the underwear and the T-shirt. "He couldn't lift the slab, for one thing."

"You didn't think that maybe he had—" God, it was hard to say "—help?"

"It never occurred to me. Did you think—?"

"No!"

"All right, then." She smiled.

He felt his muscles ease. But it wasn't all right.

"Somebody removed the well cover," he insisted.

"But not Jimmy."

"No." Marcus was sure of that.

"And no one else knows we're here?"

Marcus shook his head. "I didn't tell anybody else."

"And we couldn't have been followed?"

"No." He'd made sure of that, too.

"You must have done it yourself, then."

"No, I—" He stopped, a sick uncertainty in his gut.

Samantha raised her brows.

"I don't remember," he said helplessly.

"Well, after you disinfected the water, did you put the cover back on?"

He did. He was almost sure he did. Why didn't he remember? But every time he tried to recall the precise sequence of events, his mind went blank. It worried him.

But Samantha still shook with cold, and that worried him more.

"Hey." Alarmed, he pulled back the covers. "You've got to get in bed. Warm up."

She smiled slightly. "If you're trying to seduce me, Lieutenant, your technique needs work. Besides, it must be eighty degrees outside."

"Which is borderline in preventing further heat loss in hypothermia patients."

She slid her legs—long legs, smooth thighs, oh, man— under the covers. "Now you're a medic?"

"All SEALs have medical field training. I'm no expert, but I froze my butt off enough during Hell Week to pick up the basics on hypothermia. You need a warm environment, mild exercise and hot fluids."

She pulled the quilt around her shoulders. "How about a hot shower?"

He shook his head regretfully. "Not until the sediment in the well settles."

Her eyes rounded in dismay. "I never even thought of that. How long will it take?"

"End of the day, maybe. You can have your shower tonight."

She nodded, the covers pulled to her chin. Her hair was wet and stringy, she had no makeup on, and he still got hard imagining her naked, pink and slippery in the shower.

He cleared his throat. "You want some tea?"

"Tea would be wonderful. Thank you, Marcus."

Her voice was warm. Her gaze was perfectly sincere. And all he could think was that if he hadn't brought her here, she never would have fallen down the damn well.

"It's nothing," he said, guilt roughening his voice. "I'll get that tea for you."

He escaped downstairs and hovered by the stove, his thoughts hissing and simmering like the water in the kettle.

He had to trust Jimmy. Had to. The XO was his other self, his better-than-a-brother. There was simply no way his swim buddy had given up their hiding place.

Marcus scowled at the thick china cup that held the tea bag. But *somebody* had shifted that slab. Which meant... Which meant... Damn it, he must have forgotten to put the well cover back on yesterday. He didn't—couldn't—remember. But what other explanation was there?

He was responsible. It was his fault Samantha had nearly died.

The thought made him sweat. He'd almost failed—his mission, himself, her.

The quicker he got her back to Washington, the better.

But when he switched on his computer and accessed Baxter's secure Web site, there were no instructions and no change, only the silly little animated man in green running around against a childish backdrop. *The queen did not like him, no more did the king....*

Disgusted, Marcus shut down the laptop and went to pour Samantha's tea. He added two spoonfuls of sugar—she might complain of the taste, but she needed calories as well as fluids—and carried the hot mug carefully upstairs.

She was asleep.

He stood in the doorway watching her, feeling his heart get too big for his chest. Her lashes looked really long and dark against her pale cheeks. Her arm was tucked under the pillow at her head. She lay on her side, her knees drawn up to her body. Even in the warmth of the day, with the quilt pulled over her shoulders, she looked cold.

Marcus set the hot mug on the dresser. In rescue situations, a hypothermic patient could be zipped into a sleeping bag in contact with another, warmer body. It was a last resort, since the warm body involved tended to get pretty cold.

He looked again at the round shape huddled under the covers.

Somehow he didn't think contact with Samantha was going to make him cold. And if it did...well, it was worth sacrificing his body to the cause.

On the other hand, he didn't want her to think he was taking advantage of the situation. So after he unlaced his boots and undid the top button of his jeans for comfort, he crawled fully dressed into bed with her and pulled her into the curve of his body.

Her bottom, in thin, cotton panties, felt lush and firm and

alarmingly cool. Her damp hair smelled faintly of minerals. He put his arm around her waist, tucking her closer, and tried not to think what he'd do if he lost her.

He'd lost her.
He paddled furiously, searching the waves and the floating wreckage for his sister's small, dark head, fighting panic. Where was she?

But he knew. She was down there. Under the water.

It was his job to look after her.

He took a really deep breath and dived. When he wanted to, he could stay under a long time. Mark the shark, their mother called him. Mark the seal.

He swam back until he found the cold edge of the current that had caught him after the explosion. Only this time he let it take him, let it carry him to his sister.

Up. Breathe. Down. Search.

He was strong, but he was already growing tired. His lungs burned. His eyes stung. He forced himself to kick harder, to stay down longer. His sister wasn't strong. She needed him.

There!

Hope hurt his chest. She was there, below him, her skinny arms lifted in the water, her black hair floating around her white face like seaweed. His sister. His twin.

His heart beat about a million times a minute as he kicked toward her. Was she moving?

Was she dead?

''Marcus.'' Her voice was soft and sure. Her touch was gentle. Soothing. ''You're having a bad dream. Wake up.''

His heart was beating a million times a minute. His fists were clenched in the sheets, and he was… Oh, hell, he was crying. What a loser.

Marcus sat up in bed and dragged his hands over his face.

When he dropped his hands, Samantha was watching him with grave, sympathetic eyes. Despite the pain she must feel, all her concern was for him. "Are you all right?" she asked.

"You shouldn't do that," he told her harshly. "Wake me like that. I could—" God, this was humiliating. "I could get violent."

She arched her eyebrows. "I'm terrified."

"No, really," he insisted. "I almost killed some guy in BUD/S when he woke me up from a nightmare."

"Well, you're not going to kill me," she said positively. "This is the second time I've had to wake you, and all you do is get huffy and defensive."

He felt some of the tension ease from his muscles. "Thanks a lot. I think."

Her dimples appeared. "You're welcome." Her hand, with its broken nails, stroked his arm. "Have you ever spoken with a doctor about your dreams?"

"You mean, a shrink?" He shook his head, rejecting even the idea. "No. My father—"

"Your father?" she prompted.

Marcus stared at her, a muscle working in his jaw. This was it, he realized. The big moment in their relationship, if they were going to have one. Truth or consequences. Sink or swim. Fish or cut bait.

I can't be intimate with a man who refuses to share himself with me.

"He said my nightmares were nothing to worry about. 'A natural response to trauma,' he said." The explanation hadn't done a lot to soothe a freaked out and frightened boy living with unfamiliar parents in a strange house.

It didn't seem to satisfy Samantha, either. "What trauma?" she asked.

"I was in a…some kind of accident, I think, when I was ten. A car crash, they told me."

Except he didn't remember a car. Only the boat. And the water.

Samantha opened her lips.

"I don't really remember," he added before she could ask. He drew in a deep breath. Okay. Let her know now what she was getting into by becoming involved with him. Or rather, let her know that she could never know. Because—

"I don't remember anything before that, either," he confessed.

Samantha's eyes narrowed. "You don't remember…?"

"Anything," he repeated. "I'm a complete zero before the age of ten. The old man said my mind was repressing my memories as a way of protecting me."

"Protecting you from what?"

Her questions jabbed at an old sore. But the pain Marcus felt now was nothing compared to the hurt he was going to feel after he told her the whole truth and she rejected him. Maybe the only way to deal with it was to get it over with quickly. Like ripping off a bandage instead of peeling it back one painful inch at a time.

"That's just it. I don't know."

"What did your parents tell you?"

"They didn't like to talk about it." Which was true, as far as it went, but the sad fact was that the Evanses didn't know much more than Marcus did. He would have to come clean about the adoption bit. But he wanted to get over the worst part first.

He exhaled, not looking at her. Do it. Quickly. "I always figured I must have done something pretty damn bad to wipe out my entire childhood."

He waited for her to say, "Gee, that's sad, and by the

way, would you please get away from me?'' And that was when he knew.

Her opinion mattered too much. She mattered too much. He felt too lousy for this to be anything but love.

"That's the most ridiculous thing I ever heard in my life,'' Samantha said. "And let me tell you, as someone who has attended far too many diplomatic dinners, I've heard some amazingly ridiculous things.''

It was so not the response he was expecting that he gaped at her.

"It's not ridiculous,'' he said. "I read up on it some. Dissociative retrograde amnesia occurs when you really don't *want* to remember something.''

Samantha could picture it too clearly. Marcus as a confused little boy, as a determined young man, seeking clues to the gaps in his identity by searching medical textbooks and scholarly articles. The image moved her to admiration…and nearly reduced her to tears.

"Amnesia usually occurs in cases of abuse,'' she said gently. "Not when you do something bad. When something bad is done to you.''

His beautiful blue eyes met hers, and the uncertainty she saw there tore at her own heart.

"The key word is *usually,* babe. We don't really know. Because I can't remember.''

"*I* know. Your basic nature doesn't change from the time you're two. Your moral character is formed by the age of seven. *I* think,'' she said slowly, "that you are one of the nicest, kindest, most decent men I have ever met. If you weren't, I'd never do what I'm about to do.''

He didn't move, but she felt the tension that seized his big body. "What are you going to do?''

"Well, for starters…'' She leaned forward across the

crumpled quilt, careful not to rest her weight on her injured knee, and took his perfectly chiseled jaw between her hands. "This."

And she kissed him.

Twelve

Marcus couldn't believe it.

It was like a fantasy come true. Red-haired, hot Ambassador Samantha Barnes was kissing him, her mouth warm and seeking on his, her hands cool and seeking on his back, under his T-shirt. And they were on a bed. She was nearly naked and clearly willing, and he was so taken aback that for, oh, at least five seconds or so he didn't know what to do.

She kissed him again, a "hello, sailor" kind of kiss, deep and wet and explicit, and his body surged and his brain woke up enough to issue orders.

Kiss her back, moron. Before she changes her mind.

He kissed her back, giving it everything he had. Giving her everything he was.

And maybe she wasn't planning on changing her mind, after all, because she made this little sound deep in her throat as if she liked what he was doing. As if she *loved* what he was doing. It was the biggest turn-on.

She slid one of her hands from his back along his waist, still under his shirt, against his skin. And then—oh, man, it went beyond fantasy and into some five-star, X-rated dream. She just went for it. She touched him, cupped him, right through his jeans. He nearly shot off the bed.

"Whoa." It felt so good. Too good. He was going to lose it. "How about we slow down here, babe?"

Her busy fingers stroked and shaped him. "Why?"

She tugged at his zipper and slipped her hand inside. His eyes nearly crossed.

"I don't want to hurt you," he said.

She laughed. She actually laughed. Releasing him, she stripped her T-shirt over her head. He stared, riveted by her full, pink-tipped, perfect breasts.

"You can try," she said, and reached for him again.

After that he went a little crazy. She cooperated all the way, helping him get rid of his clothes, kicking off her own panties, touching, kissing, licking and rubbing him until they went down in a tangle of sheets and arms and legs.

He couldn't wait to fill his hands with her smooth flesh, couldn't wait to fill her with his body. She was all lush curves and soft skin. He touched her and almost groaned. She was warm and slick with wanting him. Her legs opened, her head dropped back. She watched with shining, half-closed eyes as he fell on top of her and—

Awareness hit him with the force of a call to general quarters. *Warning. Danger. Abort mission.*

Her fingers tightened on his shoulders. "Please, Marcus. Now."

The "please" nearly wrecked him, but he pulled back from the edge in time. There was fantasy, and then there was sheer stupidity. He wasn't going to screw up by losing control now. "Hang on. We need a condom."

"No."

"It's okay." Birth control was as much a part of any sailor's kit as razors or dental floss. "I'll only be a second," he promised.

She pushed her hips upward. He sucked in his breath. "You don't need to," she said. "You told me you had all your shots."

"I do, but…" He couldn't think. He could only feel her, wet and ready and—yeah, baby—right there. "You could still get pregnant."

"No, I can't."

Can't? Was she on the pill? Or—

Her hands skimmed his back to his butt and squeezed. *"Please."*

It was like a green flag at the start of a race. Like a go ahead from mission control. He was hot and throbbing and raring to go, and she was sending him all the signals to proceed. He had to be inside her. Now. Nearly violent with need, he held her down and thrust home.

The shock of it hit him like a bullet. The pleasure of it melted his bones. She was so hot and tight, pulsing around him, part of him, his. Their fingers laced. Their eyes locked. Their bodies linked, and it was beyond great, better than a fantasy, more powerful than any dream.

She was real and warm and under him, driving his body like a well-tuned machine, pumping, racing. Mouths met and devoured. Hands streaked and possessed. Every time he thought he should slow down, be cool, play nice, every time he tried to show her a little finesse, exercise a little control, she moved or moaned, gasped or bit him, and he shuddered and fell into her again, into the heat and the heart of her, into the blinding race for release.

They were way past games and a million years beyond high school. It was hot and fast and sweaty and a little rough.

"Harder," she said, her voice breaking.

His blood pumped. His breath labored. She clutched at him, tearing apart his control.

He took her harder, took her deeper, felt her clench and arch under him, felt her coil and come apart. And the explosions that rocked her blew him apart like a fuel fire detonating a load of TNT.

Racked, thankful, spent, he rested his forehead on hers and collapsed against her.

His brain didn't operate, his tongue didn't function and his body flat out refused to budge.

There was no way Marcus could manage "suave" or "smooth" right now. He would have to go with "droolingly grateful" and hope Samantha didn't deduct style points.

"Thank you," he mumbled fervently.

Her fingers combed the back of his head. He closed his eyes, loving the delicate tug of her touch against his scalp.

"What for?" she asked.

What for? Several brain cells sparked reluctantly to life and considered the question. Marcus didn't have a clue what he was supposed to say, so he went with the truth.

"For having sex with me. For wanting to have sex with me."

For climaxing before he finished without her and totally humiliated himself.

Her lips curved against his cheek. He raised his head so he could see her smile. He loved her smile.

"Since I wanted to have sex with you, you hardly need to thank me. Maybe I should be thanking you."

Fortunately, he didn't need working brain cells to respond to that one. "Nope. God, no. I owe you."

Her brows arched. "What is it you think you owe me?"

"Well… If you won't accept thanks, how about an apology?"

"Unnecessary."

"I was rough."

Her dimples deepened. "So was I."

Her obvious satisfaction made him grin. But he persisted stubbornly, "I didn't mean to take advantage. After your accident and everything."

She raised her chin, a gesture that kind of lost its effectiveness when she was lying naked under him. "Marcus, I am not going to let you cast me as the victim here."

"Not a victim," he agreed. "But…"

Oh, man, he was such a loser. What was he doing, looking for a fight after the best sex of his life?

Except Samantha wasn't fighting. She didn't ask questions, either. She just lay there, waiting, watching him with warm concern.

So of course he opened his big fat mouth and made things worse.

"Look, we had to study hostage psychology in our antiterrorist training, okay? And there's this thing called Stockholm Syndrome, after this Swedish bank robbery that happened, like, thirty years ago, where—"

"I'm familiar with the Stockholm Syndrome," she interrupted gently.

"Yeah. Okay. Anyway, the instructor told us that the hostages in that case were totally dependent on their kidnappers to supply their basic needs. Food. Information. Human contact. And after three, four days of that, they began to identify with their kidnappers as a method of survival."

Samantha stiffened under him. But her voice was still mild. "Are you suggesting that I'm dependent on you for sex? Or that I slept with you as a means of ensuring my survival?"

He was sweating again, and not from the heat of their two bodies pressed together under the quilt.

"No, I just meant…"

He didn't know what he meant. He felt like he was in eleventh grade again and being grilled by Mrs. Crane, the English teacher, after volunteering some stupid answer in class. Except unlike Mrs. Crane, Samantha had mercy on him.

"You left something out," she said. "The robbery hostages were afraid their captors would kill them. The threat of death is one of the four defining characteristics of the syndrome." She wriggled her hand from under his arm and began to count them off on her fingers. "Isolation, dependence, arbitrary kindness and fear of death."

He loved it. Ambassador Barnes, naked and glowing from sex, lecturing him on hostage psychology. He was impressed, amused and touched.

She held up all four fingers and waggled them in his face. "So unless you believe that you threatened me and I slept with you simply to appease you, you'll have to accept that I wanted you."

Okay, touched *and* turned on. Call him a pervert, but the contrast between the bad-girl body rubbing intimately against his and her earnest teacher's tone was beginning to have an unexpected effect.

"That's a relief," he said. "Because I want you, too."

Her dark lashes dropped. She smiled, a secret, feminine smile that made him want to conquer worlds for her. "I noticed."

He nuzzled the side of her face. "So what do you think we should do?"

She inhaled as he nibbled her earlobe. "We could change the subject."

"Nah. I think you should lecture me some more."

She pulled her head back against the pillow. Confused, she repeated, "I should lecture you?"

He smiled down into her eyes. "Yeah. It makes me hot."

As he'd hoped, her dimples reappeared. "Really?"

"I swear."

"I could discuss nonproliferation and arms control in Eastern Europe."

He rocked against her suggestively. "I love it when you use big words."

She laughed, but he felt her breathing quicken. She raised one hand and touched his cheek. "Unless you'd rather hear my proposed incentives for the creation of a broad-based, market-oriented democracy in Rebelia."

''Oh, baby.'' He turned his head and bit her fingers gently.

She lifted herself to meet his mouth.

And for a long time after that, they said everything they needed to without any words at all.

Samantha hiked her towel under her arms and tucked it between her breasts. In Delmonico, she lived with seventy-four staffers, an army of housekeepers, a team of gardeners and a small detachment of marines. She certainly shouldn't feel shy about sharing quarters with one Navy SEAL.

Especially since he'd already seen her naked.

But something about sharing the small domestic routines of the farmhouse felt almost more intimate than sharing a bed. She thought of Marcus, hard on top of her, moving quick and thick inside of her, and flushed.

All right, not more intimate, she acknowledged. Different intimate. Unfamiliar. Scary.

She anchored the towel more firmly around her and called down the stairs. ''I found a hair dryer in the bathroom. Is it okay to plug it in?''

Marcus strode from the direction of the kitchen, carrying some kind of gadget and looking hot and distracted.

''Yeah, I ran a wire up there this—'' He caught sight of her standing above him and stopped dead on the faded carpet. ''Well, hello, Ambassador Babe. Am I too late to scrub your back?''

She laughed, which he probably intended, and eased her death grip on the towel. Yet even as she relaxed in response to his teasing, she was trembling, tense, weak with wanting him. It was amazing—embarrassing, really—to be thirty-six years old and suddenly giddy with lust.

Did he intend that, too? Did he know? Could he guess?

It was the result of proximity, she told herself. The novelty of sex after a year of drought. Her reactions were probably heightened by the thrill or the danger or the chance finally to feel alive again after so many months of living cocooned by work and grief.

He grinned at her, his blue eyes bright in his tanned face, and she realized she was lying to herself.

It was him. Marcus. He did this to her.

"You're overthinking," he said. "Yes or no?"

She blinked. "Yes to…?"

"Did you shower already?"

"Oh. Yes. Thank you."

He nodded. "Later on the water conservation thing, then. I've got to get these cameras set up anyway."

She resisted the urge to tug on her towel. "Cameras?"

"Digital surveillance cameras." He held up a black device scarcely bigger than a matchbox. "I don't want any more close calls."

She felt a chill that had nothing to do with standing in the drafty hallway wrapped in a towel. "They were accidents."

"Probably. The camera will tell us for sure."

"How?"

"This camera responds to changes in the picture. When anything new sneaks into its viewfinder, it takes a shot and stores it on its memory card. I can download and inspect the images on my computer. If I see anything suspicious, I can send photos to DS as e-mail attachments."

"That's very—" she struggled for a word that would encompass both her admiration for his expertise and her dismay that he felt it was necessary "—ingenious of you."

He shrugged. "It's my job."

It *was* his job, she realized.

She didn't doubt for a minute that the sex was genuine. She even believed the affection was real. But first and foremost, above all else, she was a job to him. While she was weak-kneed and breathless at the prospect of playing house with Superman, he was already out saving Metropolis.

She straightened her spine. ''Where did you get the cameras?''

''I gave Garcia—he's in my squad—a supplies list.'' Marcus stopped fiddling with the device in his hands long enough to give her a crooked smile. ''Kind of hoped I'd never need them, though.''

Her heart beat faster. Was she really in danger? Or could he simply not accept that he had forgotten to cover the well? ''You may not need them now. I was careless. I fell. It was an accident.''

''Maybe. But it wasn't your fault. I was the one who was careless.''

''Marcus, you're only human. People make mistakes.''

''I don't.''

She didn't question his commitment to his job. She was sure he would lay down his life to protect her. And equally certain it would kill her to see him die. But he was over-reacting.

''Moving a well cover seems a pretty inefficient way for some unknown assassin to try to kill me,'' she said.

''You wouldn't say that if it had worked.''

Frustrated, she pulled the towel tighter. ''I wouldn't say anything if it had worked. I'd be dead.''

He turned red under his tan. ''Do you want to go back to D.C.?''

No, she didn't. The realization shook her. For over a year, the provisions and ramifications of the Delmonico Accord had consumed her, waking and sleeping. She ought to be fretting over the time and opportunities being lost in Washington while she tumbled down wells and into—

Oh, no. Not love.

She was not falling into the female trap of equating sex with love. Although the sex had been wonderful. Forget the big macho stud good looks. Forget that he was honorable and kind, with a devotion to duty and a practical intelligence that made every other man she knew seem like an ineffectual wimp. Forget that when she was with him, the knots in her stomach eased and the burden on her shoulders lightened and the whole world seemed a brighter, more hopeful place.

None of that was enough to make her disregard her purpose in coming to Washington. It wasn't enough to make her fall in love.

Was it?

"I said, do you want to go back to D.C.?" he repeated.

Her throat tightened. "Do you?" she countered.

He met her gaze somberly. "We have to, don't we? Eventually."

At least he didn't sound too happy about it. She wasn't the only one suffering from unrequited— Well, anyway, she wasn't the only one suffering.

She drew a deep breath and felt the towel strain across her breasts. He noticed. She watched a muscle in his jaw bunch before he dragged his gaze back to her face, letting her see the heat and the need that burned in his eyes.

Suffering was highly overrated, she decided.

Why shouldn't they take this time they'd been given? Why shouldn't she treasure it as the precious gift it was? And when the time came for her to return to her work in Delmonico and for him to go on saving the world, maybe she would find the strength to let him go.

Eventually. Not today. Not yet.

"Do you think it will be soon?" she asked.

He shrugged. "As soon as it's safe."

She stood above him in the drafty hall, trembling with cold and the force of longing and the certainty of loss, and looked him straight in the eyes.

"Then let's not waste any time," she said, and dropped
the towel.

He was running out of time.

In the shadows of the barn, he made a pouch of yellow
newspaper and poured his mix of chemical fertilizer and
diesel fuel inside.

She was leaving, the bitch. Maybe not today, maybe not
tomorrow, but eventually. And he couldn't let that happen.
His instructions were clear. The target must not return to
Washington. Must never return to Delmonico.

He snipped the insulation from the end of a wire. For
three dollars, he could have purchased a highly effective
and lightweight contact bomb like the Italian TS-50 or a
U.S. M14. Something plastic that would require very little
pressure to set off. But most APMs—antipersonnel
mines—were designed to maim, not kill. Take a life, and
you neutralized one enemy. Take a limb, and you neutralized two—the victim and the buddy whose job it was to
drag the guy to safety.

He was a professional. He rigged his bomb to kill. But
only one target, only one victim.

Presumably the SEAL was still of some use to
somebody.

Thirteen

All his life, he'd wanted to be accepted.

Which was pretty pathetic, if you thought about it, but Marcus wasn't a thinking man, so he was generally okay with it. Most of the time.

Even now that he *was* thinking about it he was still okay, because Samantha was on the other side of his best friend's kitchen table, wearing his kid sister's skimpy shirt and eating the peaches Marcus had picked for her.

I'm Yours, her breasts proclaimed in bright-gold letters on bright-blue cloth, and every time he looked across the kitchen table, he thought, *Damn straight.*

"That was wonderful." She smiled at him, licking peach juice from her fingers, and his lower body tightened.

"You're wonderful," he told her honestly.

"So are you." Her smile turned rueful. "But I'm sure you've been told that before."

What could he say? There had been other women, women who were attracted by his body or his uniform or his parents' money. But no one like her.

"Not by you," he said.

She grimaced slightly. "Thank you. It's nice to be special. Is that because I'm older than the others or because you've been assigned to me?"

The edge in her voice surprised him. Her insecurity surprised him. Didn't she know she was perfect?

"It's because…" He swore, frustrated. "Look, I'm no good with words."

She touched his arm, instantly reassuring. "It doesn't matter."

But it did matter. It mattered to her. And because it did, he had to try to put into words things he would normally rather die than say.

"With the others… It was physical, all right? I've always been good at the physical stuff. With you—" He shook his head. "I'm not saying this right. It's more, okay?"

"I think you said it perfectly." There was humor in her eyes, and understanding, and something else. Something that made his heart pound. "It's more for me, too."

He wanted to ask her how much more. Only he couldn't. She depended on him to keep her safe. This was a hell of a time to put her in the position of telling him she wanted to be just friends.

It would be easier if he could take her back to bed. When they made love, he could show her the things he could not say. He wanted to peel that skimpy shirt off her, inch by inch. He wanted to have her, take her, keep her….

He shook his head to clear it. He didn't get to keep her. That wasn't the assignment. His mission was to protect her.

"I should check the cameras," he said abruptly, pushing back from the table. "Are you okay here?"

"Just peachy," she assured him.

She dimpled, pleased with her small joke, and his need for her pressed on his chest until he could hardly breathe.

If he lost her…

But he wouldn't. He couldn't. He would do whatever he had to do to protect her.

He went to inspect the cameras.

Two of them had been triggered during the night, one at the side window facing the barn and one on the front porch. Well, hell. He retrieved the digital film cards and returned to the kitchen.

Samantha stood at the sink, washing the lunch dishes, up

to her smooth white elbows in lemon-scented suds. She took one look at his face and asked, "Problem?"

He didn't want to scare her before he'd even had a look at the cards. "Naw." He booted up the laptop. "Got some pictures, though. Probably some real nice shots of shadows. Or rats. Plenty of rats in a barnyard."

"How lovely." She dried her hands. "May I see?"

His instincts and his training both said no. If he had captured an intruder on camera, he didn't want her to panic. If he'd made another mistake, he didn't want her to know. But if some lowlife was this close to her, then she had the right to know.

Even if it was a rat. God, he hoped it was a rat.

He plugged in the card-reader, buying time, and began to download images. "Nothing to see."

That much at least was true. Even with the cameras' low light requirements, the thumbnail images were dark. He adjusted the brightness, trying to find whatever visual changes had triggered the camera.

He missed Garcia. Missed Jimmy. His equipment was good, but it couldn't replace the resources and know-how of his squad.

There, maybe. What was that in the shelter of the barn? He zoomed in and recentered, but the details remained stubbornly in shadow. Frustrated, he clicked on the next image.

Samantha leaned over his shoulder—*Hello, breast*—and pointed. "What's that?"

He jerked his attention back to the screen. Garcia's cameras could refocus and take a new frame every five seconds. They hadn't captured much: a deeper darkness here, an inconsistent angle there, a blur that might have been movement. But the gaps told more than the images themselves. Whoever, whatever, was out there didn't want to be seen by anyone watching from the house. Marcus scowled. Or else their nighttime visitor knew exactly where the cameras were placed and how to avoid them.

Son of a bitch.

"Hard to say," he lied.

Samantha didn't look back at the screen. She watched his face instead, like a good poker player, trying to figure out what he was holding and what he wasn't telling. "All right, fine. But if you decide to share, I'll be in the living room."

With a mixture of relief and regret he watched her go, the back pockets of her jeans swaying.

And then he loaded the memory card from the other camera into his computer. *Click,* download. *Click,* view. *Click,* enlarge.

Behind him, he could hear Samantha moving through the room, the slight shuffle of her feet, the scrape of the piano bench. The hair at the back of his neck lifted in warning. The tap of his keys was overwhelmed by the opening ripple of hers.

Tada tada tada tada dum—

Something was wrong. Cold foreboding snaked down his spine. Clenched in his gut.

—tada dum, tada dum.

He stood, jerked to his feet. "Samantha?"

Tada tada tada tada dum—

He lunged for the living room. "Samantha! Stop!"

She turned her laughing face toward the doorway, puzzled and amused. "I thought you liked my playing."

He was sweating. Shaking. "I do. It's just—"

Her fingers still hovered over the keys.

The words burst out of him. "Christ, stop it!"

Her smile faded. Her hands dropped to her lap. She didn't understand.

He didn't understand himself.

"What's wrong?" she asked quietly.

He didn't know. His mouth was dry. His heart was pounding. His muscles were rigid. His body was in full flight-or-fight response, and he didn't know where to run or who the enemy was.

"Could you…" He inhaled carefully. Combat breathing. "Get away from the piano."

"All right." She raised her hands to push herself away.

"No!"

She froze.

His soldier's sense was screaming. *Why?* Why? Nothing was wrong. She wasn't doing anything wrong, just sitting there at the piano….

He felt something twist and shift inside him.

The piano.

He didn't stop to question how he knew. In battle, survival depended on reaction time, on that mix of observation, insight and training so ingrained that warriors called it instinct.

Something about her hands above the piano keys, ready to strike…

"Don't. Touch. The. Piano," he ordered. "Get up and get over here."

Her brows lifted, but she obeyed without question. She probably thought he was crazy.

Hell, he probably *was* crazy.

He resisted the urge to grab her, to hold her, to reassure himself that she was safe. She wasn't safe. Not yet, anyway.

He couldn't send her outside—not alone into the open. Shifting his laptop to a chair, he tipped the heavy kitchen table onto its side.

"Behind here. Kneel down."

Graceful, reluctant, she lowered herself to her knees. "Marcus, what's happening?"

He didn't know. He only felt…something. Something big. Something bad.

"Stay," he commanded, as if she were a dog, and crossed the plank floor to the piano.

Well.

Samantha pressed her lips together. She wasn't stupid. She wasn't about to ignore a direct order from the man responsible for protecting her life. But when this was over—whatever it was—he had some explaining to do.

What *was* he doing?

She raised her head above the edge of the table to watch. Marcus was examining the piano, with his eyes and with his hands. He felt along the cracks on the top and sides, and then, very cautiously, he lifted the lid.

His breath hissed.

Her stomach churned. Her trepidation grew. "What is it?"

He didn't look at her. All his attention was focused on whatever lay beneath the lid of the old upright.

"It's a bomb," he said flatly. "Wired to the keyboard."

"A bomb?" Her voice squeaked. She bit her lip.

"Looks like it." He angled his head above the narrow opening to peer inside. "There's this little piece of metal tape on one of the hammers. Hit the right key, and it completes an electrical connection to the battery—yeah, here it is—and that sets off the detonator."

Both his hands were inside the piano.

She winced, unable to watch, unable to look away. "What key?"

"How should I know?" His shoulder moved as he reached for something. She held her breath.

"It's in the middle somewhere," he added.

In the middle? In her mind, she ran through the piece she'd been playing. "Fur Elise." E above middle C with the right hand. Another three measures, and she'd have been dead.

She shuddered.

She heard the sound of tape ripping. Then Marcus set something on the bench where she'd sat to play less than two minutes ago. It looked like an ordinary C battery with black and white wire attached.

Not a mistake. Her heart tripped. A bomb.

He turned. There were deep creases between his eyebrows. His jaw was tight. His mouth was grim. He looked safe and sane and angry, and more than anything she wanted to run to his arms so he could hold her. Except that probably was a really bad idea right now, since he was holding this little plastic bag covered with duct tape and if she threw herself into his arms, she'd probably set it off.

Her stomach crowded her throat. "Is that it? The bomb?"

"Would you get down behind the table, please?"

She crouched there, listening to his footsteps cross the kitchen. He wasn't behind the table. He wasn't protected at all.

Silence. She waited, ears straining, nerves stretched. "Marcus?"

Water sloshed and dribbled in the sink. "Yeah?"

"What are you doing?"

"I'm diluting the chemical components of the explosive so it doesn't blow us up."

"Oh." That seemed pitifully inadequate, so she added brightly, "That's good."

"Babe, there is nothing good about this situation. Somebody knows you're here."

"I already figured that out."

"He was in the house."

She swallowed. "Yes."

"He knows you play the piano."

Samantha stood, supporting herself with one hand on the overturned table. Her knees were shaking. "Philip ordered a piano for my suite at the hotel. My piano playing is hardly a state secret. It may even be in my official bio.''

Marcus's eyes were dark with disbelief and fear. "Right. 'Ambassador Barnes earned her master's degree in public policy from Harvard's Kennedy School of Government. She likes taking bubble baths and playing the piano.'''

She attempted a smile. "I don't, actually. Like to take baths.''

"That's not the point. The point is this guy is too close.''

"What do you want to do about it?'' she asked quietly.

He ran a hand through his dark hair, leaving it streaked with moisture. "I've got to move you.''

"Where?''

"I don't know.''

"We could go back to D.C.,'' she suggested.

Marcus shook his head. "No good. I had to get you out of D.C. Baxter warned me there's a mole in his department.''

"Baxter is your contact at the Bureau of Diplomatic Security?''

"Special Agent in Charge Jerry Baxter. Yeah.''

"But you said no one at DS knew where you were taking me. No one knew at all, you said. Except for…''

Except for James Robinson. His swim buddy. Jimmy.

Marcus swung away from her, his shoulders rigid. "I'll contact Baxter.''

"We don't have a phone.''

He gave her a get-real look, and she flushed. Of course he had a phone. Navy SEALs were always prepared. Or was that the Boy Scouts?

He reached for the black leather briefcase that held his computer. Slipping a cellphone from a side pocket, he turned it on.

Well, wasn't that just dandy. She felt like a fool. She might have a master's degree from Harvard, but she had clearly flunked Hostages 101. She could have called Philip at any time. She could still call him.

Marcus spoke into the phone, his voice low. "Sir, we have a situation here."

She couldn't hear the other side of the conversation, so she watched Marcus's face instead.

He looked taken aback. "No. No, she's still alive. But—" His jaw set. "I understand, sir. But there's been an attempt."

He listened in silence, his free hand clenched at his side. "Very seriously, sir. I want to bring her in. No, sir. Now."

Tension coiled in the pit of Samantha's stomach. Her hands trembled. She laced her fingers together, forcing herself to concentrate, forcing herself to listen.

Marcus's voice was tight with frustration. "Over, how? Over, when? With all due respect, sir— Yes, I'll continue to monitor the Web site. But—"

He paced the kitchen, increasingly agitated. "No. No. What about backup, then? Yes, sir, I understand that the more people who know… Damn it, *somebody* knows she's here."

He stood very still by the sink, then slowly lowered the hand holding the phone. He clicked it off and swore.

Samantha raised her eyebrows, deliberately cool. "I take it that didn't go well."

He scowled at her. "Son of a bitch hung up on me."

"I'm sorry," she said sincerely.

"He said they were 'very close to achieving their objectives.'" His mimicry was savage. "Fat lot of good it will do them to dig up their mole if you're already dead."

She couldn't help it. She winced.

He saw and swore again. "Sorry. My God, I'm sorry."

He came to her and pulled her into his arms. He felt hearteningly solid, reassuringly strong. She turned her face to his shirt and breathed him in, the scents of clean cotton and dish soap and hot, frustrated male.

"We've tried your contacts," she mumbled. "Want to try mine?"

He snorted. "Pansy Phil?"

She lay her cheek against his chest. "You're wrong about Philip. But as a matter of fact, I was thinking of someone with a little more influence than my secretary."

"We've got to be careful who you talk to, babe. According to Baxter, the problem goes across the board and pretty high up."

"As high as the White House?"

His arms tightened around her. "What are you thinking?"

"I could call Matt Tynan."

"And who would he call? We don't know who the bad guys are. Assuming we're dealing with the Coalition and not Rebelia, they could be anywhere."

She raised her head. "I'm sorry, I just can't be that paranoid."

"I can," he said grimly. "Hell, Samantha, this bastard got into the *house*."

She shivered. "Marcus, are you— Are we sure James Robinson didn't somehow let our location slip? Perhaps without knowing it or intending—"

"No. We may not know who the bad guys are, but Jimmy is one of the good guys. I'd trust him with my life."

"You are trusting him with your life."

He shrugged. "Not for the first time."

She wasn't about to dispute the bonds forged by duty, danger and friendship. They were comrades. Swim buddies. And yet it had to be said. "You're also trusting him with mine."

"You think I don't know that? I know." He sounded

miserable. Miserable and determined. "But it's not Jimmy. It can't be. I'd just as soon suspect myself."

She drew back to look into his face, his strong, honest, handsome, utterly unhappy face.

She'd told him she trusted him. Did she trust his judgment, as well?

"All right," she said slowly. "It's not Jimmy. It's someone else who knows my movements, who knows my habits and who knows how to rig a bomb. Any ideas?"

"Maybe. One."

But he didn't sound very happy about it. Her declaration of faith didn't seem to have cheered him at all. In fact, he looked just as miserable and every bit as determined as before.

She waited for him to explain, but this time he wasn't drawn in by her silence. His eyes were haunted. His mouth stayed stubbornly shut.

"So are you planning to share this big idea with me?" she teased.

"No," he said flatly. "I want to position the cameras again. And this time I want you to set the ones in the house."

"Why?"

"Do you have to know everything? Can't you just trust me?"

She gaped at his unexpected, unjustified outburst. "I have been trusting you. I do trust you. Can't you trust *me?*"

"Not with this. It's too weird. Too wild." He let her go and went to the back door and stood, staring out at the yard. His shoulders were rigid. His whole body radiated tension and distress.

Her heart tripped in her chest. He pivoted and met her gaze, his blue eyes dilated and deep, pleading for...what? What did he want from her?

"Please, Sam." The words sounded torn from him. "Can you do this for me? Will you set the cameras?"

Confused, concerned, she promised, "I'll do anything you want."

But her offer failed to close the distance between them. For the rest of the day he hardly spoke to her. Barely looked at her. He demonstrated how to set the cameras and then disappeared downstairs while she rigged one in the upstairs hall and hid another in the bathroom.

Her chest aching, she watched him pretend everything was under control while the shadows shifted and the long afternoon struggled and gave way to an uneasy night.

It was his job, she told herself. She was his job, and he took his failure to protect her seriously. The reminder did not comfort her.

The night was hot, filled with dreams and sudden starts. He didn't come to bed until he thought she was asleep. Neither of them slept well. But sometime in the restless stretch of darkness, in the long and aching hours before dawn, he turned to her, frustrated and fiercely claiming, his hands abrupt and his mouth bruising. Awakened, aroused, she welcomed him with her body, took her own kisses and claimed her own territory, running her hands over his strong, solid muscles and smooth, hot skin. He thrust into her, deep and fast and hard, and she shuddered, cried out with pleasure and relief.

His weight pinned her. His strength filled her. He was inside her as deeply as he could get. There was nothing between them, no words, no light, no air. They were close, closer, urgent, moving. Swept away by the dark tide of desire, she clutched him, her knees lifting, her hands pressing his back as he plunged and pounded into her, as she gasped and arched, until his need and her pleasure coiled. Crested. Broke. Spent, they clung to each other in a sweaty tangle of arms and legs and sheets.

He kissed her cheek. She stroked his hair, tenderness raking her heart. Comforted, she slept.

But when she woke, Marcus was sitting on the side of the bed, a camera in his hands and his expression shattered.

Samantha sat up, misgiving cold in her stomach. She rested one hand on his broad back. His skin was damp. His heart thudded under her palm.

"What is it? What's wrong?"

"I was right." He turned his tortured face to her. "Somebody was in the house. Somebody is trying to kill you."

She moistened her lips. "How? Who?"

He met her gaze, hell in his eyes, and whispered, "Me."

Fourteen

Marcus wanted to cry.

Samantha was staring at him, her eyes huge and dark in her pale face, as if he'd just sprouted horns and a tail. As if he'd backhanded her across the jaw. Which he hadn't.

That he knew of.

Yet.

He winced.

"What are you talking about?" she asked.

Like there was any way in the world he could explain. Like there was one chance in hell he could make sense of the unthinkable, the incomprehensible.

His hands tightened on the empty camera. "This morning when I got up, I checked all the cameras. The ones downstairs, the ones I set, hadn't been triggered. The ones up here…after I found them, I downloaded the pictures."

She waited, her silence pressing.

If he spoke very carefully, sticking to the facts, using short sentences and little words, he could get through this. "There were eight shots. Three in the hall, five in the bathroom. In most of them, you could see the guy. The intruder—the man in the images—was me."

She swung her long, smooth, bare legs over the edge to sit beside him. The mattress sagged beneath her weight. "So you got up to use the bathroom. That does not make you an intruder. Or a killer."

She didn't get it. Or she didn't want to get it. He didn't

blame her. He didn't get it either. If there was any other explanation...

"Then why don't I remember getting up?" he asked.

"Maybe you were too tired. Maybe you were walking in your sleep."

"Maybe I did more than walk," he said grimly.

She seized his shoulder, fierce in his defense, stubborn in her denial. "Look at me. I'm fine. I'm here, aren't I? You didn't do anything."

He would not meet her eyes. "Yeah. I did."

"That's stupid."

He jerked like she'd jabbed him with an electrode. "Fine. You asked me who. I told you. You asked me how. I'll show you."

Grabbing her hand, he pulled her off the bed and out of the room after him. Her bare feet made no sound in the hall. He dragged her into the bathroom and nudged her against the sink. Their bodies crowded together in the cramped, cold space. She was warm and smooth and smelled like sleep and sex. He released her hand abruptly.

"The camera was in the tub. My back was to it most of the time. But you can still see this." He picked up the hair dryer from the side of the sink.

Samantha's deep blue eyes widened in confusion. "I don't understand."

He unscrewed the plastic cap that covered the filter. His hands were trembling. He wondered if they'd been steady last night when he did this thing. This horrible thing.

"This is batting." He dug the damp white fluff from inside the hair dryer and showed it to her. "Cotton balls, I guess, soaked with an accelerant. Not gasoline. Nail polish remover, maybe, or hair spray." He sniffed. "Yeah, hair spray. See how it was packed against the heating element? And the insulation is all peeled back here. So when the coil heats to a certain temperature, it ignites the batting and instead of a hair dryer, you've got yourself a nice little flamethrower.''

"You…" Now she got it. Her throat moved as she swallowed. She was looking at him now like he was some kind of monster. Which he was. "You did this?"

"Last night." To punish himself, to make sure there was no chance of misunderstanding what had happened, what he had done, he added, "I tried to kill you."

"No, you didn't. I don't believe it."

Gratitude slid between his ribs, unexpected and painful as a knife. It killed him to say it, but he did. "Yeah, I did. We've got it on camera."

"If you wanted to kill me, why go to all this trouble? Why not just shoot me?"

Horrified, he objected, "I couldn't."

She tilted her head to one side. "Precisely."

Standing there in her bare feet and his worn navy T-shirt, her red hair tumbled around her face, she still managed to look smarter and more confident than any woman he'd ever known. But she was wrong. About this. About him. He had to convince her. Her life depended on it.

"Look, you asked me who and how. The camera proves who. And this—" he waved a hand at the neat fire trap dismantled over the sink "—this is your how. There are your answers. Those are the only answers I can come up with."

"Then I need to ask another question."

"What? What else could you possibly need to know?"

"Why?" she asked quietly.

He stared at her. "What do you mean?"

"Do you *want* to kill me?"

"No! God, no."

"Then why would you try?"

"Does it matter?" he asked bitterly. "Because I'm crazy. I forget things, remember? I can't remember last night. Just like I can't remember anything from before the adoption.''

Samantha blinked. ''You're adopted?''

Hell. Just what she needed. Another reason to mistrust him.

He hadn't told her because she had some kind of prejudice against adoption. It was a gamble, she'd said. An adopted child could have unidentified problems. Special needs.

Well, she got that right. He definitely had problems.

He clenched his fists. ''Yeah.''

''When you were ten?''

Nothing wrong with *her* memory. ''Yeah.''

''Well.'' Her gaze clouded, refocused. Her full lips pursed. He could practically hear the wheels turning inside her pretty head. ''So you were born in, what, sixty-nine?''

''Seventy. So?''

''And you have no memory of your childhood before your adoption?''

''I told you that.''

''Yes, but... Oh, it's unbelievable.'' The pleat between her eyebrows deepened. ''On the other hand, so is the idea that you would want to hurt me.''

''Samantha.'' He strained for patience. ''What the hell are you talking about?''

''Your being adopted. It changes things.''

''That's what I was afraid of. Listen, I didn't mean to lie to you. I—''

She interrupted him. ''What do you know about the Proteus Project?''

''The what?''

''Code Proteus. Philip gave me a newspaper clipping recently—''

''I don't have time to read the paper. Isn't that the mutant kids? Secret government experiments in the sixties? Tabloid stuff.''

''Well, yes, that's been my assumption, too. But the story in the *Post* suggested that there are children who survived the dissolution of the project. If there were…special children, who needed to be hidden, who needed to be integrated somehow into society, doesn't it make sense that they would be adopted? Like you were.''

His head hurt. He didn't want to think about it. Didn't want to accept it… Didn't want…

''What difference does it make? Who cares if the government cooked up a batch of superbabies over thirty years ago? What does that have to do with—'' His breath hissed in. ''You think I'm one of them, don't you? The freak kids.''

Her eyes were deep blue wells of compassion. ''I think the time frame makes it a possibility. It would certainly explain a few things. Like your really remarkable strength. And your memory losses.''

His brain felt like it was exploding. ''But not why I'm trying to kill you,'' he said, deliberately distracting her. Deliberately brutal.

She flinched. ''No,'' she admitted. ''Not that.''

''Well, right now that's all I'm interested in. That, and keeping you alive. We need to go back to D.C. Today. Now.''

She stuck out her chin. ''No.''

He glared at her. ''What do you mean, no?''

''What are you planning to do in D.C.?''

''Turn you back over to Walker. Turn myself in.''

She shook her head. Her hair brushed the tops of her breasts. ''Absolutely not. You could be risking my life. Not to mention ruining your career.''

''Don't worry about my career.''

"Don't worry? What were you planning on telling your commanding officer?"

He sucked in his breath; released it slowly. "The truth."

"Which truth? That you brought me here to protect me? Or that you've been walking in your sleep?"

He didn't say anything. He didn't even want to think about it. The navy was his life. Turning himself in to face certain disciplinary action would be like death, worse than death. But his silence was answer enough for Samantha.

"Oh, no," she said. "They'll think you're delusional. Or they'll believe you when you tell them you tried to murder a United States ambassador. Either way, they'll lock you up and throw away the key."

"Babe, don't you get it? I deserve to be locked up. I'm dangerous to you."

"Maybe not. If we could find the reason—"

"We know the reason. I'm crazy."

"I don't believe that. What if your behavior is the result of your experiences as a child?"

She was so earnest. So sweet. So determined to find an excuse for the inexcusable.

"Yeah, that's what they say about serial killers."

She narrowed her big baby blues at him. "It's not the same thing at all. If you really are the product of some genetic engineering project—"

He'd be a freak. For real. Unnatural. Unaccepted. His mind revolted at the thought. His stomach felt queasy. "It wouldn't make a damn bit of difference. Except maybe to make things worse. Not just a psychotic killer with military training, but a psychotic killer with military training, superhuman strength and unknown genetic makeup? Oh, yeah, I can definitely see a review board making an exception in that case."

She opened her mouth to speak and then pressed her lips firmly together.

Had he finally succeeded in shutting her up?

"I need to talk to Matt," she said.

"You do that," said Marcus. "After we get to Washington."

"I want to call him first."

His throat was tight. "Fine. You can use my cellphone."

That was what he wanted, wasn't it? He needed her to recognize the seriousness of her danger. He wanted her to take steps to protect herself from him. He was thrilled she was turning to her high school boyfriend for help.

Sure he was.

"Believe me, Ambassador Barnes, Matt wouldn't mind at all being called back to Washington for an emergency." The warm, amused voice of Matt's male secretary came clearly through the phone. "He took Carey to visit the in-laws. *All* the in-laws, which means they're up to stepmother number four by now. Are you sure you don't want me to have him call you?"

Samantha watched the back of Marcus's head. He bent over his computer, his shoulders tight with strain. Love and worry closed her throat.

She coughed delicately to clear it. "No, this is something I'd rather discuss with Matt in person. You'll put me on the schedule as soon as he gets back?"

"He comes in from the coast tomorrow and gets back to the office the day after. I'll fit you in right after his meeting with the White House chief of staff," Kip assured her cheerfully. "Say, ten?"

"Ten would be wonderful. Thank you, Kip."

"Not a problem. How's the cold?"

"Excuse me?"

"Philip told me you were sick. He sounded quite worried about you, actually."

"Oh, yes. I'm feeling much better, thank you."

Or she would be once she figured out how to get through this mess with her skin and Marcus's career intact.

She exchanged another round of thanks and goodbyes with Matt's assistant before she ended the connection.

"Matt won't be back in the office until the day after tomorrow," she told Marcus. "What do you think about staying here another day?"

No answer.

He seemed transfixed by the computer. He'd told her he wanted to check in with Baxter through "regular channels," but as far as she could tell he wasn't reading e-mail. He was caught by some silly computer game with a tiny green character parading erratically across the flat screen. Boys and their toys...

She smiled and moved closer to watch.

KILL.

The word flashed upon the screen so quickly it barely registered. Samantha gasped.

The little green man resumed his jerky march.

BARNES flashed on the screen.

Her mouth was dry. Her palms were sweating. Her heart pounded in her ears.

"Marcus?"

KILL. BARNES. KILL. BARNES. KILL. BARNES.

He turned his head, his face hard, and a stranger looked out of his eyes.

"Marcus!"

He blinked, and the alien vanished. "Hey, babe. Did you reach Tynan?"

Her heart threatened to pound loose from her chest. She could barely breathe, could not force enough oxygen to her brain to think.

She worked enough moisture into her mouth to speak. "Marcus?"

He regarded her. Patient. Quizzical. Himself. "Yeah?"

He didn't see it, she realized, concerned and relieved at the same time. Why didn't he see it?

"I..." A little air returned to her lungs. A little confidence returned to her voice. "I think I know the 'why,'" she said. "It's the computer. There's a command or something on your computer that's ordering you to kill."

His gaze cut to the screen.

"Don't look!" she said sharply. "Turn it off."

He turned back to her and frowned. "Samantha—"

"I saw it. In that game. Words flashing, like a subliminal message. 'Kill Barnes.' Turn it off."

"Okay. It's okay." His voice was soothing as he pressed the keys to shut the computer down. "Honey, you're overreacting. This situation has you seeing things. I may be nuts, but there's nothing wrong with my eyesight. I've logged on to that site every day since we got here, and I've never seen those words."

"Marcus, listen to yourself. You've checked it every day since we got here?"

"Because Baxter told me to. Look, I appreciate what you're trying to do. You don't want this to be my fault. Hell, I don't want this to be my fault. But I'm still responsible."

"Baxter told you to check the Web site. Did Baxter give you the computer?"

"Yeah."

"When?"

"When he gave me the order to extract you to a safe house. He said Rebelia and the Coalition were both gunning for you, and he couldn't trust his own people because of a leak in his department."

Possibilities plucked at her. Her mind raced. "A leak? Or a traitor?"

Marcus frowned. "You're thinking it's him? He's the traitor?"

"He assigned you to me. He arranged for us to be alone. He gave you access to a site that contains commands to kill me. That puts him at the top of my list."

"Careful, babe. You're starting to sound as crazy as me." But Marcus's expression was thoughtful.

"At least admit we need to stay out of Washington until Matt gets back."

"No way. I tried to kill you."

"*Baxter's* trying to kill me. If I'm right, you're just a tool."

"Is that supposed to make me feel better? Because it's not helping."

"I'm simply saying now that we know Baxter is the culprit, I should stay with you until he's removed."

"Wrong." Marcus was angry. Emphatic. "*I'm* still the culprit. And you're not safe with me."

"I'm safer with you than anyone. At least you want to protect me."

"When I'm not hearing voices I do. And if this was a physical fight, I could. But these weird mind games... I don't know." He looked at her, and the uncertainty in his eyes broke her heart. "Mental battles have never been my strong suit."

He'd told her he'd struggled in school. She knew she was asking for more than he felt he could give. But the alternative would leave him discharged and disgraced.

The alternative could leave her dead.

"This isn't about IQ scores or test grades," she argued. "This is about willpower. I trust your mental toughness. And your honor. Two days, Marcus. Give us two more days, until Matt gets back. He'll know how to deal with Baxter, and we'll have time to figure out how to deal with these subliminal suggestions. Maybe a good psychiatrist—"

"No psychiatrist," Marcus said.

She was genuinely surprised. "Why not? If it's the only way to...to—"

"Fix me?"

She flushed. "You're clearly vulnerable to some kind of mental suggestion. A competent psychiatrist could identify the cause and help you overcome it."

"And being evaluated as mentally unfit could cost me my career."

"Oh, and you going in to your commanding officer and telling him you feel compelled to kill me isn't going to do the same thing?"

His head jerked as her point struck home. Still, he muttered, "I don't want some shrink messing with my head."

She ached for him. But she said, "Your head has already been messed with. You need help to clean up the mess."

His mouth twisted wryly. "You're not going to let me duck this, are you?"

Her heart beat faster. In hope? Or sympathy? "No. You need to know what's going on, Marcus. You need help to stop it."

"And what if your shrink finds out more than I want to know?"

"What do you mean?"

"It's not just the last couple of days that are a problem, sweetcakes. I've got ten years missing. I don't know that I want them back."

She reached out and took his hands. Strong, tanned hands, capable and kind.

"Those years are part of who you are." Part of who I love, she thought, but did not say. "I don't think you need to be afraid of what you'll find."

He turned his palms over and gripped her hands. "Maybe," was all he said.

She tried to imagine what it must be like for him, having a void where his childhood should be.

I'm a complete zero before the age of ten.

Samantha considered herself essentially alone. Husband-less. Childless. She had no brothers or sisters. Her father had died while she was still in college. Her mother lived a continent away. But Samantha had memories, good and bad, enriching and informing her life. She chose where she was going based in part on where she'd been.

What did it do to a child to have all that taken away?

I always figured I must have done something pretty damn bad to wipe out my entire childhood.

"You don't remember anything?" she asked.

"No. Sometimes— When I was a kid—" He stopped.

She waited.

"I used to pretend I had a sister," he admitted. "Not Honey. I mean, I love Honey, but I used to pretend I had somebody my own age. Somebody really smart and pretty who didn't make fun of me. Like an imaginary friend, I guess. Sometimes I'd dream about her." He shrugged. "Pretty lame, huh?"

"Maybe she wasn't imaginary," Samantha suggested softly. "Maybe you'll find her one day. Your other sister."

"Maybe," he said again, but she could tell he didn't believe it. "It's no big deal. I'm good with alone."

"Did that make it hard for you when you joined the SEALS? Did you have trouble feeling part of a squad?"

He grinned.

"What?" she asked defensively.

"That is such a girlie question."

She tried to prim her mouth and failed. "But did you?" she asked.

"Nope. I earned my spot on the Teams. It's the one place I always felt I belonged. Not to mention that when you're crammed on a rubber dinghy with six other guys, it's hard to feel alone."

This time she didn't hold back her smile. But it was

terribly, poignantly clear to her how much he was willing to sacrifice for her sake: not only his career, but his identity on the Teams.

"Well, you're not alone now, either," she said. "We're in this together."

"For the next two days."

That wasn't what she meant or what she wanted. Was his impatience to get rid of her fueled by more than concern? Were two days enough for him? More than enough?

"Two days," she agreed weakly.

Two days to neutralize the threat to her life without destroying his career. Two days before she had to return to the work she had chosen, and he went back to the life he loved.

Marcus leaned forward in his chair. "And if I wait like you want, you have to do something for me."

"Anything," she promised.

He released her hands. Reaching behind his back, he slid his gun from its holster and presented it to her, butt first.

She recoiled as if he'd just presented her with a snake. Something small and black and deadly. "Anything but that."

"You need to protect yourself."

"You can protect me."

His face was grim. "You need to protect yourself from me."

"I don't know how to shoot."

"The Glock doesn't have an external safety. You pull the trigger, it's going to go off."

"I won't hit anything."

"Women are instinctively better shots than men. If you fire at close range, you'll hit me."

"I don't want to hit you!"

"Let's hope you don't have a reason to, then." He took

her hand and folded it around the grip of the gun. ''One other thing…''

She waited, her hands shaking, her stomach curling with dread.

He held her gaze and said, very steadily, ''If you shoot, shoot to kill. You won't stop me otherwise.''

Fifteen

His chest hurt.

His head throbbed.

He moved silently along the dark, windswept beach, seeking, seeking.... His mission disappeared below the surface of his mind like a weighted explosive. The waves rushed and hissed behind him. His blood pounded in his head. His instincts were screaming.

He was still in his cold, rubber wet suit, but sweat poured down his back and stung his eyes. Something was wrong with his vision. Something was wrong. Even with the goggles, he couldn't see more than a few feet. He couldn't see his squad. He couldn't see his way.

Something was very wrong.

The enemy rose out of the darkness at his feet. He lunged to strike, to kill, but his arms wouldn't move. His body wouldn't obey him.

He was going to die.

Marcus woke with his breathing ragged in his ears.

And his fingers wrapped around Samantha's slim white throat.

He swore and flung her down on the pillows and scrambled to the other side of the mattress. This time, waking was worse than any nightmare. He couldn't stop swearing. He couldn't stop shaking. He couldn't stop praying.

"God, oh God, oh Jesus, Sam, are you all right?"

She raised herself on her elbows. Her red hair tumbled

around her shoulders. Her eyes were huge and dark in her pale face.

She was crying. But she was alive. The silver tracks of her silent tears gleamed in the light from the window.

He wanted to die.

He wanted to grab her, seize her, hold her. He wanted to comfort her and reassure himself that she was still breathing. But he had no right to soothe her. He had no right even to touch her. He was a murdering moron, a nut job....

She threw herself across the bed and into his arms.

He held her tight. He stroked her back with trembling hands, buried his face in her hair and crooned reassurances.

"It's all right. It's okay. I won't hurt you, I swear. It's all over."

She clung to him and cried, and he kissed the top of her head and wished a lightning bolt from heaven would come right down and kill him.

"For God's sake, why didn't you shoot me?"

Her fingers tightened on his shoulders. "I didn't have a chance," she mumbled.

He looked for his gun. It was right there on her bedside table within easy reach of her hand. She'd had the chance, all right. She just hadn't made the choice.

Although what did he expect? She was smart and resourceful, but she was no match for a combat-trained, combat-ready Navy SEAL. And he'd known that, damn it, when he'd given her his gun. Would have known it if he'd been thinking with his brain instead of his glands.

"It's okay," he said again, stroking her hair. "Everything's going to be all right."

Which was pretty much a lie, but he figured she needed to hear it right now.

He held her a long time, until her trembling eased. Until her weight on his leg cut off the circulation to his foot.

Even then, the smell and feel of her in his arms made the blood pool in his groin.

She shifted and sighed. He gritted his teeth. Her face was damp against his neck. Her lush, round bottom nestled against his hip. He told himself he was some kind of sick, perverted bastard, getting turned on when she depended on him for comfort, but that didn't stop his body from reacting. Frustrated adrenaline flooded his muscles. He steamed with heat. Her soft breasts pressed against his chest.

Deliberate? No, it couldn't be. She didn't mean... She couldn't possibly want...

She kissed his throat, her mouth warm and seeking, and he realized she could.

"Samantha." He inhaled sharply as she rocked against him. "We can't do this." His voice was hoarse. It was a total giveaway. He was a total loser. "Not now."

She raised her head. Her hair brushed his jaw. "Do you want to talk about what happened?"

"Hell, no." He didn't want to talk almost as much as he did want to bury himself inside her. "We need to go. As soon as you're ready."

"Go where?"

He didn't answer her directly. "I called Jimmy this afternoon. He said he could meet us. I just have to tell him when."

"Where, Marcus?"

"Jimmy will help keep you safe until your friend Matt gets back."

"But—"

Marcus knew what she was going to say. It was too late at night. It was too soon in the game. She was still in danger. He was deep-sixing his career.

He knew all that. And none of it mattered against the one, overwhelming fact: He had nearly killed her. With his bare hands, as she slept beside him.

He shuddered. "No buts," he said fiercely. "No more delays. No talking. I'm not risking you again. I won't risk you again."

Which explained why, twenty minutes later, instead of dragging her down on the sheets and giving her the hot, mindless distraction she was looking for, he was loading her bag into the trunk and reconnecting the distributor cap so he could drive her back to the city and her good buddy Matt Tynan.

That proved it. Marcus made sure she was safely tucked inside the car—legs, fingers, seat belt—before he slammed the passenger side door.

He really was crazy.

After Stan died, Samantha hadn't wanted to feel too deeply, to care too passionately, to risk too much. For the past thirteen months, she had protected her heart by wrapping herself in a soft, impenetrable cocoon of courtesy and work.

She turned her face to the window. Outside the car, the gray Virginia countryside rolled and stretched like a waking cat. Low clouds streaked the horizon ahead, their undersides pregnant with gold. Mere days with Marcus Evans had stripped her protective batting away. Despite her near exhaustion, she was physically alert, emotionally aware.

She felt things now.

She hurt.

She glanced over at Marcus's hands on the steering wheel, his strong, tanned, square-palmed, long-fingered hands. Hands that had stroked, coaxed and caressed her. Hands that had closed on her neck and throttled her.

She swallowed, her throat still raw. It was going to be really hard to enlist Matt's help if she was wearing a string of bruises around her throat like a necklace. Explanations were going to be tough enough already.

Yes, Marcus Evans kidnapped me, but he thought he was acting under orders.

He set traps to kill me, but he rescued me every time.

He's responding to subliminal commands sent to him on his laptop, but he's not really crazy.

Oh, dear. Matt Tynan, cynical White House advisor, was definitely going to have trouble accepting that one. Samantha had trouble accepting it herself. And yet she believed in her heart that Marcus was sane and honorable.

Now all she had to do was convince Matt.

And Marcus himself.

Yellow lights winked on in distant farmhouses. A few cars passed them on the road, their headlights sharp in the lingering darkness. Gradually the farmers' trucks and battered pickups were replaced with early morning commuters in sedans and tourists in RVs and rental cars anxious to get the jump on capital traffic. Samantha watched the city's haze spread on the horizon and wondered what time Matt's flight arrived from the West Coast.

"Almost there," Marcus said, breaking the silence of miles.

She leaned forward. "Where?"

They were nowhere near her hotel in Georgetown and miles south of Bethesda. Marcus turned onto Memorial Drive, heading toward the national cemetery.

Arlington?

It was still very early. The traffic guard wasn't on duty. The gates to the public parking lot were closed. But on the side of the road in front of the gates, a light-colored vehicle was parked. As Marcus pulled onto the shoulder behind it, one of the doors swung open and Jimmy Robinson got out, supporting his slight weight on crutches.

One worry eased. Marcus wasn't going to turn over the task of protecting her to a man who could barely stand. Which meant he must be going with her to see Matt. Which meant he wasn't planning to do anything precipitous that could end his career. With a sigh of relief, Samantha climbed stiffly from their car and followed Marcus across the tarmac.

Except as they approached the other car, the driver's side door opened, and then a door in back. Two tall, strapping, obviously healthy men, in unremarkable civilian clothes with unmistakable military haircuts, wedged through the doors and unfolded themselves to stand by Jimmy. Her heart sank.

Marcus introduced them with careful formality, as if she actually cared about their credentials.

"May I present Ensign David Skillman—that's Slick to most of us—our team medic?"

Skillman, blond, smiling, with a firm handshake and watchful eyes, could have run for senior class president. Or doctor of the month at some tony women's clinic. Samantha murmured hello.

"Petty Officer Third Class Buzz Walters, our explosives expert."

Walters proffered a wide grin and a massive paw.

Marcus jerked his head toward the third man. "And you remember James Robinson."

"Pleasure to see you again, ma'am."

"So I'm leaving you in good hands," Marcus said, not meeting her eyes.

Oh, no. Samantha squared her shoulders and set her mouth. At four o'clock this morning, she'd dressed hastily in yesterday's clothes, too-tight jeans that rubbed her abraded knee and a tiny T-shirt that exposed her bruised arms and announced I'm Yours across the bust. Not at all the outfit she would have chosen to meet a military escort. But as far as she was concerned, Marcus had chosen the shirt. Marcus had chosen the slogan. Marcus could live with the consequences.

"You're not leaving," she said.

Skillman's sharp gaze darted between them. A faint flush crept under Walters's tan.

Marcus looked unhappy. That was good. And determined, which was not so good.

He moved a few yards away, so they could speak without being overheard.

"I don't have a choice," he said, his voice lowered.

"Yes, you do."

"No, I don't. I'm a danger to myself and others. I'm reporting to Little Creek." The Naval Amphibious Base in Little Creek, Virginia, three hours away.

Dismay shook her. She wanted to touch him, to reassure him, to persuade him. But she couldn't. Not in front of an audience. Not in front of his men. "Don't do that. Not yet. At least wait until I've talked to Matt."

"I need to talk with my CO."

"And if he locks you up?"

"Than at least I can go to sleep without worrying I'll wake up with my hands around somebody's throat."

"Marcus!"

He smiled, but his eyes were deep with pain. "Goodbye, Ambassador."

Samantha was ambushed. Outnumbered. Surrounded. There was no way she could force him to go with her into Washington. But she could make it damn hard for him to walk away.

She reached out and she—well, she grabbed him, threw her arms around his thick neck, plastered herself against his chiseled body and planted a kiss right on his stubborn, unhappy mouth. Not a polite thanks-and-goodbye peck, either, but a full penetration, I-want-you-need-you-love-you kind of kiss.

And, miracle of miracles, he wrapped his arms around

her just as tightly and kissed her back just as fiercely, hot and wet and deep.

When he finally let her go, he was hard and she was shaking. James Robinson had averted his gaze. Buzz Walters gaped until Skillman elbowed him in the ribs.

"Don't give up," Samantha whispered. "Don't you dare give up on me."

Marcus turned without a word and walked back to his car.

The Potomac flowed by, pewter and gold in the early morning light. The sun quickened the silent green hills and threw slanting shadows under the small white grave markers, row on row. Samantha watched until the view dissolved in a blur of tears.

But he never looked back.

The interview with his commanding officer was every bit as bad as Marcus feared it would be.

He sat in a cushy, fake leather chair in a comfortably air-conditioned office with sunlight streaking through the slatted blinds and sweat pouring down his back. He would rather have been driving a rubber raft onto the rocks at Coronado or crawling on his belly under a spray of live ammo from an M-16.

Navy Commander Greg Woods was tall, bald and lean, with a razor-sharp mind and a total poker face. He did not make buddies with the men in his command. He was seriously married, for one thing, which limited the hours he spent tossing back a few in the bar with the boys. And he had this strictly business and by-the-book attitude that discouraged warm and fuzzy confidences from his junior officers. Marcus had always respected the guy, though. Even felt comfortable during their dry, mission-focused exchanges.

He wasn't comfortable now.

"So what you're telling me," said Woods, speaking slowly, like a college prof summing up for a roomful of not-very-bright freshmen, "is that you aren't able to control your actions."

"Yes, sir," Marcus said woodenly.

"If that's the case, you do know what I have to do."

Lockup. Psych eval. Review board and discharge. Or worse, although discharge was pretty much the end of life as Marcus knew and loved it. What was the penalty for attempted assassination of a United States ambassador?

"Yes, sir. That's why I'm here."

But Woods surprised him. "It might interest you to know that I've already fielded a call this morning from Ambassador Barnes."

Marcus sat straighter in his chair. "Sir?"

"The ambassador made it clear to me that she accompanied you willingly, that she had no complaints about your conduct and that she placed the utmost confidence in your abilities."

"With all due respect, sir—"

"Prior to this episode, Lieutenant, I would have said the same."

"Thank you, sir. But—"

Woods leveled a look at him and he shut up. "However, despite your friends in high places and your previous record, I cannot ignore the fact that in the course of conducting your mission, you knowingly and unlawfully removed naval property from this base. Do you understand what I'm telling you, son?"

"I..." Marcus gave up. "No, sir. Not at all."

"You admitted to taking cameras and weapons with you when you *escorted* the ambassador on her *vacation*. Theft of military property is an offense under Article 15 of the Uniform Code of Military Justice carrying a nonjudicial punishment. That means I can suspend you from duty and confine you to quarters for a period of up to thirty days pending further action and investigation. Do you get it now, sailor?''

And he did.

His CO was actually offering him a reprieve. It was an enormous act of trust. Woods was relying on him not only to comply with his punishment but to keep his mouth shut while the commander got to the bottom of this mess.

Marcus was grateful. Stunned. Terrified. The CO's action could save his career.

It could also endanger Samantha's life.

''Sir, yes, sir. But—''

''I'm not in the mood for objections, Lieutenant,'' Woods warned him.

Hell, his career was probably shot, anyway.

''No, sir. But may I request a guard be placed on my door, sir?''

Woods regarded him with narrowed brown eyes for a moment. He nodded once. ''I'll have Garcia and Jacobs escort you to quarters.''

It wasn't until Marcus got up to go that he heard his commanding officer mutter, ''And God help us all if you get past them.''

Sixteen

"Thank God that's over."

Matt Tynan's heartfelt exclamation jerked Samantha from sleep on his leather sofa.

Flanked by her Navy SEAL escort, she had coaxed, charmed and intimidated the building superintendent into admitting her to Matt's bachelor pad. "I'm on his list," she had claimed, which was fortunately true. "And I promise you I have absolutely no designs on Mr. Tynan's stereo equipment." She remembered his playboy reputation. "Or his body."

Also true, on both counts. But from the sounds escaping from Matt's foyer, somebody else might.

Was that a suitcase hitting the floor? Or a shoe?

Samantha struggled upright on the deep leather couch and looked at Skillman and Walters, both fully awake and totally alert. Please let it be a suitcase.

"But I liked your family. All your family." The woman with Matt sounded sweet and mischievous at the same time. And very young.

"Family, fine," Matt said huskily. "But I'm glad to finally have you to myself. I've spent the past three days thinking of all the things I'd like to do to you when we were alone."

The young woman sighed and whispered something that sounded like encouragement.

The two SEALs exchanged glances. Oh, goodness. After Samantha's exhibition this morning with Marcus at the cemetery, they must be forming quite an impression of life in the capital.

Samantha stood, tugged her shirt to cover her midriff and hurried into the hall before the situation got any more out of hand, so to speak.

Her old chum Matt Tynan and a sweet young thing were locked together just inside the door of his high-end condo. Her fingers were in his hair. His hands were on her behind. One of her legs was wrapped around his thigh.

Samantha cleared her throat and said, ''Not quite alone, I'm afraid.''

In a practiced move, Matt put his fiancée—Samantha certainly hoped she was his fiancée—behind him while she did something to her blouse.

''Princess!'' His welcoming smile and the use of her high school nickname did not disguise the fact that Matt was seriously put out.

Samantha smiled back apologetically. ''Hello, brat.''

He ran his fingers through his disordered hair. ''You're supposed to be in— Where the hell have you been, anyway? Philip wouldn't tell me anything.''

Samantha's gaze traveled past him to the pretty brown-haired woman tucking her blouse into the waistband of her jeans. Presumably this was Carey, Matt's choice of life partner. But how well did he know her? And how much could Samantha trust her?

Aware of her attention, Matt turned and drew the young woman smoothly to his side. ''This is Carey,'' he said simply, with evident pride. ''Care, Samantha Barnes.''

Samantha extended her hand. ''It's a pleasure to finally meet you. I'm sorry to have missed you at the dinner the other night. I've been on a little…vacation.''

''Well, that's good,'' Matt said heartily. ''You needed a break. You look much…'' For the first time, his quick dark eyes swept over her, taking in the details of her appearance. "Actually, princess, you look like hell."

"That's Honey's T-shirt," Carey said. When Matt cocked an eyebrow at her, she said, "That is, I have a friend who has a T-shirt just like it."

Samantha felt some of the tension leach from her shoulders. "Honey Evans?"

"Yes." Carey sounded surprised. "She works in the White House. Do you know her?"

"No. Her brother." Samantha heard Skillman and Walters moving around in the other room, and turned to Matt. "It's complicated."

He looked over her shoulder to her SEAL escort, looming in the entrance to his living room. "Obviously," he drawled.

Samantha bit her lip. "Ensign David Skillman, Petty Officer Third Class Buzz Walters. Carey Benton and White House advisor Matt Tynan, whom you brought me here to see."

And that was when Carey forever won Samantha's friendship by stepping forward and saying brightly, "It's nice to meet you, gentlemen. Why don't we go see what we can scrounge up in the kitchen while these two old friends talk?"

"Baxter's on vacation," Matt said, hanging up the phone. "So that's a dead end, too."

"But don't you find that suspicious?" Samantha demanded.

He raised one eyebrow. "Not really. I was on vacation. You were on vacation."

"I was kidnapped by an honorable man who was receiving subliminal instructions through his computer to kill me. That was suspicious, too."

Matt sighed. "Sam..." He was using his let's-be-reasonable voice. She hated that voice. She had never felt less like being reasonable. "Have you considered the possibility that this Evans guy is suffering from some kind of post-traumatic stress disorder? You mentioned he got back last month from a mission in the Gulf. I'm not saying he's a bad guy, I'm just saying maybe he needs a different kind of help than you're looking for."

"I thought about that," she admitted reluctantly. Recent incidents with returning Army Rangers had made everyone sensitive to the connection between combat stress and domestic violence. And there was Marcus's distressing loss of memory to consider, and his troubling nightmares…. She shivered. "But, Matt, if he's crazy, then I'm crazy, too. Remember that so-called secure Web site Baxter directed him to? It said 'Kill Barnes.' I'm sure of that. I saw it."

"Then why didn't Evans see it?"

"I don't know," she snapped, miserable. Frustrated. "Maybe he was hypnotized or something."

Matt's head jerked like a puppet's on a string. "Say that again."

She blinked. "What?"

"You think Evans was hypnotized?"

"Well, can you come up with a better explanation for why a dedicated, decorated Navy SEAL would jeopardize his career by claiming he feels compelled to assassinate a United States ambassador?"

Matt rubbed his jaw. "And you're sure he has no history of mental problems?"

She hesitated. She wanted to present Marcus's case in the best possible light. That was one reason she hadn't confessed to Matt that her interest in the handsome naval lieutenant wasn't exactly platonic. She wanted to convince Matt with facts, not feelings; and yet what did she have to go on, in the end, except the conviction of her own heart?

And the truth.

If she truly believed in Marcus's innocence, then she should trust Matt with the truth.

She took a deep breath. "Marcus has a…little problem with long-term memory," she admitted. "His adoptive father said his mind was repressing certain memories as a response to trauma."

Matt's usually mercurial gaze fixed on her face. "What kind of trauma?"

"A car crash, I think he said. When he was ten."

"That fits," he said slowly. "My God. And with the hypnosis thing… Carey!" he shouted in the direction of the kitchen.

Samantha's heart beat faster. "Matt, what's going on?"

"That's exactly what Jake Ingram's adoptive parents told him. Carey!"

Samantha sat there, stunned. Confused.

Jake Ingram? She knew Jake Ingram. But what did he have to do with this? What did he have to do with Marcus?

"Who the hell is Jake Ingram?" Marcus asked.

He was doing push-ups in his room. One hundred one-arm push-ups with his left arm and one hundred with his right, and then a hundred handstand push-ups with his legs straight in the air. Jacobs and some fresh-faced kid named Weasel kept count. Garcia had organized a pot in the bachelors' quarters, and he and Jacobs were looking to clean up. Marcus figured the bet was payback for the time they were putting in baby-sitting him. Anyway, the exercise helped with the boredom.

It didn't do a damn thing for his frustration.

Or the ache of wanting, missing, needing Samantha—her cool intelligence, her warm understanding, her hot body under and around him.

"Seventy-eight," said Jacobs. "Seventy-nine."

Garcia, who had hall duty today, shrugged. "Ingram? Some big financial guy. He told the CO to tell you he was a friend of Samantha Barnes, if that's any use to you."

No use at all.

Marcus had a TV in his room. He watched CNN. He knew Samantha had been confirmed by the president and was scheduled to fly across the Atlantic tomorrow to address the Euro-Atlantic Partnership Council on the implications of the Delmonico Accord. She totally did not need to be tied up with a navy nutcase with a stalled career who might wake up one night and decide to play psycho. So for the past five days, he'd ignored her calls. He'd refused her visit the one time she drove down from Washington.

And now she was sending Jake Ingram?

Jacobs counted. "Eighty-four. Eighty-five."

"He a lawyer?" Marcus asked to distract himself from the burn in his shoulders.

Garcia leaned against the government-issue dresser. "Nope. I read in the paper he was helping the FBI investigate the World Bank heist."

Marcus lowered himself to the floor and pushed back up. "And I should care because…?"

"He's loaded, man. And he wants to see you. Maybe he's your long-lost brother or something and he wants to leave you all his money."

Jacobs laughed.

"You lost count," accused Weasel.

"I didn't," Marcus said. "Ninety-one."

Jacobs picked up the count again. "Ninety-two. Ninety-three."

"He does kind of look like you," said Garcia.

Marcus grunted. "Upside down? Sweaty?"

"CO said you should see him, sir."

Marcus thought about it as he pushed his body up, balancing all one hundred ninety-seven pounds on his palms and forearms. He owed the CO. Big time.

"Where is he? Ingram?" he asked at last.

Garcia smiled thinly. "Waiting in the hall. Him and his bodyguards."

"Ninety-nine, one hundred!" Jacobs finished in triumph. "You saw it, Weasel. You tell your guys to pay up."

Marcus lowered his feet to the floor and stood. "What does a banker need with bodyguards on a military base?"

"I told you, he's not really a banker. He's some kind of financial genius they recruited to catch the World Bank robbers. And one of the suits with him is a fed."

Marcus wiped the sweat from his chest with his discarded shirt. "Well, if they want my help, they've got lousy intel. I barely made it through algebra."

Garcia straightened away from the dresser. "You want me to get rid of him, Lieutenant?"

Marcus pulled a clean T-shirt from his drawer—gray, with Property of the U.S. Navy stamped across the front. He had an instant memory of Samantha lying next to him in bed, laughter in her voice and desire in her eyes.

Do I get to take off your shirt, too?

Well…in the interest of fairness.

His hands clenched on the shirt.

"Sir?"

"What? Oh." Hell. Garcia was going to think he was losing his hearing. Or his mind. "No, I'll see him."

Garcia nodded and crossed to the door. "Hoo yah, sir."

Ingram came in with the fed and the other guy. Jacobs stood. Weasel scrambled from the floor. With Marcus's men and Ingram's bodyguards jockeying for position, it took longer than it should have to get the greetings over with and clear the room. Marcus used the time to size up his visitor, and noted with respect that Ingram did the same.

He does kind of look like you.

Maybe.

Black hair, blue eyes, mid-thirties. Ingram was maybe a couple of years older. Marcus had more muscle, but Ingram had an extra inch of height. And better clothes. The financier held his own in the staring match, then grimaced slightly when they tested grips with a handshake.

"You want to sit down?" Marcus asked, gesturing to one of the room's two chairs.

"Thanks." Ingram took the nearest one.

Marcus sat on the edge of his mattress. It was his room. His turf. "Sorry to keep you waiting."

Ingram smiled faintly. "I think that's my line. You've been here five days already. I was out of town when Samantha first called."

Marcus wasn't discussing Samantha with this suit. "The investigation?"

"No, I was in Arizona on business." Ingram paused. "Family business."

Marcus grinned. "Funny, you don't look Italian."

Ingram's eyes narrowed. "You're not what I expected."

"Yeah, well, I wasn't expecting you at all, pal. Why don't you tell me what you're doing here?"

But instead of answering, Ingram asked his own question. "What have you heard about Code Proteus?"

Proteus. That was the name of the project Samantha had wanted to talk about. Marcus felt his muscles tense, and deliberately relaxed them.

"Enough to know you shouldn't believe everything you hear," he said.

Jake Ingram nodded. "Fair enough. Let me tell you what I know, and then you can tell me what you believe.

"Back in the 1960s, a scientist named Henry Bloomfield was determined to eliminate birth defects and inherited diseases through genetic engineering. Eventually, he decided to design 'perfect' human beings. And he was respected enough that he obtained funding for his efforts through the Medusa research branch of the CIA. Are you with me so far?''

"Yeah. Mad scientist wants superbabies. Government pays. Did he get them?''

"Yes, he did, although not entirely in the manner he originally intended. He actually fell in love with one of his assistants on the project, a young woman named Violet.'' Something—sadness? regret?—momentarily deepened Ingram's eyes and roughened his voice. "We know that Violet carried a number of genetically manipulated babies to term. Unfortunately, some of the other scientists connected with the project lacked Henry Bloomfield's talent. And his scruples. They murdered Henry, hoping to claim the credit for and profits from his work. Violet fled with Henry's notes and their children, who were sent into hiding. And our government, suspicious of the murder and alarmed by the direction the research was taking, pulled the plug on the project. The whole thing was hushed up.''

Marcus's pulse was too fast. His stomach was churning. He crossed his arms against his chest. "If this project was so hush-hush, how come you know so much about it?''

"Because I am one of the products of Code Proteus,'' Jake Ingram replied. "So—we now believe—was the perpetrator of the World Bank heist. My sister Gretchen, who deciphered Violet's clues to the hiding place of Henry Bloomfield's notes, is another.''

"Bloomfield left notes? On what? How to build a superbaby in seven simple steps?''

"Bloomfield documented his research, yes. He recorded his notes on old reel-to-reel computer tapes. I retrieved the tapes from a safety deposit box in Bluewater, Arizona. And Gretchen is currently working in a safe location to decode them.''

"Great. Why are you telling me this?''

Jake Ingram held Marcus's eyes for a long moment. "Because you are the fourth surviving child of the project."

Marcus recoiled. All his life he'd wanted to be accepted. Normal. "Whoa. No. No way."

"I had you investigated," Jake Ingram said. "And I've talked to Samantha Barnes. Your special strength, the timing of your adoption, your memory loss, your nightmares—they all fit the profile."

It was too much to deal with. Too much to take in. Marcus seized on the one thing that offered hope. "You said…you have a sister?"

"*We* have a sister," Ingram corrected gently. "Two, actually. Dr. Gretchen Wagner Miller, the noted cryptologist. And Faith. We haven't found her yet."

Marcus didn't want to accept it. Couldn't believe it. And yet he had to ask, had to know if the sister Ingram was talking about matched the child in his dreams. "Is one of them kind of small? Dark-haired? Bossy and really smart?"

"Compared to you, I imagine most women seem small. And both the girls were always smart. But it sounds to me as if you're describing Faith. The two of you always had a special bond."

Marcus eyed this stranger, Jake Ingram, sitting at ease in the ordinary, durable, navy-issue armchair and talking comfortably about genetic engineering and government cover-ups and murder.

Marcus jerked his chin up, disguising his fear and curiosity as rudeness. "So if you're the product of genetic engineering, what can you do, exactly? Walk on water? Fly?"

"I'm good with numbers," Ingram said. "I manipulate figures."

Marcus snorted. "That's a superpower?"

For the first time, humor gleamed in the other man's eyes. "It is the way I do it."

Marcus almost smiled. "And the others?" he asked abruptly.

"Gretchen, as I told you, is an extraordinary cryptologist. We believe we'll find Faith working in some branch of medicine. She was always gifted that way. Gideon—our missing brother—is a technological genius."

"So, if you're right, I'm not only a freak," Marcus said, "I'm the dumb freak in a family of freaks."

Jake Ingram looked taken aback. "That's certainly one way to put it. Another way would be to say you are the only one of the Code Proteus survivors to receive amazing physical gifts."

Marcus stood and stuffed his hands in his pockets. "I'm also nuts. Or didn't Samantha tell you that?"

His brother—God, could he really have a brother?—watched him warily as he paced the room. "What makes you think you're nuts?"

"I tried to kill her. Repeatedly. First I practically threw her down a well and then I booby-trapped the house, and when that didn't work I tried to strangle her with my bare hands. *Not* the perfect child our scientist father probably had in mind when he started his little test tube experiments."

"Actually, you're not crazy. You're hypnotized."

Marcus pivoted. "You want to run that by me again?"

"Baxter took advantage of deep hypnotic conditioning that was implanted in you—in me, in all of us—when we were children. "Frankly, I'm surprised you held out against it as long and as well as you did. The other scientists associated with the original Code Proteus project were always worried about you. Apparently they feared your strength would make you difficult to control. So they persuaded Bloomfield and Violet to allow them to implant you—and eventually, all of us—with hypnotic triggers."

"What kind of triggers?"

"Nursery rhymes."

Hector Protector was dressed all in green....

Hell.

"So I hear Mother Goose and go around killing people?"

Ingram looked startled. "No. No, the triggers were designed to induce a state of hypersuggestibility that made the subjects—us—responsive to commands."

Marcus frowned, still trying to fit the pieces together. "So, who would know about these triggers?"

"The scientists allied themselves into the Coalition. They know."

"Baxter said there was a Coalition mole within DS."

"Yes. Baxter was that mole."

"And where is he now?"

"He got away from us," Ingram admitted. "By the time Samantha talked to Matt Tynan and Matt got hold of me, Baxter had already cleared out. But we're sure now he was on the payroll of the Coalition."

Fear cramped Marcus's gut. "Then Samantha is still in danger."

"Not as much as she was."

"Because I'm locked up," he said flatly.

"Because she's a less attractive target. The treaty is already ratified. Once she makes her presentation to the Euro-Atlantic Partnership Council meeting this week, her death is less likely to derail the Delmonico Accord. You're probably a bigger target now than she is."

"Why?"

"Because you could still be useful to the Coalition. As long as you respond to your hypnotic trigger, they can activate a state where you're vulnerable to their commands. We believe that's what happened to Gideon."

Marcus absorbed the horrible implications of that. To live forever as the unwitting tool of a shadowy criminal organization, never knowing what you might have done or might be forced to do... It was unthinkable. Unacceptable.

He squared his shoulders. "So what do I do now? Fall on my sword?"

"Would you?" Ingram asked. It didn't sound like a challenge. More like he genuinely wanted to know.

"Die for the good of my country?" Marcus took a deep breath. Here, at last, was a question he could answer all by himself. Deep regret weighted his chest for the life he would not have, for the love he would not share with Samantha. But it didn't change his answer. "Yeah. I would."

Jake Ingram smiled. "Then isn't it a good thing that you don't have to?"

Seventeen

Time healed all wounds. Work was the great analgesic.

Unfortunately, time and work didn't do much for a bruised heart.

Or, apparently, an upset stomach.

Samantha took a cautious sip of tea. She had returned from addressing the EAPC meeting in Brussels with instructions for a new diplomatic initiative, and a mild stomach virus. Until this morning she'd never attended a meeting with crackers in her briefcase. Yesterday she'd actually had to ask her information officer not to wear perfume to staff briefings because the scent made her nauseous.

Philip Scott put a sheaf of letters at her right hand and frowned at her tea tray. "You didn't eat."

She held the phone in place with her jaw and waved a hard roll in his direction. "I'm working on it. Oh, drat, I got crumbs on tomorrow's guest list— Yes, yes, I'll hold," she said into the receiver.

Philip shifted the guest list to the top of a stack of reports on land mine proliferation. "Would you like me to place a call for you?"

She smiled at him gratefully. "No, thank you, Philip. This is personal."

"Still trying to reach Lieutenant Evans?"

Ouch.

"No, I— Jake?" But it was only his answering machine. She glanced at the ornate clock keeping time above the marble fireplace. Five o'clock. Which made it right before lunch in Washington. Where the heck was he?

"Ma'am, are you trying to reach Jake Ingram?"

She depressed the button on her phone. "Yes. Do you know where he is?"

"He called this morning while you were at the Ministry of Trade. The message is there on your desk. He said to tell you he was leaving with his fiancée for Texas tonight, but the situation is basically unchanged."

"Unchanged," she repeated flatly.

Philip nodded. "He said you would know what that meant."

Unfortunately, she did.

It meant Marcus was still undergoing extensive psychological evaluation, counseling and deprogramming with the psychiatrist Jake had recommended—his sister-in-law, Dr. Maisy Dalton.

It meant despite the intervention of Matt Tynan in the White House to ensure that Marcus wasn't actually charged with anything, he was still clinging to his confinement to quarters.

It meant he was still refusing to see her or speak with her.

She knew all that. She just didn't want to accept it.

"Thank you, Philip."

Her stomach lurched. Grimly, she tore another chunk from her hard roll, put it in her mouth and chewed.

Marcus felt sick. He stared at the two photos on the CO's desk: a smiling matte color portrait from the Bureau of Diplomatic Security and a glossy black-and-white photo lifted from a security camera in the Munich International Airport. Despite the superficial differences—hair color, eyeglasses, cheek pads—the subject was obviously the same man.

"It took awhile for the Germans to make the connection," Commander Woods explained. "He's traveling under a different name with what we now assume is a fake passport. But intel ran a computer analysis of his bone configuration with the images from the airport. I just got the report. There's an almost seventy percent probability this guy is Jerry Baxter."

"You'll get him at the border," Marcus said. As much as he tried, the comment came out sounding like a question.

Greg Woods wouldn't quite meet his eyes. "We'll certainly give the Delmonicans every assistance we can in securing their known points of entry. *If* that's Baxter's destination. He could be planning to join DeBruzkya in Rebelia—although what kind of welcome he receives may depend on whether he achieves his objectives first."

Marcus remembered Baxter's smooth assurances the last time he'd talked to the son of a bitch on the phone. *We are very close to achieving our objectives.* His hands clenched in his lap.

"You think Samantha Barnes is still a target."

"If I didn't," Woods said frankly, "I wouldn't have called you in here."

"Embassy security is not the responsibility of the Navy SEALs, sir."

"No," Woods admitted. "But I hoped you would make it yours."

Marcus stared again at the two photos on his commander's desk. His heart was thudding. His palms were sweating. "I'm not sure I can be responsible for anything, sir. Including my own behavior."

"That doctor of yours thinks otherwise. She told me you're fit to return to duty."

"With all due respect, sir, she's not a navy doctor."

"Which is the only reason you're still in the navy, son, so spare us both the pity party."

At some point you must accept that you are not responsible for the attempts on Samantha Barnes's life, Dr. Dalton had lectured him only yesterday. *Whether you choose to be a part of that life... Well, that's up to you, isn't it?*

Maybe. Or maybe Samantha would take a good look at his dangerous job, his time-consuming deployments, his blemished record, his total lack of family tree and his freakozoid gene pool and figure out he didn't have a lot to offer a rising diplomatic star with baby-making aspirations. Once she got over feeling guilty about the way he'd screwed up his career, she could probably have a nice life.

Assuming she lived.

Marcus looked down at the smirking publicity still and up at his commander. "I'd like to request two weeks' personal leave, sir. Effective immediately."

"Granted." Woods smiled. "There's a C-130 prop transport taking off for Gaeta at nineteen-hundred hours. Assuming you can be ready to leave tonight."

Tonight was good. The sooner the better.

Marcus just hoped it would be soon enough.

It was too soon to know.

The limo pulled away from the gray-and-white edifice of the National Assembly in Belagna. Red roofs flashed in the hot sun. The narrow streets were bright with flower boxes and kiosk signs, noisy with scooter motors and bicycle bells.

In the cool, closed interior of the car, Samantha leaned back against the cushioned headrest and shut her eyes, holding the silence inside her like a secret.

Did she even want to know? Maybe it was better to hope. And plan. And dream...

"Madam Ambassador? Ma'am?"

She blinked, disoriented. She must have fallen asleep.

Her driver raised his voice. "We're here, ma'am. Do you need any assistance?"

She tightened her grip on her briefcase and her dignity, and smiled at the young marine holding open her limo door. She was so tired lately.

And she still had to get through the party tonight. Ostensibly, the two hundred thirty-nine guests had been invited to toast her official confirmation as United States ambassador to the Republic of Delmonico. But the real purpose of the evening was to wine, dine and flatter the accord's supporters in the National Assembly. Thankfully, the bulk of the preparations had fallen on Nancy Vandercourt, Samantha's steel-willed, iron-haired social secretary. But Samantha was the one who would be judged by the success of the evening. And the evening's success depended on more than the food or the flowers or the band. It depended on Samantha's ability to charm, to connect, to observe and to communicate with her guests.

She needed a nap.

She trudged up the stairs and crossed the marble foyer, stepping out of the way of a junior staffer wheeling a potted orange tree into the ballroom. With appreciation, she noted the sparkling crystal drops on the chandeliers, the fresh flower arrangements on the tables.

Philip and Nancy pounced as she approached her suite on the second floor.

"Ma'am, if you could sign this…"

"Ma'am, would you approve this…."

"Ma'am, do you want this…"

She signed, approved, excused, dismissed. Then she opened the door to her suite with a sense of escape, unbuttoned her jacket with a sigh of relief.

And whirled, her heart pounding in her chest, as a voice rumbled from the direction of her French windows.

"You've got to be more careful, babe. The security in this place sucks."

She looked good.

Yeah, good and scared.

And maybe in the back of his mind, in some shadowed corner of his soul, he wanted to scare her. Maybe that was why he'd climbed to her room like a thief, like an assassin, testing the limits of the embassy's security and his own heart's defenses. Testing the limits of her trust.

But after that one second of shock, when her eyes went wide and her face went white, she whispered his name. "Marcus?"

Her hand went to her heart. She said it again, louder. "Marcus."

And then, before he could apologize, before he could begin to retreat or explain, she flew across the room and flung herself in his arms.

She was smiling, crying, touching him, his chest, his shoulders, his face. "You're here. Marcus, I'm so glad you're here."

She embraced him like a wife, like a sweetheart waiting for her sailor lover after a six-month tour at sea.

It was the welcome he'd watched and never had.

The acceptance he'd yearned for and never felt.

The love he'd craved and never expected.

It washed his disciplined, lonely soul and flooded his aching, empty heart. He could no more resist her than the restless tide could resist the pull of the moon.

Wrapping his arms around her, he buried his face in her hair.

Samantha felt his surrender. It thrilled her. She held him tight with both hands, trying to reassure herself that he was safe, that he was here, that he was hers.

She had thought—feared—that his pride and guilt would

combine to keep him away. She hadn't reckoned on the power of her love and the force of his need. She felt him pulse against her, heard the ragged rasp of his breath and the pounding of her own heart. Love and need coupled and twined inside her. She threaded her fingers with his and drew him toward the bed.

"Nice bed." His voice was husky.

It was a great bed, a square four-poster from the seventeenth century with white silk hangings and a white down duvet like a cloud. But she would have taken him on the floor of Jimmy's barn.

"I'm glad you like it." She tugged on his shirt.

"I didn't come here for this."

Her hands stilled. His skin was so warm under her hands. His breath shuddered in and out.

"Why did you come?" she asked.

"I forget." His smile almost crept into his eyes. "When you touch me, I forget my name."

"I'll have to keep touching you, then," she whispered, and did.

She twined her arms around his neck. She sought his mouth with hers. His kiss was hard and deep, but his hands trembled. He skimmed his wide palms up her back, slipped the jacket from her arms and the skirt from her hips. She didn't feel tired anymore, or nauseated or lonely or afraid. All she felt, all she wanted, was him.

They sank onto the mattress. Outside the high double doors that protected her suite, she heard music playing, a vacuum humming, the clink of glassware and a murmured instruction. Inside, there was only this. Only him, moving over her and then inside her, hot and urgent.

She cried out, it was so lovely, and he kissed her to keep her quiet. He covered her with his incredible body, filling her with his power, sheltering her with his strength. Pleasure coiled deep within her. Her breathing hitched, and her heart pounded. He was moving inside her, thick and slow, and the intimacy of it, the intensity of it, reached along all her nerves and shattered her. She cried out once more and felt him shake with his own release.

When Samantha pulled herself together—how many minutes later? two? twenty?—she was draped over Marcus like a wet sheet.

"I told you security sucked." He sounded disgusted. "You screamed and nobody came."

She smiled against his hard, damp chest. "You did."

But he was not amused. "Besides me."

She pushed her hair out of her eyes, trying to gauge his mood. "That's probably a good thing. It would have been awkward if half a dozen marines burst into the room and I had to explain what you were doing here."

"I think they could have figured out what I was doing here," he said grimly.

"It still would have spoiled the mood."

Sudden, silent laughter expanded his chest. His arms tightened around her. "Yeah."

She rubbed her cheek against his warm, hair-roughened skin. His heartbeat was sure and strong. "Marcus?"

He stroked her back. "Yeah?"

"What *are* you doing here?"

"I came to protect you."

It wasn't the answer she wanted. Not all of the answer. "Why?"

"Two days ago German police photographed a man who could be Jerry Baxter at an airport in Munich. That's less than two hundred miles from here."

She raised her head from his chest. "Is that your only reason?"

He held her gaze for several long seconds. A muscle worked in his jaw. "It ought to be."

Her throat closed. She swallowed. "You know, one of

these days you're going to figure out you could offer me a lot more than protection."

"No," he said. "I can't."

"Why not?"

He didn't answer her directly. "Did Jake Ingram tell you about me? About us?"

"About Code Proteus?" She waited until Marcus nodded before she said, "Yes."

They were lying naked, pressed together, but she already felt him drawing away from her, retreating into himself.

"So you know I'm a freak. I have freak genes."

Her heart stuttered. "You have normal genes. Maybe the way they were put together wasn't completely conventional, but—"

"You can say that again."

"But you had a mother and a father. Siblings. Marcus—"

"My birth name is Mark. I just found that out. About the same time I found out that I'm genetically manipulated and hypnotically controlled. Kind of makes me a bad relationship risk."

"But with deprogramming—"

"Deprogramming can counteract the effects of indoctrination. In my case, my hypnotic trigger. It can't predict how I'll react in any given situation. And it doesn't change my genetic makeup."

Fear churned under her breastbone. "What's wrong with your genetic makeup?"

"I'm different. Any child I could have might be different, too."

"Faster? Stronger?"

"Different," he insisted.

"Special."

"Not normal."

She sat up, the sheet sliding down her naked back. She

watched his gaze darken as he looked at her breasts, and was fiercely glad. She was fighting this battle with every weapon at her disposal.

"You want to be normal? Why? You're a U.S. Navy SEAL. You think normal people make choices like that? You think your average guy just waltzes through BUD/S? Or do you think you have to have something extra? Not superhuman strength or speed, but loyalty and courage and honor and heart. Commitment. Those things may make you different, Marcus, but they don't make you a bad relationship risk."

He cupped the back of her head with his hand and drew her down to him. He kissed her, with need and sweetness. But he didn't answer her. He didn't believe her.

Hope struggled with panic in her chest. Maybe in time— Oh, Lord, the *time*.

She bolted upright. "What time is it?"

He narrowed his eyes. "About twenty-hundred hours. Why?"

"I have a party. There's a party at the embassy. Tonight. At nine."

"You're kidding, right?"

"No. I know the timing is inconvenient—"

"The timing stinks. Didn't you hear what I said about Baxter? He could be out there gunning for you."

"Oh, I don't think so." Samantha slid out of bed. "Nancy Vandercourt went over the guest list very carefully."

Marcus scowled. "Honey, this guy infiltrated the State Department's Bureau of Diplomatic Security. He's not going to have a real hard time crashing your little party."

Eighteen

The party was on. Marcus understood that neither the hospitality of the United States nor the arrangements of Nancy Vandercourt yielded to the threat of terrorism.

Samantha was on. What had she said when he'd kidnapped her weeks ago? *I am willing to assume the risks of my job. Just as you are willing to assume the risks of yours.* Okay. He could accept that, too.

But he didn't have to like it.

Before she went downstairs, stunning and composed in a floor-length blue silk gown and full ambassador mode, Samantha tried to reassure him. "I'm not being careless. We have four DS agents, a detachment of marines and half the Delmonican police force providing security this evening."

Marcus didn't remind her that he'd gotten by all of them, undetected, to reach her room. Scaring her wouldn't help her do her job. But it sure as hell motivated him to do his.

While Samantha dressed, he made copies of both Baxter photos and distributed them to embassy security. He got a copy of the guest list from Nancy Vandercourt and asked Philip to check off the name of every guest he wasn't able to vouch for personally.

As limos began to pull up to the compound walls, Marcus faxed that list to Jimmy. He hung his uniform in the bathroom to get the wrinkles out while he showered. Dried, dressed, armed and prepared, he left the residence suite.

The marine guard posted outside the door smirked when

he saw him coming out of the ambassador's room. "How do you like Delmonico, Lieutenant?"

Marcus flashed the kid a look that wiped the smile from his face and made him snap to attention. "Beats Baghdad for duty," he replied pleasantly. "Doesn't it."

"Sir, yes, sir."

Satisfied that one mouth at least wouldn't be yapping in the mess tonight, Marcus made his way down the broad staircase.

But the exchange made him think. He was living in the ambassador's house now. He was sleeping in her bed. Somebody was going to notice. Somebody was going to talk.

Did his presence compromise her mission? Would their involvement hurt her?

He would give his life to protect her. But death might be preferable to the fishbowl of embassy existence.

Then he got another look at her under the full glow of the chandeliers, as sparkling as the other women's diamonds, as smooth and gleaming as the pearls at her own ears.

She took his breath away.

She smiled as she saw him coming down the stairs, and it wasn't the warm, polite curve of her lips every other guy got, either. It was her "hello, sailor" grin, the one that made him shove his hands into his uniform pockets to keep from grabbing her. If she smiled at him like that, it didn't matter how much he glowered at baby-faced marines, people were going to talk.

The idea didn't bother him as much as it should have.

"Having a good time?" she asked as he reached her.

"Absolutely," he lied.

She rewarded him with another smile and turned to greet some short, bearded diplomat with a ribbon across his chest.

And actually, Marcus thought later as he prowled the perimeter of the room, it wasn't so bad for a black-tie-and-champagne affair. He'd grown up with wealth. He respected the rituals of protocol, even if he was more familiar with the military kind. The women were easy on the eye, in the way of women who had the money to make the most of their looks, and some of the men weren't boring.

He scanned the room again, looking for anything—a package, a sudden movement, an expression—that could signal danger. Looking for Baxter. The women's gowns swayed in time to the music. The curtains framing the French doors rippled in the breeze. Marcus watched while a pretty blonde retrieved her purse from a table, tensed when a stiff-faced officer on the terrace reached for a cigar. A waiter dropped a fork and was practically wrestled to the ground by an overzealous security agent.

Marcus grinned as the luckless waiter bolted for the kitchen and the agent straightened his jacket.

The crowd cleared for a moment, giving Marcus a good view of Samantha on the other side of the room standing with… Who was that guy? He was leaning forward, like he was really interested in what she was saying, and looking down the front of her dress. Marcus started toward them.

Movement registered in the corner of his vision, at the edge of the dance floor. Another figure moving toward Samantha, gliding through the crowd.

Marcus turned his head and lengthened his stride, trying to get a step ahead of the guy to get a look at his face. There was nothing suspicious about him; he was just another paunchy, gray-haired diplomat in a monkey suit, with his hand under his jacket like Napoleon.

Or a killer reaching for his gun.

There was barely time to observe. No time to evaluate. No time to intervene.

In one smooth move, in three short seconds, the guest withdrew his hand from his jacket, pointed a gun at Samantha's head and fired.

Samantha spotted Marcus cutting across the ballroom, and her heart skipped in pleased anticipation. Her womb quickened. Among the black-clad men and gorgeously gowned women, he sailed like a great white swan through a flock of geese and ducks.

And wouldn't he be annoyed, she thought, amused, to be compared to a swan?

And then he took off. With incredible speed, he sprinted—no, he flew—toward her. And stopped five yards away.

A terrible anguish tore her heart.

She did not need to hear the muffled pop to know he'd been shot.

She saw it in the widening of his eyes, in the stiffening of his shoulders, in the jerk of his big body an instant before the bright blood blossomed across the front of his white dress uniform.

He'd been shot. For her. Taken a bullet meant for her.

The room erupted. Women screamed. Chairs crashed and glasses shattered as guests jumped to their feet or dived for cover. Another agent slammed Samantha to the floor, knocking the wind from her lungs. The nine-piece jazz band wailed and stuttered to silence.

"No!" She fought to rise, struggled to see.

The agent's hard weight pressed her to the cold marble floor. His jacket smelled of fear and dry-cleaning fluid. "Ma'am, please."

She shoved at his shoulder. "Marcus!"

"It's all right, ma'am," the agent said breathlessly in her ear. "We got him."

"Marcus?"

"The shooter."

"If you don't get off me," Samantha said through clenched teeth, "*I* will shoot *you*."

It was possibly the most undiplomatic statement she'd made in her life. She didn't care. Panic pressed on her lungs, heavier and more unyielding than her bodyguard. She had to get to Marcus. Had to see… Had to know… Had to tell him…

The agent's weight eased. She struggled out from under him. Ignoring the hands that reached out to help her, she scrambled up and across the floor toward the huddle around Marcus. Pushing past the black jackets, she fell to her knees. A woman in a silver gown—a doctor, apparently—rapped out orders in German while she pressed a napkin to Marcus's chest.

The napkin was scarlet with his blood.

"Marcus?" Samantha whispered.

His eyes opened, his blue, blue eyes. They met hers, and his mouth crooked in a smile.

"Faster than a speeding bullet," he said weakly.

And then he was gone.

A silent cry of anguish swelled inside Samantha, too horrible to voice, too huge to contain.

She had never told him. And the things she had not said burned in her throat like tears and raged in her chest like fire.

An assemblyman touched her arm. "I am sorry, madam. Perhaps—"

She jerked her elbow from his grasp. "He's not dead," she said fiercely.

The agent who had followed her cleared his throat. "Ma'am, he took a .22 caliber bullet fired at close range through the upper right quadrant of the chest. Even if it missed his heart, that's not good."

The doctor in the silver gown continued to apply pressure

to the exit wound in Marcus's chest. Her hands were slippery. Her dress was stained. One of the waiters had brought her some kind of plastic bag, which she slapped over the sucking hole of Marcus's chest.

Hope tore fresh wounds in Samantha's soul. He was still bleeding. He was still breathing. He was still alive.

She stood. "Philip!"

Her secretary was at her shoulder, his neat brown hair disordered and his face white.

"I want doctors. I want surgeons. Get me the 86th at Ramstein. We need aeromedical evacuation to the naval hospital in Naples as soon as it can be arranged."

"He's strong," Jake Ingram offered from his post by the waiting room door. "He'll pull through. Hell, any other man would be dead by now."

Samantha knew Jake meant well. But his words made her shiver in the climate-controlled room.

Any other man...

Stan had died like this. Died at the hospital while she paced cold linoleum halls that smelled of steel and sweat, of pain and disinfectant. Died while she sat upright on a rigid chair in a brightly lit room with her hands in her lap and her heart like a stone in her chest. Died while she waited.

She had been waiting, this time, more than thirty-six hours. Long enough to find Jake Ingram at his future father-in-law's ranch in Texas, to field an anxious phone call from Marcus's adoptive parents in Maryland, to fend off a visit from his nearly hysterical sister Honey.

There's nothing to be done. Samantha mentally repeated what the doctors had told her. Once the surgery was over, there was nothing to do but wait.

And pray.

The Evanses were still making arrangements to fly out.

Jake had beaten them, using his connections to wangle a seat on an air force jet.

"Can I get you some coffee?" he asked.

Her stomach lurched. She pressed her lips together. "No, thanks."

"That surgeon—Wilson—said they'd repaired the lung."

She didn't want to talk about the surgery. She didn't want to talk at all. Her composure was eggshell thin. Too much conversation would crack it. But she appreciated his efforts anyway. "Thank you for being here, Jake."

He shrugged, and for one poignant moment, she saw Marcus in the gesture. "He's my brother."

"Long-lost brother."

"Maybe that's why I felt I had to come. I just found him. I don't want to lose him again."

"I'm sure he'll be glad you're here," she said.

If he ever wakes up, she thought, fear like an acid burning her stomach and the back of her throat. Please, God, let him wake up.

"To tell the truth…"

She waited. She'd known Jake Ingram for years. He was friends with Matt and Ethan. He'd done business with her husband.

"It was kind of a relief to get away," he admitted at last.

"The pressures of the investigation?" she asked sympathetically.

"No. More like pressure from my fiancée."

"Tara?"

"She wants to set a wedding date."

Samantha arched her eyebrows. "Well, is that so surprising?"

"No. We should get married. I want to get married. I just…" He thrust his fingers through his dark hair. "I didn't even tell her where I was going," he confessed. "I couldn't. I haven't told her yet who—what—I am."

Dismayed, Samantha stared at him. "You need to tell her."

"Eventually."

"Now."

"Samantha, things are complicated enough without my burdening Tara with this. My plane barely touched down here when I got a phone call about some trouble in Chicago. As soon as Mark—Marcus—comes around, I've got to fly back. Any big confession will have to wait."

"Are you sure it can wait? What if something happened—" what if you were shot, bleeding, dying, dead "—and you never told her until it was too late? Maybe sharing the truth would drive you apart. But not sharing the truth divides you now. And now may be all the time the two of you have."

Her voice trembled. So did her chin. Damn. And she'd been doing so well.

Jake moved toward her. "Samantha…"

"Ambassador Barnes?" A tall, black corpsman stood in the entrance to the waiting room. "We've moved Lieutenant Evans to the unit. Would you like to see him for a few minutes?"

Hope speared her. "Is he awake?"

"No, ma'am." And then, obviously taking pity on her, he added, "But his vitals are real good. To be honest with you, the doctors are amazed."

She got up to follow the corpsmen and then thought of Jake. She looked back over her shoulder. "You're his brother. Do you want to—"

"Long-lost brother," he interrupted gently. "You're the one he's going to want to see when he opens his eyes."

When was a nice word. A much nicer word than *if*. She clung to it on the short walk to intensive care, using it like a talisman to hold the smells and the fears at bay. The corpsman talked to her quietly along the way, trying to prepare her for the sight of Marcus.

But no charm in the world, no murmured reassurances, could stop her heart from breaking when she finally saw him.

Despite his incredible strength and his extraordinary beginnings, she had always perceived Marcus as fully and completely human. He hardly looked human now. He was totally hooked up to machines, machines that pumped and monitored, blinked and bleeped. His big, vital body looked gaunt and still. Some kind of tube stuck out from his powerful chest. Thinner tubes ran from his arm and under his nose. His firm, tanned cheeks were slack and gray, his mouth drawn tight as a scar with pain, his eye sockets bruised and hollow.

Her mouth dried with fear and pity.

"I can give you five minutes," the corpsman said, and rattled the striped curtain closed behind her.

Five minutes. She wanted a lifetime.

She took Marcus's hand, careful to avoid the tubes and cords that connected him to his high-tech life-support systems. His skin was cool. His grip was unresponsive. Tears stung her eyes. She ignored them.

There were no chairs in the tiny curtained cubicle, so she leaned over the metal side of the bed and pressed her cheek to his forehead.

Five minutes.

If this was all she had, if this was all they would ever have, then by God she would make the most of it. She turned her head slightly, so that her lips brushed his ear. Hot tears streaked her face and slid into his hair.

But her voice was steady as she whispered, "Listen, sailor. I love you. And I'm pregnant. So you have to come back to me now, because if you think I'm raising Super-baby by myself, you really are crazy.''

She waited. The machines bleeped. The blinking monitors blurred. This was it, then. This really was all they had.

Samantha drew a shaky breath and straightened to ease the ache in her back. There wasn't a thing she could do about the pain in her heart.

But when she lifted her head, Marcus had opened his eyes.

''You told me you were on the pill,'' Marcus said three days later. His voice was still raspy from a combination of narcotics and the breathing tube, but he sounded wonderful to Samantha. And not particularly upset.

''I told you I couldn't get pregnant,'' Samantha corrected him. She lifted the silver cover from his plate of scrambled eggs. Three days in the hospital—and yesterday's visit from his adoptive parents—had gone a long way toward restoring his health. And his appetite. Samantha heard they were taking bets in the nurses' lounge on how much he would eat and how quickly he would be discharged.

''And I couldn't, before.'' She smiled at him. ''I think it was your supersperm that did the trick.''

Marcus scowled and slathered jelly on a piece of toast. ''We have to get married.''

Her heart beat faster. ''Do we?''

''Yeah, of course we do. You're not planning on giving this kid up for adoption.''

''No,'' she agreed quietly. ''I'm not planning to do that.''

''So we get married.'' He shrugged. ''Simple.''

''It's not simple at all.''

''If you're worried about my job, I've already talked with Commander Woods. Since I was technically guarding you, I won't be charged with an unauthorized absence for the time we were in Virginia. So my record is clean, and I'm fit for duty.''

''As soon as you get out of the hospital.''

He grinned at her, making her insides go all warm and mushy. ''Yeah.'' He shoveled in eggs.

''I'm happy for you,'' she said sincerely. ''I know how much it means to you to continue with the Teams. But—''

He waved his fork at her. ''And it's not like I'll have to be away when the baby is born, either. Now that Delmonico isn't a Rebelian ally, they need to beef up their own forces. My squad can be deployed here to conduct military training, and I can keep an eye on you.''

She wanted to be more to him than a job or an obligation. She bit into his leftover toast. ''You don't need to keep an eye on me. Baxter is in custody now.''

''But he's admitted he was working for the Coalition. There's still a chance you could be a target.''

She licked jelly from her fingers. ''Are you trying to frighten me into saying yes?''

He put down his napkin. ''If that's what it takes. That bastard actually boasted—'' He broke off.

''What?''

Marcus shook his head. Swore. ''There's a chance that the accident that killed your husband... There's a good chance it wasn't an accident. I'm sorry.''

She sat, stunned. ''Baxter...?''

''Not Baxter. Not personally. But he claims the Coalition arranged for that truck to pull across the intersection in the path of your husband's car. They wanted to kill the treaty.''

The truth hit her like a stone. ''So they murdered Stan.''

''But they didn't count on you. You gave your husband the best revenge and the best memorial he could ask for.''

''The Delmonico Accord.''

''The accord is part of it. As long as the treaty exists,

the bad guys lose. And as long as you live, so does your husband. You know, in your memories. And in your heart."

Tears, so long suppressed, welled up and sparkled in her eyes. Trust Marcus to put things in the most practical, personal terms.

"You got to live, babe," he said. He reached out and covered her hand with his. "As long as you're living, you win."

She tried to find her smile. "I have a lot to live for."

"You bet."

"The baby."

Marcus nodded, encouraged that she was looking forward again. "And me."

She was silent.

Panic time. He tightened his grip on her hand. "The baby *and me.*"

She avoided his gaze. "You're not obliged to marry me because I'm pregnant."

He was insulted. "Yeah, I am."

Now she looked at him, and that was worse, because her eyes were miserable and determined. "I don't want you to marry me because you feel obliged."

He'd thought his chest had taken as hard a hurt as a man could stand. He'd been wrong. "You don't want to marry me," he repeated flatly.

She raised her chin. "Not if you don't love me."

Immediately he started to feel a whole lot better. "Right. I'm a moron. And for a brilliant woman, you have some pretty stupid ideas, too."

He pushed the tray table out of the way and swung his bare legs over the side of the hospital bed.

Samantha's eyes narrowed. "What are you doing?"

"Something I should have done three days ago, only I couldn't get out of bed."

"You shouldn't get out of bed now. Marcus!" She tried

to look stern and only succeeded in looking flustered. "Do you want me to call a corpsman?"

"Not unless you want an audience."

Enough get-well bouquets crammed his hospital room to supply an admiral's funeral. He looked them all over carefully and finally selected a rose. A big, red one.

He knelt, which was tough because he still had a tube in his arm attached to a stupid bag on a pole, and tougher because the shorty hospital gown flapped around his bare ass. He took her hand. It trembled, but that was okay, because he was trembling, too.

"Okay, let me see if I can get it right this time. Listen up, babe, and I'll use real little words so you understand. I love you. I want you. I want to make a family with you and spend the rest of my life with you. Will you please marry me?"

Samantha's eyes were still shiny with tears. But she smiled at him then, the kind of smile that made him lightheaded even when he wasn't fighting off blood loss and painkillers.

"I love you, too," she said clearly. "And I'll marry you and make a family with you and spend the rest of our lives together. Now will you get back in bed?"

He grinned at her foolishly and lurched to his feet. "If that's an invitation, honey, the answer is yes."

She snorted and drew back the covers for him. "I don't care how impressed the doctors are with your rapid recovery, I think you're overestimating your amazing physical powers, Clark."

But she was going to be surprised.

*There are more secrets to reveal—
don't miss out!
Coming in November 2003 to
Silhouette Books*

*Framed for the World Bank heist, Eric Jones
has lost all hope of clearing his name, until
he discovers his new attorney is his long-lost
love, whom he shared one passionate night
with nine years ago...*

*A VERDICT OF LOVE
by
Jenna Mills*

FAMILY SECRETS: *Five extraordinary
siblings. One dangerous past.
Unlimited potential.*

*And now, for a sneak peek,
just turn the page...*

One

Jake picked up the remote and zapped the television. "You've been following the World Bank heist investigation?"

Eric's tension eased a fraction. Whatever bomb his friend Jake Ingram had to drop, it pertained to business. For over four months he'd been following his friend's progress as he and the federal government worked to solve the ultimate April Fool's joke—the theft of $350 billion from the influential World Bank. Achilles, they called the culprit who single-handedly had sent the stock market into decline and small banks into failure. Eric, an investment banker, had been dealing with panicky clients ever since, worried about the security of their college funds and retirement plans.

"Kind of hard not to, when your name and picture have been splashed across the newspaper on an almost daily basis." Even the *Wall Street Journal* was tracking Jake's progress. "Are you closer to finding Achilles?"

The planes of Jake's face tightened. "The son of a bitch has the FBI running in circles like a dog chasing its tail. He's planted endless dead-end trails and false leads."

Eric heard that. It blew his mind that hundreds of billions of dollars could simply vanish into thin air. "Do they think he was working alone?"

"No. They're pretty sure he's on someone's bankroll, probably a struggling Eastern European country, like Rebelia."

"But there's no evidence?" Eric guessed, reaching for his beer.

"Nothing concrete. Nothing they can nail him with."

For the first time, Eric realized the magnitude of responsibility sitting on Jake's shoulders. He wasn't just investigating the largest theft in history—he was potentially tracking a madman who posed a risk to the entire free world. No wonder he'd put his wedding on hold.

"Christ, man, you're in deep, aren't you?"

Jake pinched the bridge of his nose, then met Eric's gaze. "The feds and I aren't seeing eye-to-eye anymore," he said levelly. "Daniel Venturi, the agent assigned to the case after the first agent, Lennox, went down, is an old-school hard-liner who sees this as his opportunity to make a lasting name for himself."

Eric rolled the beer can in his hands. "Not exactly an unassuming Fox Mulder type, I'm guessing."

A hard sound broke from Jake's throat. "Hardly." He leaned forward and balanced his elbows on his knees. "Communication has broken down since he came onto the scene. At first I thought it was because Venturi doesn't appreciate an outsider being involved."

"And now?"

Jake glanced toward the sliding glass door, then back at Eric. "Now I know it's because before Lennox died, a suspect surfaced. When Venturi took over, he was under instructions to hold quiet until the case was almost completely buttoned-up."

The resentment in Jake's voice was impossible to miss. "Does that mean this mess is almost over?"

Jake frowned. "I'm afraid it's just starting."

It wasn't like Jake to talk in circles. "How so?"

"Dammit," Jake said. "There's absolutely no easy way to tell you this. Their suspect, Eric. Their suspect is you."

Eric went very still. "Come again?"

Jake stood, started to pace. "The feds, Indy. The feds have fingered you as the mastermind behind Achilles."

"That's ridiculous," Eric said, slamming his beer down and surging to his feet. "I can't program my way out of a paper bag."

Jake frowned. "I know that, and you know that, but right now that doesn't make a damn bit of difference."

Incredulity blasted him. "Why me?" he bit out, fumbling savagely at the silk tie cutting off his oxygen flow. "Why would the feds even look at me?"

"They're looking because someone wants them to," Jake said grimly. "Because you're my friend." His eyes took on an ominous glitter. "Ever since this investigation started, someone has been playing fast and loose with my life. Did you know my brother Zach was kidnapped? That they thought he was me? Sought to silence him—*me*—before I could finger the real bastard behind Achilles?"

Eric just stared. It sounded as if his friend was discussing some complex action thriller, not their lives.

"They want me off the case," Jake continued, clearly angry and agitated. "Whoever is behind the World Bank heist, they're well connected and they're powerful, and they'll stop at nothing to make sure I don't expose their house of cards. Now any claim I make of your innocence will be written off as friendship and loyalty."

"They're that scared you're going to find the real culprit?"

"They're that determined to make sure I don't. With the feds focused on you—"

"The real trail goes cold." Eric sucked in a rough breath. With stunning speed, pieces and implications were falling into place, hard and fast and with brutal clarity. "How bad is it? How strong of a case do they have against me?"

"Strong enough that you need a lawyer. You need one now. That's why I'm here."

"A lawyer," he muttered. "Christ." He didn't even know any defense attorneys. "You really think that's necessary?"

"I wouldn't be here if I didn't."

Shock was slowly giving way to cold shards of anger, but Eric forced back both emotions. He needed a clear head. "Okay. I'll make a few phone calls," he said, opening a drawer for his address book, "see if I can come up with a recommendation."

"You don't need to make any phone calls," Jake said quietly. "You need Leigh."

Eric went very still. For just a heartbeat. Then he turned slowly, looked at his friend standing in front of the sliding glass door, the late-day sun streaming in behind him and casting him in silhouette. "What did you just say?"

Jake stepped into the shadow of an enormous banana plant. "I said Leigh, Eric. You need Leigh."

Her name came at him through a dark tunnel of time and space, blasted him like a gust of warm tropical air. He'd not heard it spoken aloud for close to ten years, since shortly after she'd left Oxford, when Jake and Ethan and Matt had ganged up on him, tried to convince him to go after her. Eric had been keeping everything bottled up inside, all his frustration and anger, the regret and guilt, the sense of helplessness he'd never before experienced. He'd exploded, slammed his fist through a wall and shocked his friends into silence. *Don't say her name to me,* he'd roared. *Just let it go.*

As he'd let her go.

And they had.

Until now.

Where love comes alive™

Five extraordinary siblings.
One dangerous past.
Unlimited potential.

FAMILY SECRETS

**Collect four (4) original proofs of purchase from
the back pages of four (4) Family Secrets titles
and receive a specialty themed free gift
valued at over $20.00 U.S.!**

Just complete the order form and send it, along with four (4) proofs of
purchase from four (4) different Family Secrets titles to: Family Secrets, P.O. Box
9047, Buffalo, NY 14269-9047, or P.O. Box 613, Fort Erie, Ontario L2A 5X3.

Name (PLEASE PRINT)

Address   Apt. #

City   State/Prov.   Zip/Postal Code

Please specify which themed gift package(s)
you would like to receive:

❑ PASSION
❑ HOME AND FAMILY
❑ TENDER AND LIGHTHEARTED

❑ Have you enclosed your proofs of purchase?

FAMILY SECRETS

One Proof
Of Purchase
FSPOP5

Remember—for each package selected, you must send four (4)
original proofs of purchase. To receive all three (3) gifts, just send
in twelve (12) proofs of purchase, one from each of the 12
Family Secrets titles.

Please allow 4-6 weeks for delivery. Shipping and handling included. Offer good
only while quantities last. Offer available in Canada and the U.S. only. Request
should be received no later than July 31, 2004. Each proof of purchase should
be cut out of the back page ad featuring this offer.

FAMILY
SECRETS

Five extraordinary siblings.
One dangerous past.
Unlimited potential.

If you missed the first riveting stories
from Family Secrets,
here's a chance to order your copies today!

0-373-61368-7	ENEMY MIND by Maggie Shayne	___ \$4.99 U.S. ___ \$5.99 CAN.
0-373-61369-5	PYRAMID OF LIES by Anne Marie Winston	___ \$4.99 U.S. ___ \$5.99 CAN.
0-373-61370-9	THE PLAYER by Evelyn Vaughn	___ \$4.99 U.S. ___ \$5.99 CAN.
0-373-61371-7	THE BLUEWATER AFFAIR by Cindy Gerard	___ \$4.99 U.S. ___ \$5.99 CAN.

(limited quantities available)

TOTAL AMOUNT	\$_____
POSTAGE & HANDLING	\$_____
(\$1.00 for one book; 50¢ for each additional)	
APPLICABLE TAXES*	\$_____
TOTAL PAYABLE	\$_____

(Check or money order—please do not send cash)

To order, complete this form and send it, along with a check or money order for the total above, payable to **Family Secrets,** to:

In the U.S.: 3010 Walden Avenue, P.O. Box 9077, Buffalo, NY 14269-9077;
In Canada: P.O. Box 636, Fort Erie, Ontario L2A 5X3

Name:_____
Address:_____ City:_____
State/Prov.:_____ Zip/Postal Code:_____
Account # (if applicable):_____
075 CSAS

*New York residents remit applicable sales taxes.
*Canadian residents remit applicable GST and provincial taxes.

Visit us at www.silhouettefamilysecrets.com   FSBACK4

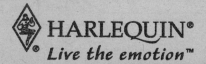